# Forever with You

BY BARB CURTIS

A Sapphire Springs Novel

FOREVER

NEW YORK BOSTON

This book is a work of fiction. Names, characters, places, and incidents are the product of the author's imagination or are used fictitiously. Any resemblance to actual events, locales, or persons, living or dead, is coincidental.



Forever

Hachette Book Group

1290 Avenue of the Americas, New York, NY 10104

read-forever.com

twitter.com/readforeverpub

First Edition: November 2020

Forever is an imprint of Grand Central Publishing. The Forever name and logo are trademarks of Hachette Book Group, Inc.

The publisher is not responsible for websites (or their content) that are not owned by the publisher.

The Hachette Speakers Bureau provides a wide range of authors for speaking events. To find out more, go to www.hachettespeakersbureau.com or call (866) 376-6591.

ISBNs: 978-1-5387-0307-6 (mass market), 978-1-5387-0306-9 (ebook)

Printed in the United States of America

OPM

10 9 8 7 6 5 4 3 2 1

**"Do you still hate me that much after all these years?"**

Suddenly her fingernails required close inspection. "Please. Don't flatter yourself by thinking you were so significant that I carry some eighteen-year grudge." She pretended to flick something away before meeting his gaze, because if she didn't, he'd call her out on it.

The light breeze lifted her hair and tousled it into her face. Jay inched forward and swept it away with a gentle brush of warm fingertips. His fingers hovered over her cheek a couple of seconds, and maybe, just *maybe* she leaned into his touch a little, yearning for that contact again, but he was already dropping his hand to his side. Like he'd surprised even himself by touching her.

His gaze narrowed, though, and she knew her impulsive reaction hadn't gone unnoticed. His brooding eyes filled with awareness and locked on hers.

She glanced away, but just that one second of broken contact already made her crave his dark stare again. *Screw it.* She lifted her gaze. The closer he got, the darker his eyes looked, and they drew her in with a force of magnetism. Her eyes fell on his full bottom lip, and her breath hitched.

"Jay," she warned through clenched teeth, as his fingers circled her wrist. But their surroundings blurred and her lips were already parting.

*For Keira*
*My sun, moon, and stars*

# Acknowledgments

Where to begin, when so many people have contributed to this book becoming a reality.

First, to my family, in particular my mother. You've been offering your unwavering support for nearly fifteen years, even though I've never let you read a single word. What can I say, I was worried you'd sugarcoat your feedback! To my aunt Daphne, for offering up the camp any time I needed to escape to a quiet place to work. There's just something about that place, isn't there? And all the rest of you—there are too many to list here—but thank you from the bottom of my heart for sitting through the many "I think *this* draft is the one" late-night conversations. I'm sure I sounded like a broken record.

To Brenda Drake's Pitch Wars organization for helping strengthen my craft. I never actually got in, but I credit the community with connecting me to my writing tribe. To those early readers: Allison Marie Silver, Maia

Kumari Gilman, and Jessica Holt, for reading my manuscript before I even really knew what I was doing, and still giving me honest and supportive advice. My critique partners: Tara Martin, Janet Walden-West, Kat Turner, and Amy Kidd. "Meeting" all of you was a turning point for me. You suffered through some seriously shitty drafts and encouraged me to keep going. I can only hope I've returned the favor, at least in part.

To Joel Williams for your input in the earliest of drafts. If I've managed to come across at all seeming as though I know anything about grape growing, it's because of you—I tip my glass. And to Brian Schmidt of Vineland Estates. Your "Twactor Tweets" were an invaluable resource in the research for this book.

Thank you to the team at Forever / Grand Central: Daniela Medina, cover designer; Lori Paximadis, copyeditor; Bob Castillo, production editor; Estelle Hallick, my publicist; and most notably Junessa Viloria, my editor, for "finding" me in some forgotten inbox and loving my words just as I had begun to lose faith.

To my agent, Stacey Graham. If I've said it once, I've said it a hundred times—I cannot imagine this roller coaster without you riding shotgun. No way could I navigate this crazy world of publishing without your wisdom and expertise. You took a chance on me, talked me off ledges, and cheered me on. Seriously, you are so stuck with me!

And most of all, to Chris. You're my sounding board and my cheerleader, and you've talked me through more self-doubt than anyone should ever have to listen to. I could not and would not be holding this book in print without your support. And to my daughter, Keira, the kick in the pants I needed to take a long look at the things that matter most to me in life and the kind of example I want to set, which ultimately led me to take this manuscript off the shelf, wipe the dust off of it, and pursue this crazy dream with a little more purpose. You, my sweet girl, are what it's all for.

# *Forever with You*

# Chapter One

"Three catastrophes before breakfast has got to be a record." Leyna Milan answered the phone call via Bluetooth without taking her eyes off the narrow winding road.

Her best friend, Emily, offered a cheerful laugh. "Your day is off to a great start, obviously."

"Another liquor order screw-up nobody seems to be able to straighten out. Twenty-seven draft beers, and they still manage to deliver two kegs I don't carry on tap." She'd resisted the urge to kick one of the kegs for being stuck in the middle of the restaurant, where it didn't belong. There was a strong possibility it would break her foot. Plus, it would ruin the toe of her favorite Louboutins, and she'd stopped wasting money on footwear the price of a car payment after she broke off her engagement to Richard. "What's up with you?"

Leyna could hear Emily's heels tapping against pavement, and she pictured the petite blonde crossing town square from her apartment over her cake shop, head tipped back, breathing in the fragrant spring air.

"On my way to the coffee house. I had an epiphany at three a.m. while brainstorming ideas for fresh new local events." She lowered her voice before continuing. "I think I might run for a seat on town council." A bell jingled as Emily entered Jolt Café. "I can already see it," she whispered. "Elect Emily Holland for Sapphire Springs town council. Am I crazy? You think I'm crazy, don't you?"

"No way, it's the best news I've heard this week. I'll be your campaign manager." Town council needed new blood, and Emily was full of great ideas. Leyna slowed and turned down a long driveway. "Let's strategize over lunch."

"Definitely. But while it may be the best news you've heard this week, it's not the biggest. You're not going to believe what Nana heard at book club last night."

Emily's Nana was the source of all their gossip. Normally Leyna would've been eager to hear the news, but she was distracted as a couple of reporters ducked out of the way when she drove around the bend. She lifted her hands from the steering wheel long enough to shake the tension out of her fingers. "Save it for lunch, I gotta go. Duty calls."

"Wait—"

A weather report on the local radio station replaced Emily's protesting.

Leyna parked her black Jetta in front of the gray

stone building that housed Wynter Estate headquarters. A breeze stirred the bed of ornamental grass surrounding the company sign, bending the long blades toward the manicured lawn.

Home of her new restaurant.

When Leyna inherited her grandfather's Italian bistro, part of the deal was to open a second location of Rosalia's at his best friend's winery, her own plans be damned.

She grabbed her laptop bag out of the back seat and, with her hand resting on the car door, paused. Thick smoke trailed from brushfires ablaze on the edges of the vineyard, and a deafening helicopter circled overhead—a desperate ploy to raise the temperature. According to the morning news, all of Niagara wine country scrambled to try to save their grape vines from a late bout of spring frost.

Given the weather debacle and Stefan Wynter's recent stroke, she'd been banking on today's meeting being postponed so she'd have more time to prepare for next week's catering job at the art gallery. No such luck. On the tail of the liquor order screw-up and one of her servers quitting via text message, Stefan had sent a cryptic email that it was crucial (in caps) that everyone attend today's meeting, as there would be an important announcement.

Previous meetings had been in the winter, before Stefan got sick, when a thick blanket of snow still covered the sleeping vineyard. Now the greening fields bustled with crew members. A reporter and cameraman paced the parking lot, asking anyone who resembled an employee if frost damage would compromise the year's vintage, and if the helicopter pushing down the warm air from the fires would really give them enough heat to save the vines.

To ward off questions, she allowed her long dark hair to fall over her face and chanced a glance past headquarters to Stefan's large house, nestled among sycamore trees, and the smaller guesthouse, with its dock on the lake.

Memories of swimming there with friends, of falling in love, flickered in her mind, and as always, she pushed them away. Though a mere fifteen minutes from downtown, she'd avoided wine country for years before this business arrangement.

Tearing her gaze away from the house, she made her way inside. Her arches already throbbed from the height of her heels, so she skipped the stairs and rode the elevator. Those damn heels were a great idea when she'd left the house, envisioning a day in her office.

With a ping, the elevator doors slid open, and Leyna stepped off into the reception area, already alive with ringing telephones and the buzzing of printers.

"Good morning, Ms. Milan," Stefan's assistant, Carolyn, said, punching a button on the phone and setting down the receiver. "Can I get you a coffee?"

"I'd love one, thank you."

Carolyn poured the hot brew into a paper cup and passed it to Leyna. "There's cream and sugar around the corner and blueberry scones I baked last night. I nuked them when I came in, so grab one while they're still warm," she added with a wink before turning back to the caller on hold.

A few staff members mingled in the boardroom,

whispering among themselves, so Leyna waved hello and chose a chair next to Les from accounting. He was too preoccupied with punching numbers into a calculator to offer small talk, which was perfect. She'd have a few minutes to look over her notes in case Stefan called on her to speak.

A hush fell over the room when Stefan surfaced in the doorway and hovered there. He spoke on his cell phone, jabbing his finger toward the ground with each quiet order he gave the person on the other end. Normally his deep complexion popped against his thin white cap of hair, but today he was pale. It was only a little over a week since he'd gotten out of the hospital. He stabbed at the screen of his phone before shoving it into the breast pocket of the sport coat that hung loose around his chest. With a sigh, he gripped his cane and hobbled into the room.

Not out of the woods yet. Her heart ached for the man who was the closest thing to a grandparent she had left.

Stefan surprised Leyna by taking the seat next to her, instead of his usual spot at the head of the table.

"Good morning, love." His deep eyes wrinkled with the warm greeting, and he placed a hand on her shoulder to ease into the chair while the others trickled to seats around the long conference table.

"You're looking well," she whispered. "I'm glad you're on the mend."

Stefan leaned his cane against the table and retrieved a stack of papers from his briefcase. "I'm tougher than a burnt steak." He winked before raising his voice to address the room. "We're waiting for one more to arrive."

Pushing up his sleeve to look at his watch, he let out a long, drawn-out sigh before plucking the phone from his pocket again and hammering out a message.

His daughter, Danielle, no doubt held up in a session with her personal trainer. It'd be too easy to get through a meeting without her constant interrupting.

Leyna tapped her pen against the lined paper in her notebook, smattering a constellation of blue dots across the page. Damn delayed meeting. Mondays were too busy for this. Maybe she could convince Stefan to stall on the restaurant a little longer—at least until she and her brother, Rob, could put their heads together to come up with a financial miracle so she could not only open the second restaurant but also buy the building next to Rosalia's on town square. She pulled out the realty information on the Blackhorse Theatre and the designs she'd been working on for a logo.

A risky idea—maybe even foolish, considering she had next to zero capital left after taking ownership of Rosalia's last summer and overhauling the tired restaurant to bring it into the twenty-first century, both structurally and aesthetically. But ever since a FOR SALE sign went up in the window next door, the building haunted her dreams. It shared a pedestrian alley with Rosalia's, which meant she could expand her back courtyard and double her patio seating, not to mention the perfect concert venue to host bigger acts than she could feasibly bring into a restaurant-lounge setting.

Securing the space wouldn't be such a pipe dream if it weren't for needing to solve the first problem at hand—pulling off this new restaurant at Wynter Estate.

"Stefan, since we have a minute, I wondered if we could talk about the timeline for the new restaurant. There's some stuff on my end I'd like to fig—"

"Hold that thought," he apologized, pulling the vibrating cell phone out of his jacket, and turning away from her to answer the call. After a short conversation, he turned back to face the group.

"We'll begin," he bellowed, silencing the whispers that had morphed to a low murmur in the short time he'd been on the phone. "All hell is breaking loose here today, and we've all got other things to get to."

Stefan passed Leyna a stack of agendas. She took one off the top before passing the pile to Les. She glanced down at the document and noticed the last topic of discussion was "announcement."

Way to keep it cryptic.

Stefan recapped the previous meeting and worked through the first few points on his agenda, ticking each one off the list.

The end of April was still too chilly to warrant air-conditioning—and for the low neckline of her camisole. She pinched her pale pink cardigan closed at the neck, sipped her coffee, and tuned back in to Stefan, who discussed ideas for upcoming summer events. He was a man to be admired. He'd famously built Wynter Estate from the ground up, planting his first rows of cabernet sauvignon after his land proved to be too grainy and low in nutrients for growing pear trees. Or something to that effect.

"The Sip and Savor Festival is fast approaching,"

Stefan was saying. He placed a chilly wrinkled hand over Leyna's. "We are thrilled to have Rosalia's new chef, Marcel, catering our summer solstice tasting in the vineyard, and Carolyn informed me on my way in this morning that the event is officially sold out."

A mumble of approval erupted, and Leyna's eyebrows shot upward. Sold out already? She'd barely promoted it. The Sip and Savor Festival took over Sapphire Springs for two weeks each June. Local wineries hosted special events to launch their latest vintages. Wynter's summer solstice tasting was always one of the highlights of the festival.

Stefan turned to her. "It's all thanks to your savvy business sense and that glowing review in *The Post*. Leyna, is there any chance Marcel can bend on his numbers, so we can open up more tickets?"

She scrawled a reminder to send a thank-you note to Marcel's buddy at the newspaper for the favor. "I'll ask him and get back to you, but I'm sure we can handle an extra fifty people." They would whether he liked it or not.

"Excellent." Stefan beamed, and jotted something down on his agenda. "Get back to me when you've discussed it with him. There's a case of samples waiting for you downstairs. I've suggested pairings to go with each wine but will leave the final menu selections up to you and your team. The sooner you can get back to me with confirmation, the better, so we can move forward with print material."

She nodded, flipping her day planner to the end of the week to task herself with following up.

Stefan went on to other matters. “Many have expressed concerns about this cold snap in the weather and the effect it could have on our yields.” He pushed his chair away from the table a little and adjusted his posture. “I’ll tell you all the same thing I’ve been saying for forty years. Any farmer worth the dirt under his nails understands one thing.”

“Mother Nature will always have you by the balls.” The voice, low and husky, came from the doorway.

Midsentence, Leyna stopped writing. She’d know that voice anywhere.

“Nice of you to join us, Jason,” Stefan said, turning toward the door.

She stopped breathing.

A drum solo couldn’t have drowned out the hammering of her heart.

“Sorry I’m late.” He pushed off the door jamb. “It’s a shit show out there.”

He mumbled something else, too low to detect.

Obviously she’d turned the alarm off this morning instead of hitting snooze and somehow the ex of all exes scored a cameo appearance in her dream, because this could not be happening.

“Sit down,” Stefan commanded, kicking an empty chair under the table so it rolled toward Jay.

The chair directly across from her. Okay, call it a nightmare, actually.

His brown eyes fell on Leyna, and he hesitated before raking his fingers through his chestnut hair and crossing the room. Dirt fell from his Blundstone boots, leaving a trail across the gleaming floors.

Leyna jerked her head down to stare at her notebook, the words blurring together. Jay Wynter rising to the surface after eighteen years and strolling into a staff meeting at Wynter Estate? No way in hell. Heat crept up the back of her neck and pulsated in her cheeks. Why was it so damn hot in here all of a sudden?

Without raising her head, she rolled her gaze toward Stefan. His mouth formed a crease, and he looked away.

"Most of you know my grandson, Jason," Stefan began, glancing around the room at everyone but Leyna. "For those who don't, I'll give a brief introduction. Jason's been working in this industry since he used to toddle around behind me in the vineyard. The last eighteen years he's divided his time between Wynter Estate and various wineries throughout France—mostly Burgundy, experimenting with organic growing practices and modern irrigation systems—things I considered fluff until a few years back, when his efforts started winning him awards in the wine world. He's late, didn't bother to shave, and couldn't have dressed less professionally if he'd tried…but he's a hell of a vintner."

Jay's back went straight, and he glanced down at his worn Pearl Jam T-shirt and the tanned knee poking out of his faded jeans.

The smoke that had been curling over the vineyard when she arrived wafted off of him, wrapping its bony fingers around Leyna's throat. She reached for her coffee.

"Given my recent health scare, he's come back to help out," Stefan said. "Please excuse his appearance. He arrived just in time to be up all night dealing with this weather fiasco on my behalf." He clasped his hands together on the table and paused a moment before going on. "Which brings me to my announcement—after the Sip and Savor Festival in June, I'll be retiring as CEO of Wynter Estate and naming Jason as my successor."

Leyna's coffee lodged somewhere in the back of her throat, refusing to go down and leaving her no choice but to give into a fit of coughing. Les scrambled to pound her back.

Jay's mouth dropped open, and his wide eyes stared at Stefan.

The hum of the air conditioner kicking in nearly catapulted Leyna from her chair. Successor? Jay? No. Nope. Nope. Nope. The only successor worse than Danielle was her fickle son.

"I know my decision to retire comes as a shock to everyone," Stefan said, "but I'm following the advice of my doctors."

"The place won't be the same without you," one of the vineyard crew said from the far end of the table.

"Don't worry, I'll still be around. I'm just handing over the responsibilities. Now," he slapped the stack of papers in front of him. "I've reversed the order of our agenda. The next item to be discussed was the progress on Rosalia's new restaurant at Wynter Estate."

Jay inched forward in his chair, and the sleeve of his T-shirt crept up to reveal the edge of a small tattoo. "New restaurant?" He studied Stefan and then Leyna.

"I'll catch you up later," Stefan said, before focusing on the group. "Most of you have heard the buzz about the new restaurant, but we've yet to discuss it in a full staff meeting." He turned to Leyna, his smile warm. "Unless you've been living under a rock, you'd have heard about Leyna Milan stepping up to revamp her grandfather's Italian restaurant. Joe Leone was my best friend for fifty years. Two years ago, we got to talking about our ailing health, the future of our family businesses, and the future of the economy in general. Both businesses were stable, but Joe and I brainstormed ideas and began considering how the two companies could complement one another."

The room remained silent while Stefan went on. "We've decided to use a section of the Renaissance Road vineyard for the new restaurant. There's more than enough untouched land for the building and parking lot."

Though she'd been in on the planning since her grandfather's death a year ago, none of Stefan's words sunk in. Mouths moved, but the words were drowned out by flooding in her ears, like she struggled underwater.

Jay's brow was furrowed, and he had yet to close his mouth. Clearly, he thought his grandfather went off the deep end. "Renaissance Road? Last time I checked that land belonged to me."

"I will catch you up *later*," Stefan repeated with a force that silenced Jay. Speaking to the group again, his voice softened. "We'll be using the same designer who oversaw Rosalia's rebranding last year, for a look and feel that will complement the existing restaurant."

Breathe, nod, repeat.

Jay Wynter—her first boyfriend, first love, first everything was stepping up as head of the company she was partnering with. He also occupied the chair opposite her, and his presence hung in the air, robbing her of oxygen, like the smoke from the smoldering fires outside.

Stefan wrapped things up, and Leyna chanced a glance at Jay. Deep-set eyes, dark as chocolate, bore across the table.

"That's all for today. Meeting adjourned," Stefan announced, pounding his fist against the oak table like a judge, earning a few chuckles from around the table.

Leyna snapped out of the daze and shoved her chair away from the table. "Stefan, a word?"

"Me first," Jay said, already standing with his arms crossed.

"We have much to discuss," Stefan said, buttoning his sport coat with some difficulty. "But it'll have to wait." He closed his fingers around his cane as staff trickled out of the room. "I have a conference call." He hoisted his bag onto his shoulder and headed for the door, the room constricting with each measured step he took toward the elevator.

Jay rubbed his fingers across the scruff on his chin before starting around the table toward her. "Look—"

"Don't," she warned. She preferred the distance of the table between them. Hands trembling, she gathered her papers, shoving them into her laptop bag in no particular order. To her dismay, a few scattered across the table onto the floor, and Jay bent down.

From her side, she knelt under the table and froze, inches from his face. "I've got it."

He leaned back, squatting, and picked the pages off the floor. His gaze traveled partway up her legs before he darted his eyes away and glanced down at the realty information and her logo designs.

Her face burned, and she tugged on her gray pencil skirt, willing it to be a few inches longer. "I said I've got it."

Saying nothing, he passed her the pages, his callused fingertips brushing against hers, sending a shiver from her ankles all the way up to her neck.

Fisting the gaping opening of her cardigan again, she fumbled to zip the papers inside her bag with her free hand. Over the years, she'd envisioned all sorts of scenarios where she ran into Jay Wynter—rehearsed what she'd say if she ever saw him again. She'd be calm and collected, confident, indifferent. Why were all those calculated snubs escaping her the moment she laid eyes on those gentle hands that used to comb through her hair until she fell asleep?

She had to break the silence. Say something. Anything. Clearing her throat, she forced her gaze to his. "So you're back."

"Seems that way."

He held the eye contact—a silent challenge, she was certain. Under the layer of smoke, he smelled like the outdoors, and immediately she knew he was one of the crew members she'd paused to watch on her way in to the meeting. The scruff on his face glinted with silver, a rough contrast to his soft lips. He'd grown his hair out a little, too, and wore it sort of messy. It suited him.

Enough with the small talk. The hardwood floor was

cold on her bare knees, and the last thing she expected to be doing today was crawling under a table with Jay Wynter. She pushed off the floor, smacking her head against the table, hard.

"Agh," she groaned, cupping the back of her head with her hand.

"Whoa," Jay's lazy smile morphed into a worried frown. Leaning forward, he gripped her shoulders, steadying her. Are you okay?"

It hurt. Almost as much as her pride. "I'm fine," she said through clenched teeth.

He released his hold, but not before his thumb grazed her collarbone, igniting her nerve endings again. Rising cautiously, she smoothed her skirt. "I'm late for another meeting."

He surfaced on his side of the table, lips parting into a grin.

With what little confidence she could muster, she held her head high and marched toward the door, heels clacking against the floor.

"Leyna," Jay called behind her.

She whirled back around. "What?"

He lowered into the chair and spun half a turn so he faced her, propped an elbow on the armrest, and lowered his chin into his hand. His fingers failed to mask the smirk tugging at the corners of his mouth. "It's really good to see you."

On a long sigh, she whipped back around and marched out the door, eyes set on the elevator.

And that made four catastrophes before breakfast.

# Chapter Two

Jay pounded his fist against Stefan's office door.

"It's open."

Turning the knob, he stepped inside the bright corner office and closed the door behind him.

"Jason, we're going to have to work on your punctuality." Stefan folded his hands on the desk. "When you're running the show, you can't be late for your own meetings."

The stroke had twisted the left side of his mouth into an almost permanent grin, and the slight slur in Stefan's speech made Jay's chest ache. The sport coat he'd been wearing in the meeting hung on the back of his chair, and he'd rolled up the sleeves of his shirt, revealing a plethora of purple bruises from the poking and prodding he'd received in the hospital. A tingling crept into Jay's legs, cementing them in place, but he pushed forward, despite growing weaker with each uneven step toward the heavy armchair opposite Stefan's desk.

Stefan Wynter was the strongest man in the world to Jay. But now…gone was the tall, rugged man who'd been a constant in his life since his mother unloaded him at eight years old. In the five months since Jay had seen him, he'd withered away to a gaunt shadow of his former self.

Growing up without a father was something that damaged some kids—leaving them with voids they could spend their whole lives trying to fill, but Jay never took any interest in learning about the biological father who hadn't wanted him or the seventeen-year-old girl carrying his child. The man meant nothing to him, of that he was certain. Jay was definitely one hundred percent Wynter.

Stefan picked up a remote off his desk and pressed a button, bringing classical music to the speakers—a sure sign he wanted to drown out their conversation to potential eavesdroppers.

"What can I do for you?"

Jay leaned forward in the chair and cleared his throat, opting to approach the issue with a bit less force than he'd earlier imagined. "You can start by explaining this retirement curve ball, and then tell me how you and Joe dreamed up a new restaurant on *my land* that I already had marked for syrah. That might catch me up, as you said back there in the meeting."

"Lose the attitude." Stefan pointed a stubby finger at Jay. "My retirement shouldn't come as a surprise. I'm damn near eighty years old."

Jay shrank a little and softened his voice. "I get that, and if we were talking about anyone else, I wouldn't be surprised, but Wynter Estate is your life. I guess I thought you'd have a harder time walking away."

Stefan rolled away from the desk and got up to peer out the floor-to-ceiling window overlooking the cabernet franc plot. He jingled change in his pants pocket and spoke with his back to Jay. "I'm hardly walking away. I'll still be here for guidance. Besides, I meant what I said back there." He turned now and gave Jay a long look. "You're a brilliant vintner—the best there is. There's nobody I have more faith in to carry on my legacy."

Jay swallowed hard, face burning from the compliment, as it had in the meeting. "I'm good out *there*." He raised an arm and pointed to the vineyard sprawling outside the window. "I don't know the first thing about finance, or marketing, or running a company. Not to mention the way my brain scrambles every single thing I try to read."

"We've got people managing those departments," Stefan offered, skipping over the dyslexia remark. "Besides, you know who is good at those things? Your Leyna."

The mention of her name sparked an image of her long, slim legs in that prim skirt. He cleared his throat. "You shouldn't call her *my* Leyna. She hasn't been that in a very long time. And you didn't mention anything about a restaurant the last time we discussed the future of Wynter Estate." In fact, it seemed it had been mentioned to everybody *but* him. "Given your recent health scare, the timing couldn't be worse. The idea is ludicrous."

"That's where you're wrong." Stefan moved back to the desk and sat. "People like to spend a day touring wine country, but this area lacks options to bridge afternoon into evening. More wineries need a restaurant on site, so I decided if nobody else was going to seize the opportunity, we would. But it's got to be reputable—a place that's tried and true. That," he said, pointing his finger on the desk, "is why I want Rosalia's. And now, with the makeover, it's got marquee value that will up our destination factor.

"Leyna overhauled the place after Joe passed. Big-shot chef, classy atmosphere. Your culinary experience will benefit her, and the second location in wine country opens her doors to an entirely different clientele than downtown. It will raise the profiles of both businesses. I can already see it." He gazed past an outstretched hand, toward the sleek black sofa on the far side of the room. "It's the best idea I've had in years."

Jay eyed his grandfather. He was seriously suggesting they partner with the former love of Jay's life—the girl he let get away. More like set free. Christ, had the man lost his mind in the stroke, too?

"She's still a sore spot for you."

That was one way of putting it. Rather than confirm the suspicion, Jay plugged on. "You've set us up as business partners without even bothering to include us in any of the planning."

"Until I was faced with retirement, it didn't concern you, Jason, and Leyna's been in on the planning since Joe passed." Stefan smirked. "Joe wasn't on board with her taking over at first, believe me, but her parents already had their hands full with the bed and breakfast. I think he hoped Rob would step up, being the grandson and all that, but Rob's dedicated to his job at the bank." Rubbing his chin, he went on. "He underestimated Leyna. Nothing against Joe, but he was an old-fashioned sort. Not a hipster like me."

He slapped his thick hand on the desk to reinforce the joke, and laughter worked up his throat. "That Leyna…She's got what it takes. I could see that a long time ago."

Still hung up on Stefan's use of the word *hipster*, Jay gave his head a shake. "Has it even occurred to you that she probably still hates me more than anyone on this planet after the way I treated her when I left?"

When he was twenty years old, Leyna Milan had been his entire world, and that scared Jay to death. She'd started to hint about not going away to school—staying in Sapphire Springs so they could be closer to each other—and had practically been naming their kids, for God's sake. Breaking up with Leyna was by far the hardest thing he'd ever done. He'd told himself he put her first, but no amount of justifying could ever erase the anguish and betrayal in her eyes or her sobs of despair when he told her he was leaving Sapphire Springs. She'd begged him not to go, and it gutted him, but in the end he'd turned his back on her and walked away. Little wonder she'd spent the next eighteen years hating his guts.

The longer he stayed away, the harder it became to come back.

Stefan's distorted face didn't hide his smirk. "There's a fine line between love and hate, Jason."

Not from Leyna's perspective, apparently.

"We need to reinvent ourselves. The past few vintages were gems, but we were out of the playing field a long time after the ice storm and replant. The world went on without us. Joe and I were concerned that the businesses in their current states would be something of a burden. Times are changing, and both businesses required reviving." Stefan tented his hands like Mr. Burns. "Rosalia's needs to branch out and expand their market. Wynter Estate needs a leg up on our competitors. The new restaurant will do that for us both."

Headaches. The jet lag hadn't even hit him yet, and there were already headaches.

Stefan continued to fill him in. "With festival season approaching, we should be focusing on local business, and we need more of a social media presence, too. Do you know anything about this Twittle, or whatever they call that damn thing on the internet?"

Jay eyed the ceiling in disbelief. "You've heard of Twitter?"

"I'm old, I'm not dead."

For the second time in mere minutes, Jay gave his head a shake. "Look, Pop, I have no problem helping out, but I'm no good behind a desk or in front of a computer. Besides, are you sure partnering with Wynter is how Leyna wants to expand her market? Because from what I gather, she wants to buy the Blackhorse and turn it into a concert venue." At least according to the notes she dropped on the floor.

Stefan's eyes darted left before his forehead folded into a mass of wrinkles. "She's mentioned those ideas in passing, but it's castles in the sky. This restaurant is a win-win, and it's a done deal. The decision was made before Leyna inherited Rosalia's and I decided to retire. We're all legally bound. Whether the two of you like it or not, it's happening."

Jay had been working at Wynter Estate since he was old enough to hold a pair of pruning shears, and he spent his teenage years pruning obsessively from dawn until dusk, every single day Stefan let him take off school. His hands, blistered raw, would sting with every flex, and beads of sweat would drip down his spine, dampening his worn T-shirt. It was tough, but he'd loved every agonizing second.

He gazed out the window, past the vineyard, where the lake glistened in the sunlight. In a lot of ways, what Stefan proposed epitomized everything he'd ever wanted at twenty years old. But his grandfather, though a brilliant winemaker, had been set in his ways and quick to shrug off a lot of the organic vineyard practices Jay wanted to pursue. Bitterness had begun to build and left him fed up with being treated like an inadequate kid.

His mother and stepfather Cass, on one of their brief stints living back in Sapphire Springs when Cass's investments had gone south, had gotten wind that he and Leyna were sneaking out sometimes to spend the night together. She threw a fit, calling Leyna a tramp and going on about how she wanted more for her son than to ruin his life by knocking up Joe Leone's granddaughter.

*Like I ruined yours?* A few days later, his grandfather surprised him with the news that he'd scored Jay an apprenticeship in France. Conveniently, Cass had sprung for a backpacking trip so Jay could go away and "find himself hair" before it started. It had felt to Jay like everyone just wanted to be rid of him.

In France he'd climbed his way from vineyard to vineyard to the very impressive top, without anyone ever suspecting his dyslexia. Moving there gave him a clean slate. He wasn't typecast as some screwed-up teenager who only had a job because he was the boss's grandson. They respected his knowledge and valued his skills, and that mattered.

Jay shrugged. "This only affects me if I decide to step up as head of Wynter."

Stefan's eyes narrowed. *"If?"*

Before leaving Burgundy, Jay's boss, Frank, had hinted at offering him a position as head of vineyard operations. If they nabbed the international award their estate pinot noir vied for, Jay's stock would go through the roof and the promotion would be in the bag.

Still, it wasn't Wynter Estate.

The answer to this dilemma would've been a simple no, had he not been facing the man who taught him everything or gotten nose to nose with the woman who had held his heart as long as he could remember. Pushing his hands into his pockets, Jay turned away to pace across the plush rug in the middle of the floor. "I've got a job in Burgundy, Pop. A life."

One without baggage.

Stefan rose from the chair, sending it reeling back against the wall. "You're hiding in Burgundy, and we both know it. You came back here ten years ago after the ice storm and dealt with the damage and the replant, no questions asked. You told me you wanted this company someday—hell, you saved it single-handedly. *Five* years ago, you told me you were ready to commit, and then you just took off the moment Leyna's engagement announcement hit the newspaper. I looked the other way that time, because I knew what that did to you, but this time, I need you to man up."

Stunned, Jay turned to face Stefan. Not once had his grandfather ever called him out on his reasons for his abrupt departure five years ago. He fumbled to come up with a response. "We both know there're a lot of people—family and crew—who think I don't deserve what you're trying to hand me. That I don't have what it takes."

"Nonsense." Stefan silenced him. "I don't give a rat's ass what anyone thinks, and neither should you."

Jay peered into Stefan's dark eyes. "But they're not wrong."

"They *are* wrong," Stefan snapped, drilling his cane into the rug. "I won't listen to you belittle yourself. Our single vineyard pinot noir won a gold medal last year. Whose idea was it all those years ago to expand on pinot noir because New World pinot was becoming a *big deal* and he didn't want Wynter to miss that boat?"

He moved ahead, closing in on Jay's space. "Who convinced me we had the perfect conditions to produce something that could rival Burgundy? Who planted those vines with his very own hands, nurtured them, and practically monitored their pulse while coaxing them to grow?"

Stefan's voice grew louder with each step forward, until he jabbed his finger into Jay's chest. "When this cold snap threatened, who jumped into action from halfway across the world to arrange a helicopter and then waited up all night in his truck monitoring the temperature and stoking fires to gain us enough heat to save this vintage?"

"Okay, okay, calm down." The last thing he needed was Pop getting worked up and having a setback because of him. He tossed his hands in the air. "I'll think about giving it a shot."

His grandfather's lip pulled up at the corner and his expression softened. "I blame your mother for your insecurities. She filled your head with doubts about yourself and your abilities all those years ago, and made you believe being dyslexic meant that you weren't good enough—for the winery, for Leyna, for anything... My only regret in life is that I didn't try harder to convince you that you were. That you *are*. I'll rectify that mistake if it's the last thing I do."

Jay raised a hand to halt the conversation. "Stop with the *lasts*. You sound all cryptic, and I don't like you talking that way."

Stefan put an arm around Jay's shoulder and led him back to the window. "All I ask is that you at least take time to think things through before you turn down my offer. After harvest, if you decide you don't want Wynter Estate, then I'll accept that, but don't back down because you're afraid you can't handle it. If I believed that, I wouldn't be handing it to you."

Wanting it wasn't the issue. He wanted it more than anything—had since he was eight years old—but he wasn't cut out to run a company. As if severe dyslexia weren't enough of a hindrance, he was nowhere near good enough to fill his grandfather's shoes. If he dropped the ball this time, a legacy forty years in the making was at stake.

"What's the other option?" he asked, stealing a glance at Stefan, and bracing himself for the answer.

Stefan's mouth formed a tight crease. "Your mother and Cass have been cozying up to me. Of course, having no training in the business, they would be forced to hand over vineyard control to outside sources."

Jay's stomach plummeted. His stepfather, Cass, was a sly businessman. He could run a company, but he didn't have the first clue about growing grapes. Hell, his mother probably knew more about it than Cass. Their interest was no doubt based on Wynter having achieved a certain level of prestige the last few years. They'd never give a second thought to the integrity of the wine. Instead of keeping yields down to ensure a higher-quality product, they'd cut corners and overproduce. Their biggest concern would be how fast they could get it from the vine to the dinner table. In Cass Nixon's world, the bottom line was measured in dollars and cents.

No way in hell would Jay stand by while they corrupted Wynter Estate, and his grandfather had banked on that fact.

Taking the season to make up his mind seemed like a

fair compromise for them both. He'd be around to run the vineyard while his grandfather got back on his feet—plus he would have time to get used to the idea of working with Leyna.

"Okay," he said, tilting his head down to meet Stefan's gaze. "I'll stay until after harvest. I won't commit to anything more until we see how the season goes, but you need wind machines before next spring—no matter how much it costs. Considering what you're going to pay for these helicopters, it would be worth it in the long run."

Stefan grinned and opened his bottom drawer, where he kept his stash of cigars. "That's my boy." He struck a match and smoke curled out the corner of his mouth, drifting past the cigar.

Jay plucked it from his mouth to steal a puff. He eyed him through the thick gray smoke. "Thought they told you to quit."

"They tell everyone to quit," Stefan grumbled. "Old Grandfather David smoked till he was a hundred. Damn doctors don't know what they're talking about half the time anyway. To hell with them all!"

Well, there you had it. Whatever lasting effects the stroke had had, his grandfather's spirit remained the same. There was no point in arguing with Stefan Wynter. The man had a mind of his own. "Someone should have called me the minute they took you in the ambulance. There's no excuse for it taking almost a week."

"Your mother wanted to wait until she had more details." He slapped him on the shoulder. "Besides, you're a busy guy."

Busy, sure, gallivanting around Amsterdam, sweet-talking Nadia, the sexy bartender who mixed him sidecars all night, while his grandfather recovered in a hospital bed. The whole thing infuriated him, and he made a mental note to have a little chat with his mother. "I'll get the lowdown straight from the horse's mouth at your next doctor appointment, so I can keep you on track."

Stefan rubbed his hand over the butt of his cane. "You've got bigger things to worry about than keeping me on track. Leyna was fired up after the meeting and sent me an angry email. You know how she can be. I'm going to need you to smooth things over. There's a gallery opening next week down at the harbor, and Rosalia's is catering. Take my invitation and find a way to talk to her. Get us back in her good graces."

More headaches. Jay nodded, visualizing her full glossy lips, inches from his under that boardroom table. He pulled out his phone and sent a quick text to his boss, Frank, saying that he'd be in Sapphire Springs a little longer than planned. He owed his grandfather that much. Besides, when Stefan Wynter wanted something, he didn't let up until it was a done deal.

Halfway to his truck, Jay caught sight of his mother and stepfather emerging from their BMW. Her heels clacked against the pavement at a rapid pace as she approached.

"Jason." She came at him with open arms. "You're looking... worn, but well. It's great to see you."

"Hi, Mom." Jay returned the hug, hands resting on her bony back. She'd lost weight again.

"You've been smoking cigars with Dad."

Cass winked. "Oh, sweetheart, lay off the boy. The smell is coming from the fires in the vineyard."

Jay extended an arm to Cass and offered a handshake.

"Good to see you, Jay." Cass removed his sunglasses. More gray flecked his dark hair than the last time Jay had seen them. His mother, of course, still went to great lengths to mask her age.

Danielle met Cass after growing bored with her hometown and leaving Jay in the care of his grandfather. They married quickly and traveled the world on Cass's dime, at least while his investments ran hot. The rare times she visited were clouded by turmoil. Danielle Nixon thrived on melodrama.

Still, Jay had always made excuses for his mother's absence—she traveled all the time for her charity work, brought him back lavish souvenirs. In reality, she lived less than two hours away.

"We were just coming to have a chat with Dad. We weren't made aware of this morning's meeting." Danielle pushed her dark sunglasses up the bridge of her nose. "I guess we missed the retirement announcement."

Pop had had the foresight to avoid a scene over his choice of successors.

"Retiring, my ass." Cass draped an arm around Danielle's waist and rested his hand on her hip. "I'll believe it when I see it. His recovery from the stroke has been amazing."

"Yeah, about that." Jay folded his arms. "I wish you would've called me sooner, Mom. Finding out after

Pop had already spent days in the hospital was pretty unsettling."

She reached out and clasped his hand. "I know, Jason, but we didn't want to alarm you before we had all the details. The clot buster the paramedics administered on the way to the hospital worked wonders. If he's diligent with his therapy, he'll have few lasting effects. It didn't seem worth upsetting you."

Jay's shoulders tensed. "I don't need protecting. I'm not a child."

"Well now that you're here, you'll be kept in the loop." Danielle patted his arm. "Don't worry about this retirement stuff or let Dad talk you into committing to anything here with the winery. I know he plans to try to involve you, but sometimes he forgets you've got a life of your own. Cass and I will do our best to rein him in."

Doting like this wasn't her style. Something was up. "No need to rein him in. We're on the same page, at least for the time being. Now, if you'll excuse me, I've neglected the crew half the morning."

When Jay reached his truck, he glanced back at headquarters, where his mother and Cass hurried toward the main entrance.

# Chapter Three

Leyna ducked under the black awning of Rosalia's and unlocked the heavy glass door. A layer of tension brought on by Jay Wynter receded the moment she stepped inside the cozy restaurant. Roasted garlic mingled with tomato and basil, the intoxicating aroma drawing her across the wide plank floors and back toward the bar.

Propped against one of the wooden stools was the day's specials board, presented in the chef's creative penmanship. Nona's signature minestrone soup wafted from the kitchen, reminding her she'd skipped breakfast. No need for the vibrant chalk to spell it out. That mouthwatering smell had been meeting her off the school bus since she was six, spending after-school hours at the restaurant until her parents finished work.

With the chalkboard in tow, she hurried toward the entrance to set it up on the brick sidewalk. Laughter trickled down the tree-lined street from where a team of guys unloaded wrought iron benches from a municipal truck and set to work positioning them next to the oversized flowerpots placed next to every lamppost.

In just a few weeks, tourists would flood quaint little Sapphire Springs to tour vineyards, enjoy live theater, shop local businesses, and dine on outdoor patios on their way to and from Niagara Falls.

Turning on her heel, she headed back inside and glanced at her vibrating phone. The text from her mother invited her to dinner. At least from what she could tell.

Sinner Tomoro? Spaghettil and mestballs

Nina Milan had just gotten her first smartphone and was still a little sloppy with the typing. She never bothered texting on her old dinosaur flip phone, but since the novelty of upgrading, she checked in several times throughout the day. Leyna texted back to say she'd be there. As if she'd miss out on Mom's spicy spin on the family's signature dish. Family dinners were just one of the perks of being back home in Sapphire Springs.

Because her nerves vibrated like she'd already had four coffees, she opted for hot water and lemon. Cradling her favorite red mug with both hands, Leyna nudged one of the dark wooden chairs away from the nearest table and lowered onto it. Determined to shake off the image of Jay, she ran a finger over the embossed calligraphy on the front of the new black leather menu. ROSALIA'S—EST. 1968.

She'd been helping out in the restaurant since she was old enough to know a cucumber from a tomato, and by sixteen, knew she wanted to run it someday. She loved the rapid pace of working in a restaurant and the idea of carrying on a business with such a history in the community. Still, it had taken a lot of convincing for her grandfather to entrust her with Rosalia's. It seemed he'd rather have left it to anyone else, but his cancer prognosis had been dire, and since he wanted to work alongside the new owner to ease the transition, he'd had to make a decision.

Not that her grandfather didn't love her dearly; he was just a product of a different generation, one where women were expected to raise children, not take over the family business. For months, her parents and Rob rallied for her, until Gramp finally agreed to take a chance on her two months before he passed away.

Steam curled from her mug as she sipped her lemon water. Joe Leone may have finally given in and left his restaurant in her hands, but he was most certainly looking down, scrutinizing her every decision. In her darkest moments, she worried she couldn't pull it off. Not only did she have a lot to prove, but she intended to surpass any and all expectations.

The first step had been reviving a town fixture gone stale, and she hoped her grandparents would approve of the menu updates, the stripping of the walls down to the original brick, and the funky industrial lighting she'd chosen to modernize the atmosphere. Leyna needed to take measures to make Rosalia's her own. After all, the family business came with several conditions, the newest of which appeared to be working alongside her most significant ex.

And there she was, thinking about him again. She drummed her glossy black fingernails on the side of her mug and then grabbed the remote to change the music station to classic rock. Before Mick Jagger could paint a red door black, there was a tap from the front entrance, where Emily shifted from one strappy sandal to the other.

Leyna had texted her the moment her heels cleared the elevator at Wynter Estate.

"Hey." Leyna unlocked the door. "Thanks for coming so quickly."

Emily hurried past Leyna to the nearest table, where she offloaded her heavy purse. "You said it was an emergency."

On autopilot, Leyna set her cup behind the bar and checked the time on her phone. "Let's go snag a table at the coffee house before the lunch rush and I'll fill you in."

* * *

The sidewalks were filled with sunshine and the easy chatter of locals milling about town square. Magnolia petals blanketed the ground in a soft pink and white fluff, their lemony vanilla scent wafting through the air.

Leyna set her tray down across from Emily and pulled the chair away from the table, dragging the metal legs against the plank floors with a piercing scrape. "Did you know that those trees along the street are called cucumber trees? How did I not know that?"

A man with a laptop at the next table glared over his shoulder at them for the loud interruption, and Emily offered an apologetic smile. "Please tell me you aren't going to drink that coffee you ordered. You're jittery enough already. What gives?"

"I read it on one of the tourism flyers on the counter," Leyna continued, ignoring her friend's question as she lifted the top off her tuna sandwich to remove the pickle.

"Something's got you out of sorts." Emily helped herself to the pickle on Leyna's plate. "Let me guess, you decided to accept Mark Toner's business proposal."

Leyna furrowed her brow. "What?"

"I saw him leaving Rosalia's the other day with a little skip in his step. If you ask me, he wants to invest in a lot more than the restaurant." She raised her eyebrows.

Oh yes, how could she forget? Mark spent the bulk of their last conversation pitching said business proposal, declaring that somebody like him—translation: rich—was exactly what she needed to expand her restaurant.

She'd thought her inheritance would be enough to cover the renovations on the original location and front her contribution to the new restaurant, so she could use her personal savings to put a down payment on the Blackhorse. It would have been, if not for the bill from Mark's estate law office, breaking down all the fees owing from when her grandfather was sick and working on his will. Between that and the cost of the renovation, both her inheritance and personal savings were pretty much wiped out.

She wasn't completely in debt yet, but she certainly didn't have enough money left for a second restaurant, let alone the Blackhorse.

Mark had offered to invest a small fortune in Rosalia's. Seeing how the last meeting with her bookkeeper practically had her hyperventilating into a brown paper bag, she'd listened to his spiel with an open mind. The problem was, he only wanted to do so if she expanded into the Blackhorse Theatre. He wasn't the least bit interested in investing in a restaurant at Wynter Estate, and as much as she dreamed of buying the Blackhorse, it was a pipe dream. She was legally obligated to the partnership with the winery.

His touchy-feely hands suggested he wanted to invest more in their relationship than money anyway. No way would she accept an offer that came with those strings attached.

"I did not accept his business proposal. I've also told him I'm not interested in dating, and he said he's not, either," Leyna said, distracted by the Nolans, an elderly couple a few tables over, sharing one of the café's massive brownies. God, the two of them must be a hundred by now. For as long as she could remember, they walked around town square in the evenings, hand in hand. Something in her chest yearned for that kind of commitment, that kind of devotion. The kind of effortless love her parents had. Did it even exist anymore? Marsha Nolan reached across the table to rub a bit of frosting off Harold's chin, which made him tip his head back and laugh. Adorable. Her parents would be just like them in a few years.

"As far as relationships go, you could do a lot worse than Mark Toner." Emily paused to dab her mouth with her napkin and began counting on her fingers. "He's divorced, no kids, has tons of money, a stable job . . . I could go on if I put my mind to it. Plus he's a lot nicer than he was back in high school."

Leyna tore her eyes away from the Nolans and forced herself to focus. "I know, but he's still arrogant, and there's just . . ." She fluttered her fingers wishing her hands could do the explaining for her. "There's no spark."

Not a connection that spanned decades. "Besides, the last thing I need right now is a relationship."

"You're stubborn." Emily pointed a finger at Leyna. "You refuse to tell your parents you're broke, because you won't accept a handout. If you're not taking Mark up on his offer, did you at least manage to get a hold of your brother to discuss loan options for buying the theater? He was going to try to use his connections at the bank to help you figure this all out, wasn't he?"

"That didn't happen." When Leyna's hand trembled on the way to her coffee cup, she changed course and reached for the tall glass of water instead. She'd been working up to the Jay conversation and couldn't avoid it any longer. "Stefan sent a cryptic summons email first thing this morning. The meeting went on as planned. Well . . ." She shook her head to ward off the vision of Jay crouched under the table in the boardroom. "Not exactly as planned."

"Oh crap." Emily dropped her wrap onto her plate. "So you've heard the news."

"You knew?" Leyna asked through drawn eyebrows and a mouthful of tuna on rye. "Em, the return of an ex is major. How could you not have told me this?" She slapped her hand on the table, causing it to wobble from the impact, earning another harsh stare from laptop guy. "I was blindsided."

Emily poured an obscene amount of sugar into her coffee and added a copious amount of cream. She stirred until the color faded to a sickly off-white, a ploy to stall. "I tried to tell you on the phone this morning, and then when you had to go, I'd planned to break it to you over lunch."

Visions of jumping across the table and wringing Emily's neck Homer Simpson style clouded Leyna's thoughts. "Jay Wynter is code blue."

"I'm sorry, but my crystal ball was foggy, and I couldn't envision you'd get summoned to Wynter Estate before lunch. Obviously I would have sent you an emergency text, had I known where you were going."

Leyna tossed the rest of her sandwich onto the plate. She wasn't sure she could keep it down.

"You can't hide this time, Lane. We always knew he'd be back someday. You got off lucky all these years, living away and managing to avoid him on the rare occasions you did happen to be in Sapphire Springs at the same time. You could have crossed paths much sooner."

Valid. She'd hoped he'd stay away forever, though. No such luck. She drew in a long breath, pulled her chair in, and composed herself. "I know it was only a matter of time before he came back, but it really has nothing to do with me."

"Oh, come on." Emily snorted, combing her fingers through her blond hair. "Two seconds ago it was code blue. Of course it has to do with you. You guys were legendary in this town."

"Legendary for what? Going up in smoke?" The kind he smelled of, under the boardroom table.

Hot tamales.

Something fluttered in her stomach, and Leyna stirred her ice water with her straw, watching the lemon slices glide around the tall glass.

Emily waited a few beats. "Look, I'm not saying you guys will ever patch things up or anything, but his moving home has to have some impact on you, Leyna. For better or worse, the two of you have history. You never even cared about Richard the way you cared about him—and you were going to marry Richard!"

Leyna drained her water and sucked on the remaining ice cube. "Okay, even if that were true, it was a lifetime ago. The wounds have healed, and the scars have faded."

"So then why does it bug you so much?"

Oh, maybe because he was the love of her life? Because she'd let him closer than anyone, and he'd blindsided her the night after graduation by saying he didn't love her, and then immediately left town for an apprenticeship he hadn't once mentioned, never to be heard from again. "It's going to be...awkward." Leyna filled Emily in on

Stefan's retirement announcement. "Anyway, I'd like to think we could at least be civil to each other. It's not as though I still hate the guy for breaking my heart when we were nothing more than kids. He might even be married by now for all we know."

Her stomach rolled. What if he was married and she had to see him parade some perfect wife around town? She hadn't pondered that possibility and was too frazzled at the meeting to notice if he wore a wedding ring. Determined to keep her lunch down, she swallowed hard.

"He isn't married, Lane. We'd have heard about it. Haven't you ever creeped him on social media?"

"He doesn't have any social media," Leyna confirmed, embarrassed that she knew. "And whether he's single or not, I think we can both manage to live in this town and stay out of each other's way. I'm not about to let the return of Jay Wynter interfere with the life I've made. Sure, it'll be a little weird, seeing him around, but we'll have to put our differences aside, at least for the sake of business..." She trailed off as her mind began to race.

"Wait a minute." Leaning forward, Leyna braced both hands on the table. "Maybe I don't need to be anywhere near him. Maybe there's a way out of all this."

Emily cocked a brow.

Leyna rolled her gaze toward the sidewalk—for some reason people watching helped her think. "Humor me for a minute. What if Stefan stepping down negates the whole agreement somehow? The deal was, I open a restaurant with *him*, not with Jay, or anybody else." She nodded, letting the idea take shape, and stabbed a finger into the table. "This could be a loophole."

Emily's forehead wrinkled and she smirked. "Nice try, but you're grasping. You know what this whole thing sounds like to me? A matchmaking scheme between your grandfathers."

"No way." Leyna shook her head and pressed her back into the chair as music drifted through the speakers. "Stefan was all-in before the stroke. This Jay stuff is only happening because he's been given orders by his doctors to retire. It's probably the best solution he could come up with on short notice."

She gasped, bolting upright when her hand flew to her mouth. "Maybe he's not medically fit to make these kinds of decisions."

Emily covered her mouth to contain the coffee she'd just sipped and her shoulders began to shake with laughter. "Give it up. Stefan is not operating on damaged brain cells or clouded by meds. Apparently Jay's been very successful. Some wine magazine did a full spread. I also heard through the grapevine, no pun intended," she said with air quotes, "he was on vacation in Amsterdam when Stefan's stroke occurred. I guess when he heard the news he decided on the spot to come home. He dropped everything and was on the next flight out."

How noble.

"It's a good thing, too," Emily continued. "God knows Stefan isn't able to manage those vineyards anymore, even if he hadn't had the stroke. Jay must be ready to take over by now. How many years has it been?"

"Eighteen." Leyna responded without thinking. Shit. It wasn't like she kept track or anything.

Emily sat back in her chair, meeting Leyna's gaze. "Are you going to be okay?"

Leyna tucked her dark hair behind her ear. "Em, come on, the guy left me without a backward glance when I was still a kid. I'm not harboring any feelings, so don't worry about me. I got over him a million years ago."

Emily narrowed her eyes. "He was the first in a domino effect of failed relationships in your life, culminating with Richard, the sleaze. Not that I've had any better luck in the love department, but I wouldn't be a very good friend if I didn't worry. Now, having said that"—she cocked a brow and leaned forward on her elbows—"aren't you the least bit curious to find out if there's still chemistry between the two of you?"

Leyna's heart rate tripped up at the memory of Jay's thumb skimming across her collarbone. "Chemistry or not, I have no interest in Jay, or anyone else for that matter. I've got a business to focus on. Besides, there'll be tourists in town longer than him."

Emily shook her head, her crystal earrings moving back and forth like pendulums. "Not if Stefan's handing over the company."

Leyna helped herself to the glass of water Emily hadn't touched. "Sure, that's the plan, but we all know Jay has the staying power of a cheap perfume. He'll be gone the first sign of a crisis." Fingers crossed.

"Maybe," Emily said. "But the romantic in me is rooting for the two of you."

"Ha!" Leyna threw her head back with a sarcastic laugh. "Even if I were looking for a relationship, which I am not, Jay Wynter would be the absolute last person on this planet I would consider dating. Fool me once. Now." She pushed her chair away from the table and stood. "Ready to jet?"

They wormed their way around tables and onto the street. Leyna was about to change the subject to the town council when Emily tugged on her arm. "Shit, here comes Fuzzy. Don't tell him I'm considering running in the election. I haven't really thought it through yet, and you know how he gets."

Fuzzy Collins earned his nickname by going bald at age thirty. He was on his twelfth year as Sapphire Springs's mayor and showing no signs of giving up the title. He marched across the street and stepped up onto the brick sidewalk in a striped sweater layered over a dress shirt.

Before Emily could steer them into the bookstore, he waved a stack of flyers at them. "Ladies, we have important matters to discuss, and Emily, please don't kid yourself, I have the eyes of an eagle."

Despite the fact that he joined them sometimes for cocktails after work, when Fuzzy was in full-on mayor mode, it was like being addressed by the school principal.

"Oh hey, Fuzz," Emily greeted him, as though she hadn't seen him approaching.

Fuzzy gave his flyers a shake for good measure. "Town hall meeting Wednesday night to discuss events for the summer season. As small business owners, I expect you both to be in attendance." He fell into stride and followed them inside Rosalia's, waving to a few people getting seated for lunch.

Fuzzy arranged a pile of his flyers on the bar, fanning them out, like brochures at a travel agency. "If you'd been at the last meeting you'd know what a disaster I prevented with the flower pots. They wanted to put them out two weeks ago. Can you imagine, with the weather we've had? And, the committee ordered azaleas. Imagine. Of all the most ridiculous things I've ever—"

"Fuzzy, you can't leave those flyers there." Leyna gathered them up as quickly as they'd been set down. "Customers need to be able to sit at the bar. I'll find another spot for them, okay?"

"Oh, who sits at the bar anymore? It's so nineties."

If she weren't already pressed for time, his comment would have amused her. "Lots of people sit at the bar. You'd be surprised."

"Well, you better find a good spot for them, and not down that dark hallway to the washrooms, where you hang all the posters. The more people in attendance, the better. We're discussing fundraising efforts for the upgrades to the gazebo in town square and also this year's election. Need I remind you it isn't too late to throw your names in for town council? I told you both before I would nominate you, and the offer still stands."

He nudged Leyna with his elbow. "We could use somebody with your pizzazz."

Pizzazz? She'd never thought of herself as having pizzazz. Rob was the successful one of the family. The one with the stable job, the family, and the picket fence.

He had his shit together, and she'd always sort of paled in comparison.

"You must have all sorts of ideas," he continued. "All those years in the city."

She caught Emily masking a smirk and put an arm around Fuzzy to guide him back toward the front entrance. "I'll think about it, Fuzz, but things are hectic. It's coming up on tourist season."

"And if we all work together, it can be a record-breaking year for everyone," he said, backing out the door. "We can make Sapphire Springs a real destination."

"That's the spirit." She gave him a thumbs-up. "Thanks for the flyers."

She followed Fuzzy out onto the sidewalk, and something red caught her eye.

Dread kindled in the pit of her stomach as a sign on the window of the Blackhorse came into better view. SOLD. What the hell? The place had been vacant for more than six months, and out of nowhere, there were other interested buyers?

"Fuzzy, wait." Leyna pointed to the sign as Emily joined her on the sidewalk. "Who..." She fumbled to find words. "When..."

Emily eyed the sign and grabbed Leyna's arm, giving it a supportive squeeze. "Oh, Lane..."

"Oh yes, I just got the scoop at the bookstore," Fuzzy said, oblivious to Leyna's crushed heart. "It was a quick sale. Some kind of doughnut place. You know, one of those trendy new franchises that are all the rage in the cities. Everyone is up in arms. Imagine, a franchise, in Sapphire Springs. The council wasn't even consulted."

Leyna's vision of Rosalia's branching out slowly evaporated. Sure, it was a pipe dream, and she had more obvious priorities, but the place had sat vacant so long she'd begun to think it waited for her.

Doughnuts. She'd lost her concert venue to doughnuts.

# Chapter Four

Leyna drove down the gravel driveway to her little cottage on the lake and parked her car in its usual spot. The red tulips along the path to the lake had popped up about a week before, and the geraniums she'd planted in window boxes added a burst of coral to the weathered shingles of her cottage. Neither did a thing to brighten her mood. Since the SOLD sign had gone up at the Blackhorse last week, word had gotten out that a franchise was opening next to Rosalia's, and it was all anyone talked about. At least it took some focus off Jay being back.

"Doughnuts," she muttered, still hung up over it. So help her God, she'd never eat another doughnut again. She knew the type of place Fuzzy had described. There had been one down the street when she'd lived in Soho. The first few weeks it was open, crowds lined up down the block. Six months later, the novelty wore off.

The city held a special place in her heart. She'd been scared to death to move there on her own—away from her family and friends for the first time. She'd done a lot of growing there, as a person, and gained the confidence to tackle whatever life threw at her next.

"You're a long way from New York City now, Milan," she murmured, remembering her tiny loft, with its retro refrigerator and rickety fire escape. As much as she cherished her life in the city, coming home was what it had all been for. Her current digs had belonged to her grandfather and looked like something out of Martha's Vineyard.

Since Leyna was his sole beneficiary, she had inherited the cottage, along with Rosalia's and the savings he'd been stashing away for most of his life. Her family agreed it was only fair that as the one taking over responsibility for the restaurant, she get all his assets. It still baffled her that his life savings had taken such little time to spend. Since the renovations, she'd been strapped.

Plowing past a wave of nausea, she decided putting it out of her mind for the evening was best. She had all of forty-five minutes to change her clothes and get ready for the gallery opening.

She unlocked the door, and her black cat, Felix, greeted her with a yawn, stretching in the small patch of sunlight warming the floor in front of the glass doors. Beyond the doors her deck and pergola overlooked the lake. Even though she had been living in the cottage almost a year, she still caught herself stopping to admire the view sometimes.

She turned on the lamp, picked Felix up from his

sunny spot on the dark hardwood floor, and allowed him to snuggle into her neck as she paced back and forth around the room.

Word of Jay being back in town got around fast, too. People chatted about him everywhere from the gas station to the dry cleaner's. Bad news traveled at the speed of light.

In eighteen years she had almost been able to forget about Jay Wynter. Or, if not forget, at least move on. In fact, she rarely thought of him at all anymore.

When they were kids, he was little more than the jerk her older brother was attached to at the hip. Cut to tenth grade. She'd been digging books out of the bottom of her locker when she glanced up, and there he was, leaning against the brick wall. Hot tamales, he had the most gorgeous lean of any guy she'd ever seen. His good looks were effortless, straight out of a Gap ad.

No connection in her life had ever been like the one she'd had with Jay. She'd trusted him with her whole heart, and the future they spent countless nights under the stars planning was all that mattered. She'd go to college and get her business degree while he worked at Wynter Estate. Eventually they'd both be employed by their family businesses and get married and buy a house in Sapphire Springs—one of the old Queen Anne style homes they pointed out during their many drives in his truck. Before starting a family, they'd take a few nice vacations as a couple.

But as soon as she graduated he dropped his bombshell—he'd been accepted for an apprenticeship in

France for a year. After the initial shock wore off and the disappointment dissipated, she'd been supportive. One year wasn't such a long time in the grand scheme of things. She'd be away at college, and maybe knowing he wasn't in Sapphire Springs would make it easier for her to go. They'd make the distance thing work. She would wait for him, and before they knew it he'd be home again and they'd be together.

*Don't wait for me* had been his flat response. He didn't want any of those things anymore. It was just talk. *I don't love you. I don't even know what love is. We're just holding each other back, and I want more than this.* She'd been shell-shocked. The way she'd begged and pleaded with him to stay still practically made the bile rise up her throat.

A day later he took off to learn the ropes of wine-making, or whatever he'd called it, without a care in the world about what it would do to her—that she'd never in her life feel like *enough* ever again.

And now, he was back. Did it bother her? Damn right it bothered her. And the fact that it bothered her bothered her even more.

Mark Toner asking her out was like a measly puddle to an ocean now. She needed to stay away from men altogether, it seemed. As if reading her mind, Felix decided he'd had enough attention and began to squirm, a sign he wanted to get down. She let him jump to the couch, where he perched himself among the bold-colored cushions before settling onto the knit throw.

A copy of *Vines Magazine* had found its way into her

laptop bag, no doubt thanks to Emily, who had stopped by the restaurant earlier to check in. All throughout the afternoon, Leyna had found herself drifting toward it and then slinking away.

Since she was in the privacy of her own home and couldn't ignore it any longer, she whipped through the pages until she came to the infamous article titled "Heartbreak Grape," accompanied by a glossy photo of Jay standing in some French vineyard.

Interesting title.

She studied the photo with the eye of an art critic. His fashion sense hadn't evolved over the years. He wore faded jeans and a black T-shirt, which had always been typical. Behind him stretched an upward slope of vines, the myriad of greens disappearing into a molten sunset of corals and pinks.

Against her better judgment and quickening heart rate, she turned the page and began skimming through the interview about his success growing pinot noir. He talked about dividing his time between New York and Burgundy, and how he'd gone there to train under the most skilled growers in the business.

They mentioned a few awards, which he downplayed...

Blah blah blah.

On the verge of tossing the magazine aside, her eyes fell on the word *education.* She pulled the article closer to read what he had to say when they asked about training in Europe rather than going the traditional route of a formal education back home.

> Getting to grow grapes with some of the people who are the reason I grow grapes has been invaluable. All the degrees in the world can't compare to the knowledge of an eighty-year-old grower who's seen a hell of a lot more than some professor. Don't get me wrong—I have nothing against the university route, but it was never in the cards for me. Wine isn't just a result of numbers and chemistry. Some of the greatest wines on the planet, Champagne, for Christ's sake, happened by accident. For men like my grandfather, who can't give this up, wine isn't some case study they're being graded on; it's the blood running through their veins.

The local university had one of the best viticulture programs in the world, and Stefan's money easily could have paid for it. But college hadn't been in the cards for Jay because of his dyslexia, which he hadn't mentioned. He never did. He'd always accepted that it would be a hindrance to furthering his formal education.

Even back in grade school, it took Stefan months to convince Jay's teacher that he wasn't goofing off for attention because his mother abandoned him, that there was a legitimate learning disability that required experienced tutors. Jay ended up repeating second grade, but rather than admitting to the other kids that he had dyslexia, he told everyone he had failed on purpose so he could be in the same class as Rob. Most of them bought it, too, and assumed any special treatment he received was because his grandfather was a prominent man in the community.

Okay, enough with the memories of Jay. She shoved the magazine back into her bag. She had a gallery opening to cater, and if she didn't pull herself out of this funk, she'd never be ready on time.

* * *

Leyna pulled into the gallery parking lot. Three cases of wine to carry inside, and not a parking spot to be found.

"Great," she muttered, navigating around the congested parking lot. Who knew they'd get such a good turnout? She'd have to park all the way at the back of the lot, and the opening started in seven minutes. No matter how much preparing she did, things seldom went off flawlessly. She pulled into a spot, killed the engine, and got out of the car.

As her trunk popped open, a voice came from behind, startling her.

"We meet again."

She froze, eyes widening, and her heart began to thud at the recognition of Jay's voice. *I can do this.* She closed her eyes, took a deep breath, and turned around. "Jason." She nodded, her tone coated in ice. "I didn't expect to see you here." He looked more rested than the day she'd seen him at Wynter Estate.

Jay stuck his hands in his pockets and looked at the ground, pretending to kick a rock that wasn't there.

"Yeah. Pop got an invitation to the gallery opening,

but he wasn't feeling up to it, so he asked me to come in his place."

As she turned away to begin lifting boxes of wine out of her trunk, he stepped forward.

"Here, let me give you a hand carrying those inside."

His warm hand brushed against her arm when he reached for the box, and Leyna pulled away. "I've got it."

Her voice sounded nothing like her own. She forced herself to take it down an octave and lower the volume a notch. "I don't need help. I'll send someone out to get the rest."

"Don't be ridiculous, Leyna. I can carry the other two in for you. Will it kill you to let me help you?"

*Yes, actually.* "Fine." She stomped away in her high heels, not trusting herself to say anything more.

So much for getting through the gallery opening with a clear head.

"Wait a second," he called as he slammed the trunk and juggled the boxes, peering at their labels. "What are you doing, pouring this garbage?"

"You can leave it at the bar," she replied over her shoulder, ignoring his comment about the wine, smug with the knowledge that he'd probably never been more insulted in his life. Should she own up and tell him she donated wine she'd received as samples from a sales rep, or keep quiet and let it infuriate him?

No contest. The small victory gave her the upper hand long enough to pivot around to look at him one last time. "Welcome back, by the way... See you around."

By the time she delivered her case of wine to the

bar, her heartbeat had managed to slow down, but everything around her, the guests, the music, the art, all spun into a blur.

Of course he would show up when she least expected it. And he looked amazing, too, trading in the usual T-shirt and jeans for a black sport coat that accentuated his broad shoulders. Not to mention the hint of stubble highlighting his jawline again, even after Stefan had pointed it out to everyone in the meeting last week. The guy had always hated to shave.

If she didn't know him, if they didn't have a history that rivaled your pick of any primetime drama, she'd jump into gear before some other woman got her claws into him. They would, too. Even Leyna had to admit he was a catch.

Leyna's mom and dad approached, each with a glass of white wine. Leyna pulled her mom into a hug and gave her dad a quick peck on the cheek. "Thanks for coming. You both look great. Very handsome, Dad."

John ran a hand back over his slicked silver hair. "Thank you, thank you very much," he joked.

Nina snorted and elbowed him. "We wouldn't miss it, sweetheart. The food is incredible, and what a great turnout, too."

John leaned toward Leyna with his hand to his mouth, though he still spoke loud enough for Nina to hear. "Compliments to the chef. Those stuffed mushroom caps are even better than your mother's."

Nina grinned with an eye roll. "Let's not interrupt her work, John." She gave Leyna's arm a supportive squeeze.

"We know you're busy. Come see us tomorrow morning for coffee. I made biscotti."

They wandered off just as Mark waved at her.

"Leyna," he called from across the room. "You lose your phone again?"

She ignored the little dig, as she had his last few messages.

"Hi, Mark. What's up?"

"I was thinking maybe we could go for a drink later?" Mark whispered in her ear, his breathy invitation full of hope and Jack Daniel's. "You look like you've had a rough day."

He was a nice guy, but that hadn't stopped her from turning him down every time he asked her out, no matter how innocent the offer was presented. "I can't. I'm always the last to leave these things. I'll be exhausted."

"Ah, should have known. It's a valid excuse, so I can let it roll off without taking it too personally." He flashed perfectly whitened teeth. His gaze narrowed. "Have you given any more thought to my little business proposal?"

"It's a generous offer, Mark, but like I said before, I can't accept."

Unfazed, he trailed a finger down her bare arm. "I'll repeat what *I* said before…It's the answer to all your problems, and I don't see anybody else rushing to your rescue."

She backed out of his reach. "I'm surprised you haven't heard the news. The theater sold already, so I don't require rescuing." Silver lining, anyone? With the

Blackhorse off the table, she knew Mark's interest would fizzle. She needed to focus on the second restaurant anyway. It was, after all, the priority.

Out of the corner of her eye she caught a glimpse of Jay leaning against a post scowling at them from across the room. When he realized he'd been caught, he turned away, only to bump into her parents. Now they were all smiling, Mom hugging him and Dad shaking his hand.

Mark tilted his head as though he'd heard wrong, and he blinked several times before speaking. "I was away at a conference for the past week, but...That's impossible, I...Who the hell bought it?"

She stole one more glance over her shoulder at the happy reunion before shifting her gaze back to Mark. "Some doughnut franchise. I don't know any more than that."

He shook his head. "Wow, that must've happened quickly. I'm sorry, I know you kind of had your heart set on it."

Leyna forced a small smile. "Thanks. I've gotta get back to work." She wormed her way through the crowd. A breather in the ladies' room was in order. Leyna nabbed Emily on her way there.

"I need you for a minute," she muttered in Emily's ear and gave an apologetic smile to Dennis, an accountant who had Emily cornered.

"For crying out loud, I've been waiting for you to come to my rescue since you walked in the door. He was going on and on about the opera, and how he'd love for me to join him sometime. Can you imagine me at the opera? I'd pass out as soon as they dimmed the lights. What's going on?" she asked as an afterthought, noticing Leyna's tight grip on her arm.

"Two o'clock," Leyna hissed, dragging Emily into the ladies' room.

"What?" Emily looked puzzled, but at Leyna's raised eyebrow she stuck her head back out the door and scanned the room, her eyes falling on Jay brooding while he pretended to study a painting. "Ohhhhhh..."

"Stop staring!" Leyna hauled Emily back into the bathroom.

Emily adjusted the neckline of her light green dress—a color very few people would be able to pull off so well. "Wow. That's all I can come up with, Lane."

Leyna bent over and did a quick check to make sure all the stalls were empty before releasing a sharp exhale. "I ran into him in the parking lot." She leaned against the wall.

"And?" Emily prompted, "What happened?"

Leyna paced, her voice echoing throughout the empty room. "Nothing. We talked for about thirty seconds, and then I took off inside. I'd have rather had a few teeth pulled, but I survived."

"He looks amazing." Emily walked over to the mirror to smooth her hair across her forehead.

"I hadn't noticed." Her cell phone vibrated, and she checked the text message. "It's the kitchen. They need me. Look, if Jay tries to talk to me again, I need you to intercept, okay? Pretend you're having a crisis. I'll return the favor if I see Dennis corner you again."

Emily accepted the duty with a nod. "Deal. You better get to the kitchen. Let me know if you need any help."

* * *

After about thirty minutes of rubbing elbows with Sapphire Springs' finest, as well as ignoring their whispers and watching Mark Toner guard Leyna like some briefcase full of hundred-dollar bills, Jay decided his appearance at the gallery would be short-lived. He headed for the parking lot, grabbing one of Emily Holland's extravagant little cupcakes for the road.

Obviously Leyna didn't have the time or the interest to talk to him. A public event in front of half the town wasn't the place to smooth things over anyway. As he unlocked his truck a familiar voice surfaced behind him.

"Jay Wynter. Son of a bitch never calls, never writes..."

Jay grinned and shook his head before he turned. Tim Fraser, one of his oldest friends, and one of the few people he'd kept in touch with over the years, leaned on the railing of his boat shop. He sauntered down the steps and held out his hand.

"Been a while, Fraser."

Tim grabbed Jay in a bear hug. "Dude, I haven't been able to reach you for a couple of weeks. Where did you disappear to?"

"Amsterdam. I decided to take a little last-minute trip, but when I got the news Pop had a stroke I beelined it home. Aside from driving Pop to his appointments, I've been spending dawn till dark in the vineyard every day."

"How is he, anyway?"

"Well, the doctors say if he rests and follows orders, he could make a reasonable recovery, but you know how he is."

Tim shook his head. "Typical old people, huh?"

"Set in his ways and stubborn as hell."

Circling Jay's black '57 GM pickup truck, Tim ran his hand across the gleaming hood. "Damn, she's a beauty. The grille restoration is killer. Is the starter still causing you grief?"

"Depends on the day. At least I don't have to worry about it getting stolen, because nobody else can get it started."

"Just temperamental, that's all." Tim spoke to the truck as though it were a woman he tried to charm into bed.

"So how are things with you, anyway? Not attending the big gallery opening tonight?"

"I'll put in an appearance after I close up shop." Tim glanced over his shoulder at his store, a red building in the center of a strip of businesses along the marina, sided with clapboards or cedar shingles, all painted in bold colors. Locals referred to them as Crayola Row. "I've decided to run for a spot on the town council, so attending local functions is kind of expected."

Jay leaned his elbow on the hood of the truck. The engine was still warm. "Good for you, man. That's great."

Tim mirrored his pose. "Yeah, well I came into some money last year when my uncle passed away. I bought the two spaces on either side of the boat shop to expand into a year-round sporting goods store, with clothing and camping gear. The grand opening will be this fall, so it seems like a good time to get more involved in the community."

"If anyone can do it, you can," Jay offered. "I won't be surprised if you own all of Crayola Row someday." It was the truth. Tim was ambitious, and he had the drive to pull it all off.

Tim grinned, shrugging off the compliment. "I figure I might as well keep busy. Melissa's still in New York. A bunch of her auditions fell through, so she was supposed to spend the summer here, but then she scored a spot on this TV show—one of those reality series where a bunch of people share a house. They start shooting later this summer." He rubbed at a smudge on the hood of Jay's truck. "Technically I don't even know if I'm allowed to tell any details. I signed a contract not to divulge information about anything I see or hear until after the season airs."

"Wow, she must be stoked." Jay knew Melissa had been trying to break into acting for a few years now. Maybe this was her foot in the door.

"Yeah, she is, but it gives me way too much time on my hands. I guess the timing couldn't be better, though, now that you're back. I gotta tell you, man, ever since word got out you were moving back to Sapphire Springs, people have been speculating about you and Leyna, what with the new restaurant in the works. Have you seen her yet?"

Jay bit his lip. "Yeah, last week and here tonight. It hasn't been a warm welcome."

To put it mildly.

"I told you before, you crushed her when you left. Anyway, you win some, you lose some right, Romeo? Tell me about Amsterdam."

"Oh man, there is so much to tell." His voice trailed off as Mark Toner approached them.

"Hey, Tim, Wynter," Mark said. "Tim, would you mind giving me a moment with your long-lost pal? There's something he and I need to discuss."

Oh, the suspense. If this conversation didn't involve Leyna Milan, may lightning strike him down.

Tim looked from Jay to Mark and back again. "Sure, I've gotta get inside anyway." He turned toward Jay. "Things are a little hectic for me this week, but we'll get together soon. I can't wait to catch up."

When Tim was out of earshot, Jay turned back to Mark. Very few people got under his skin, but Mark had always seemed to derive a sort of pleasure from Jay having a rough time in school, calling him stupid because of his dyslexia and teasing him about becoming nothing more than a farmer like his grandfather. The two families had feuded over land a hundred years ago, and bad blood remained to this day. The years away should have softened those memories, but seeing him ogling Leyna earlier and now standing there with that smug look on his face made Jay's blood pressure rise to a roaring boil.

"There's a matter you and I need to discuss," Mark began.

"You already said that," Jay pointed out. "So why don't you get to the point?"

"Leyna Milan." Mark enunciated each syllable as though he spoke to someone who didn't speak English. "She and I are sort of starting something. I wanted to give you fair warning in case you had some ridiculous idea the two of you would rekindle some ancient flame. Just so you know, she's not interested."

Unbelievable. Jay ignored the urge to take a swing at the guy. He had a few inches on Mark in height, but since the old rival could probably bench press him with one arm, Jay decided to err on the side of caution and keep the interaction verbal.

"So, is Leyna aware you're handling matters in her personal life for her now, or is she cool with that because you two are *sort of starting something*? I knew Leyna quite well at one point in our lives, and I have to say she must've changed a hell of a lot if she's letting some washed-up quarterback fight her battles."

"I'm not fighting her battles, I'm protecting her," Mark shot back. His eyes darted around the parking lot. "I'm stating my opinion. You've got no right to swing back into town after all these years and start complicating Leyna's life. She's happy with the way things are, so stay away from her."

"She doesn't look happy." It slipped out before Jay could think better of it. Might as well roll with it. "She looks like she's going through the motions." He shrugged his shoulders and his voice softened. "But that's just *my* opinion."

"Whatever." Mark huffed. "Forget I bothered." He started toward the gallery but then turned back.

"In case you didn't know, you did a real number on her when you left town, and everybody knows it. I like Leyna. I can give her anything she wants, and most of all, I'd never hurt her. I think we both know you can't say the same." With that, he wound his way through the parked cars and disappeared back inside the gallery.

Jay stood alone in the parking lot, struggling with a bitter taste he wasn't used to. Jealousy. Maybe he and Leyna needed to settle a few things once and for all.

* * *

After sending the last bartender home, Leyna double-checked to make sure the catering staff left the gallery spotless before locking up and slipping off her strappy heels. Crossing the cool, rough concrete, she could almost hear her feet scream a relieved hallelujah.

Only two vehicles remained in the parking lot, parked side by side. For crying out loud, would this day never end?

Jay leaned against the driver's side door of the same black antique truck he'd driven since he was sixteen. Behind him, boats lined the dock.

"You always did end up barefoot by the end of the night."

She slowed to a stop about five paces from her car. "What, did you wait here the entire night?"

"No, I came back. We need to talk."

Talk. Sure. Just what she was in the mood for after a sixteen-hour day. She folded her arms over her chest and remained silent.

Jay shoved away from his truck and rested his elbows on the roof of the passenger side of her car. "So you're with Mark Toner now?"

Wouldn't that be the nail in his coffin? Though his tone hinted at humor, the slightest bit of jealousy seeped through. The glow of the streetlight in front of Tim's boat shop cast shadows over his features. Somehow it made him easier to face.

"*If* I were dating anyone, how would it be any of your business?"

"It wouldn't." Jay shrugged, relaxing his shoulders and stepping away from her car. "I'm just surprised you'd date such a jerk. Plus, he's losing his hair, and he's not even your type."

"Losing his... my... What?" Thirty seconds, and he'd already managed to frustrate her beyond words. She unlocked the car, tossed her shoes onto the passenger seat, and then faced him again. "And I suppose you know what my type is, right? Let me tell you something, Jay. You haven't known me for a very long time. In fact, you don't know me at all." Snippets of those rehearsed phrases rose to the surface. "You made it clear a long time ago how little I mattered to you, so why don't you cut the overprotective act and stop pretending there's something we need to resolve?"

He made his way around to the driver's side of her car. "Because clearly, there are things we need to resolve, if we're going to work together."

She spun around to face him. "The jury's still out on that. The second restaurant was never supposed to involve *you.*" Not that it changed anything, but it felt good to say it out loud.

"Do you still hate me that much after all these years?"

Suddenly her fingernails required close inspection. "Please. Don't flatter yourself by thinking you were so significant that I carry some eighteen-year grudge." She pretended to flick something away before meeting his gaze, because if she didn't, he'd call her out on it.

The light breeze lifted her hair and tousled it into her face. Jay inched forward and swept it away with a gentle brush of warm fingertips. His fingers hovered over her cheek a couple of seconds, and maybe, just *maybe* she leaned into his touch a little, yearning for that contact again, but he was already dropping to his hand to his side. Like he'd surprised even himself by touching her.

His gaze narrowed, though, and she knew her impulsive reaction hadn't gone unnoticed. His brooding eyes filled with awareness and locked on hers.

She glanced away, but just that one second of broken contact already made her crave his dark stare again. *Screw it.* She lifted her gaze. The closer he got, the darker his eyes looked, and they drew her in with a force of magnetism. Her eyes fell on his full bottom lip, and her breath hitched.

"Jay," she warned through clenched teeth, as his fingers circled her wrist. But their surroundings blurred and her lips were already parting. His light scruff grazed her face, a contrast to the soft lips capturing hers and clinging. When he let go of her wrist to comb his fingers through her long hair, her hand settled near his hip, gripping while their tongues swayed in a familiar dance. Deliciously familiar.

The years melted away like icicles in spring, and Leyna clung to his familiarity, his solidity, as though she were seventeen and he'd just dropped her off at the front door. Drifting apart, she studied him for a moment before placing her hand on his chest. Heat pulsed against the palm of her hand, from under his thin cotton shirt. The drumming of his heart swayed her to seek his soft lips again, but her voice of reason finally showed up, and she shoved him away.

What on earth was she doing? She sighed, the chaos of the day taking its toll. "You've got a lot of nerve, but I don't hate you, Jay. I don't even know you anymore." Her voice betrayed her, cracking before she got the last words out. "I'm not sure I ever did." She spun around and opened her car door before he could see the tears welling up in her eyes.

Slamming her car door, she started the engine and sped off, wishing the sensation of his mouth, and the memories it brought with it, would disappear as easily as he did from her rearview mirror.

* * *

With Leyna's taillights out of sight, Jay started his truck, peeled out of the gallery parking lot, and headed home. It had been a long day. On top of working in the vineyards with the crew, he'd taken Stefan to an afternoon appointment and cooked dinner, so the housekeeper, Maria, could have a break. He was tired and needed a good night's sleep.

At least Leyna hadn't gone home with her boyfriend, Mark Toner.

Not that it mattered.

The moment he saw her sitting in the boardroom last week, an eighteen-year-old ache resurrected inside his chest. He'd crossed the line, kissing her, but the way she lost herself for a moment, pulling him in, surprised him. Hell, he'd have placed better odds of getting hit by lightning.

*Jason.* Never in his entire life had she called him by his full name, and she'd spat it out, like she had sand in her teeth. Safe to assume her opinion of him hadn't softened any over the years.

He'd survived the last eighteen years without her; what difference did it make now whether she hated him or not? He'd gotten over her a long time ago.

Hadn't he?

Sure, he'd dreamt of her from time to time, only to wake up as her voice faded or her hand slipped out of reach. He'd be filled with warmth before reality sunk in that she wasn't there.

What did it matter, anyway? Harvest was a few months away. By then he'd have kept his word to his grandfather to stay on until the end of the season, and if he decided to walk away from Wynter Estate, at least he could do so knowing he'd tried.

Getting caught up in memories of Leyna would complicate things. He'd been home a week, and already he was losing himself in the depths of her immense dark eyes.

She looked so fragile standing in the dark parking lot in her bare feet, and damn it, she'd been on the verge of tears. He slammed his fist against the steering wheel. He'd done a bang-up job of skewing her opinion of him. Obviously she still hated him after all these years.

He wondered if she could ever hate him as much as he hated himself.

# Chapter Five

A stiff office chair that squeaked every time his weight shifted was the last place on earth Jay should've been sitting. He belonged on the other side of the window, where the hum of tractors and smell of freshly tilled earth taunted him from beyond the screen.

Logic would have him out there sweating with his crew and getting his hands dirty, but he was stuck inside, his legs crammed under a damn desk while a wobbly ceiling fan rattled overhead. As he slid his chair away from the desk, it gave another contrary whine.

The light rain shower that had come overnight petered out, and robins scampered around, pecking at worms slithering through the wet grass. The vines had leafed out, coaxed into a growth spurt by the rain. At least that's how it looked from this side of the window, where he tried to make sense of a blasted sales report from the previous quarter. If Pop could see the way his mind scrambled all the numbers, he'd never be trying to hand Wynter Estate over to him.

And let's not forget the endless emails regarding the summer solstice event he'd been bombarded with the last few days. They'd begun as forwards from Pop, until Leyna added him to her distribution list so he'd be in the loop with preparations.

So what if he got a little adrenaline rush each time her name popped up on his phone.

The tasting was over a month away, and she was scouting the vineyard's best vantage point of the sunset for the location of the damn tent. His crew was already booked the afternoon of the event because the boss lady insisted she needed all hands on deck to lug tables and help set up.

She wanted twinkle lights, too. More of them than Fuzzy Collins had strung up around town square. Oh, and don't forget the jazz trio that cost as much as the chopper a couple of weeks ago. Seriously, who was the boss around here, anyway?

When the phone on his desk came to life, he was grateful, yanking it off its base before the end of the first ring. "Jay Wynter."

"Jason," Stefan's voice bellowed over the line. "You've been avoiding me this past week."

Busted. He dreaded having to tell Stefan he and Leyna were still at odds.

"Did you speak with Leyna, smooth things over?"

Jay rolled his eyes toward the ceiling fan, where the

pull chain clinked against the globe with every oscillation. "Well, Pop, talking to her was kind of impossible. She was busy, running around keeping the flow of food going." And talking with Mark Toner.

"You mean you haven't spoken to her yet?"

"I did, but like I said, she was busy. Plus, it didn't really come up in conversation." What with groping her and all.

"Didn't come up in conversation." Stefan uttered an exasperated sigh. "Jason. I need you in her good graces. I thought I made that clear."

Stefan's speech was improving, so Jay could be thankful for that. He shoved off the chair and walked to the window. "You did make it clear. It's damn near transparent. But you need to get off my back about this and let me feel her out. She's saying that when the deal was made, I wasn't part of it, and it sounds like now that I am, she's not so keen to be on board. I know Leyna, and she does not like being backed into a corner. This is going to take more persistence than you realize. Let me approach this my way, please."

"Well, at this rate, your way might take decades. I want this restaurant to happen in my lifetime, so stop sulking over there in that office and go see her. She's legally bound. There's no backing out, but I could do without her dragging her heels. As you may have noticed, I am not going to be around forever."

Go, Pop. Hit where it hurts. The guilt trip trumped the frustration that had been nearing its boiling point. Jay sighed into the phone. "Fine. We'll do it your way. But don't be surprised when I come back here with my tail between my legs."

"Well, at least it'll be progress. You've got to start somewhere."

Jay waited until Stefan hung up and then slammed down the phone. He hated bickering with his grandfather, but the man could be so unreasonable sometimes. Here he was trying to decipher reports and keep Leyna Milan from backing out of a restaurant he never wanted any part of, when he should have been out firing up the tractor.

He snapped his laptop shut to get the report out of his sight. "Bigger fish to fry. Time to go grovel." He grabbed the keys to his truck and headed for the door before he lost his nerve.

* * *

From the corner booth of Rosalia's, where he sat peeling the label off his beer, Jay had the perfect vantage point to watch Leyna plow through the back door, clearly on a mission.

"Randy." She paused in front of the bar, cell phone in hand. "The band's drummer left me a voice mail while I was out—something about getting delayed and wanting to push their first set from nine to ten. Can you call Jesse and see if his mom will let him play one opening set on a school night? We'll need to figure out a drink special, too, and an appetizer. We can't have people getting bored and going home."

"No problem, boss," Randy called from behind the bar,

where he practiced some flashy bartending moves. "And by the way, your two o'clock appointment is waiting for you over at table thirteen."

"I don't have a two o'clock..." Her eyes trailed over to the far end of the restaurant and locked on Jay.

A flash of hesitation flared up before her expression turned stormy. What was she going to do, kick out a paying customer? He didn't miss the aggravation in her eyes as she approached the table, her hips swaying in her tan skirt, and the skinny strap on her black top threatening to slip off her shoulder.

She clutched her heart. "Of all the gin joints, in all the towns, in all the world."

Enjoying her theatrics, he played along. "I walked into yours."

Her shoulders fell. "Can I help you?" She stretched out her words with disdain.

Something had set her off already, and she was in the mood for a fight. He indulged in a long swig of beer before he spoke again. "Do you always greet customers with such delight?"

"Do you always invent meetings with people?"

So that's how they were playing today. Not a problem. Fired-up Leyna he could handle. Fragile Leyna on the verge of tears bothered him. "You haven't changed at all. You're still the same hot-headed girl."

"I am certainly not the same girl you used to know. Some people evolve."

He fought the grin tugging the corners of his mouth. "Okay, I stand corrected. But you've still got that spark."

She threw her head back in a throaty laugh before her tone became crystalized in another layer of frost. “Rest assured, there is no spark here.”

His chest clenched. It’d been so long since he heard her laugh. Yeah, there was a spark all right. A damn near explosive one. “I beg to differ.”

They stared at each other for another moment before Leyna broke the silence.

“What do you want?”

He shrugged. “I came to clear the air. I’m back, so you might as well get used to me.”

“Oooh, you’re back. Alert the media,” she mocked.

He set down his bottle. “What’s your problem, Leyna? You said there’s no leftover resentment from our breakup, so can’t you cut me some slack?”

“Who hasn’t changed now?” She shook her head. “You’re still selfish as ever.”

“Yeah, well you’re still stubborn as hell.”

“You’re relentless.”

“I’m *optimistic*.”

“More like delusional.”

“Think again.” God, he’d missed her.

They studied each other for another moment before Leyna folded her arms across her chest. “I have a business to run, and I don’t have time for whatever game you’re playing.”

“No problem. I’m here on business.”

“Business?” She batted her eyelashes and looked him up and down. “You don’t have an appointment, and you’re wearing a T-shirt and dirty jeans.”

Impossible. That was the only word to describe Leyna Milan. "Just sit down for five damn minutes," he snapped.

After a moment's hesitation, she sat.

He figured he had the half dozen customers scattered throughout the restaurant to thank for that. "Thank you."

Out of the corner of his eye, he saw the bartender toss a bottle into the air, then lunge forward a fraction of a second too late to catch it. The smash of broken glass had everybody's heads whipping around.

"Nice work," Jay muttered. "Hope it isn't premium liquor."

"It's water," Leyna clarified, unfazed by the disruption. "He's been using practice bottles ever since the cost of an entire case of rum was deducted from his paycheck."

"Ouch."

"So please, tell me. What's this apparent business you've come here to discuss?"

"It seems this new restaurant means you and I are destined to be business partners." He waited a beat, and when she said nothing, went on. "So I came to clear the air. We're going to have to get used to each other." He paused to look at her, letting all that implied sink in before flashing a grin. "Oh, and I looked at your menu, and came up with a few wine pairing suggestions, too."

Leyna remained silent for what felt like eternity, and then spoke suddenly.

"I'm sorry, is there a hidden camera crew, watching from the sidelines, waiting to leap out and tell me I'm going to be on TV?" She leaned forward, pressing her elbows into the wooden table. With narrowed eyes, she spoke in an ice-cold tone at a level only he would hear.

"First thing's first, *Wynter*. I don't need any suggestions from you, so save your sexy little smile for someone who doesn't see right through your act. Second, I didn't agree to go into business with you. My grandfather agreed to go into business with Stefan. There's a huge difference, and now that you're a part of the equation, I have a lot to think about, and I *will* be considering all my options."

She shoved away from the table, stormed past Randy, who pretended to focus on the broken bottle, and went back to her office, letting the door slam behind her with an echo that resonated throughout the quiet restaurant.

Jay downed the last of his beer and slapped the bottle on the table so hard it almost cracked. "Awesome." He rubbed a hand over his tired face, sick over the conversation with Stefan earlier that morning. "That's just fucking awesome."

* * *

Leyna stood at the tiny window of her office, watching from behind the curtain as Jay marched to his truck.

Who did he think he was? Did he think he was so important she could clear her schedule because he showed up wanting to smooth things over?

He tried to be casual, but there was something underneath the act. Desperation, maybe? Did he feel guilty for leaving his grandfather in a lurch all these years?

For some reason Jay's not-so-subtle approach reminded her of the first time he asked her out.

She could still picture the baggy plaid shirt he wore, still hear the swooshing of his jeans as he paced her bedroom floor, blurting out some mumbo jumbo about the two of them going to a movie together. Instinct had told her the whole thing was a cruel joke contrived by him and Rob, until she realized how nervous he was.

His tactics were no better now than they were in high school.

Reaching into her laptop bag, she picked up the magazine and flipped to Jay's interview, brushing her hand across the glossy photo.

Jay had to be dealing with a lot, with Stefan's stroke and preparing to step up as the winery's CEO and vineyard manager. Carrying on the family business was a big responsibility, a lot of pressure.

She should know.

She berated herself for being so absorbed by her own feelings she hadn't even bothered to ask him how Stefan was recovering.

Still clutching the photo, she sank into her chair. She'd been talking smack back there in the booth with Jay. Stefan was retiring, and if Jay didn't take over, it would be Cass and Danielle. Neither scenario was ideal, and no matter how much she fought it, no matter how many options she pretended to consider, the restaurant was happening—her grandfather made it a clause in his will.

There was no backing out.

But accepting it didn't mean she had to like it.

# Chapter Six

The early evening sun pulsed down on the boats bobbing along the edge of the Sapphire Springs Marina. Not even a month ago they fretted over frost damage to the vines, and now summer fast approached. Typical Upstate New York weather.

Jay idled up to the dock in front of Tim's shop and tied off his boat with a cleat hitch. One of the things he loved about Sapphire Springs was being able to use his boat to travel from the winery into town whenever the mood struck him.

He paused a moment to bask in the golden light and take in Tim's world. He'd served in the Navy for ten years before retiring and opening the boat shop. His winter months were usually spent traveling and working on cruise ships. He had even visited Jay in France a couple of times over the years. Every spring he came back to

Sapphire Springs to manage the store and share his love of boats and knowledge of sailing with others.

Tim was leaving just in time to fall into stride beside Jay. "Hey, buddy, I thought we were meeting up later. You always call it quits early on Fridays?"

"I needed the therapy of a quick boat ride after the week I had."

"I know all about that." Tim adjusted his sunglasses and gave Jay a once-over. "That button-up shirt seems a little spiffy for a boat ride. You meeting someone for dinner?" His eyebrows shot up over the rim of his aviators.

"Flying solo," Jay confirmed. "And starving."

"I could go for some food, if you want company."

Jay gave Tim a playful slap on the shoulder. "Your company is fine, but don't get the wrong idea. I didn't dress up for you."

Tim threw his head back and his laugh carried down the dock. "You should be so lucky."

Jay nearly succumbed to the scent of grilled onions and smoked sausages wafting from a food truck parked by the street entrance of the marina, but street food had a time and place, and right now he craved something else. "Where's the best place to get a steak?"

"Rosalia's." Tim circled a hand over his belly. "Bar none. Oh, and the lobster bisque is pretty stellar, too. I had it for lunch yesterday and highly recommend it."

Naturally, the best restaurant in town had to be off-limits. Images of the fiery conversation he'd had with Leyna the week before crept up, and Jay pushed past the burn in his chest, chalking it up to aggravation rather than budding desire. He gave Tim a knowing look and lowered his voice. "I'm not much of a seafood guy, and after the spat I had with Leyna last week, I'm probably banned from the premises anyway."

"Then I guess you'll have to settle for Sally's Surf and Turf. I'd tag along, but I can eat the sole of my shoe in the comfort of my own home."

Tim's dig at Sally's steaks coaxed a smile out of Jay for the first time in days. "Fine, it doesn't have to be steak. Just anywhere but Rosalia's." They rounded the corner and were met with honking horns and the revving engine of the transit bus. Jaywalking near town square was an offense Sapphire Springs' law enforcement gave up policing years ago. Nobody bothered to walk to the corner crosswalks except tourists, a constant irritation to commuters fighting traffic on busy afternoons. They passed a cluster of people milling over the outdoor menu at the pizzeria.

Tim glanced at his apartment windows above Euphoric Yoga Studio in the former Patterson Shoe Factory building. "Since we haven't agreed on a place to eat, you mind if we stop at my place? I need to change out of these rags if I'm expected to look good next to you."

"Make it snappy, and there better be a beer in it for me." Jay followed Tim up the narrow stairwell, and before the door even clicked shut behind them, Tim handed him a beer out of the refrigerator and disappeared into his bedroom.

Jay sipped his beer while checking out the snapshots of Tim and Melissa on top of a bookshelf. Most of them were selfies taken on Tim's boat, with everything from fireworks to sunsets serving as a backdrop. Tim had never been a relationship guy, but Melissa had changed him. Wide smiles and sparkling eyes stared back, and though he didn't compare his life to other people's as a rule, the photos produced a tug in his chest and left him feeling somewhat incomplete.

He'd only had that kind of connection once, back when he and Leyna were starry eyed and crazy about each other. Convinced he wasn't meant for that life, he'd tossed it all away. Leaving helped mask those memories, diminishing them to nothing more than brittle grainy Polaroids shoved into a dusty book, out of sight, out of mind. But being back, surrounded by their familiar haunts, stealing that kiss, stirred the pages of that book and coaxed old photos to flutter to the floor.

Seemed he'd been tripping over them ever since.

"Man, what a day." Tim breezed into the room wearing dark jeans and a bold Hawaiian print shirt. His blond hair curled at the ends, damp from his quick shower. He lowered into the brown leather recliner and twisted the cap off his beer. "The nice weather these last few days brought people out in droves, scrambling to rent kayaks and book tours for the weekend. What about you?"

Jay filled Tim in on Stefan's retirement bombshell, as well as the events of the past few of weeks. "He's planning to put the new restaurant on Renaissance Road, on land I had earmarked for syrah, and he didn't even bother to ask my opinion." Because his temper started to rise again, he paused for a drink. "It's just further proof that even if I did take over the company, it would never be mine. Somebody else will always call the shots."

Tim pressed a button on the side of his chair that catapulted him back into a reclining position. "Ahh, that's better. Can I play devil's advocate for a minute?"

"I'd expect nothing less." Jay glanced at the time on his phone. His stomach was eating itself. He took another swig of beer to squash the hunger.

"You keep saying you don't want the responsibility of running the company, or to be forced to settle down in Sapphire Springs—which everyone knows is bullshit, by the way—yet you don't want to give up your precious land for a restaurant. If none of it matters to you, then why worry about what happens to the land?"

Jay processed Tim's opinion. Why *did* it matter what happened to the land on Renaissance Road if he went back to France at the end of the season and washed his hands of Wynter Estate? If nothing else, he could sell the plot of land back to his grandfather and make a little extra money. "You're right. Let them bulldoze the syrah plot and open a restaurant, if that's what they feel is the profitable thing to do. Pave paradise, put up a parking lot, as the song goes." What did he know? Nothing, apparently. He waved his hand to downplay the situation, because he regretted bringing it up. "In a few months I could be out of here, anyway, for all I know."

Tim rubbed his chin, studying him for a few seconds. "You sure about that? You'll be willing to give up Wynter Estate and just hand it off to who, your mom and Cass?"

Setting his drink to the side, Jay leaned back on the couch and stared at the ceiling, willing it to drop answers into his lap. "I don't know. That's why I agreed to stay for the summer. Of course I don't want Cass running the company, and I don't want to disappoint my grandfather again, either, but maybe settling down is not in my blood. Look at my mom, she couldn't even stick around until I made it through elementary school." Not to mention his father, who took off before he was even born.

"You're not your mom, but you do have a lot on your plate, when you add Leyna to the mix. Speaking of Leyna…" Tim tucked the footrest of his chair back in so he could sit up. "Some guys at the golf course were teasing Mark about getting shot down by her. I don't think there's too much going on between them. He'll never crack her shell. Better men have tried."

Jay wondered about Leyna's shell. "She was engaged for a while, wasn't she?" How could he forget the beaming couple in the *Sapphire Star*—Leyna's diamond-clad finger, resting on the chest of some older guy with too much gel in his hair and a patchy excuse for a beard. He radiated privilege and prominence. Jay always imagined Leyna would end up with someone like that. Distinguished. Smart.

Tim nodded, draining his beer. "Yep, to some bigshot restaurant guy in New York. Old money. Rob said she got cold feet or something."

"Well, if she's not interested in Mark, he better back off."

"Easy." Tim grinned. "One thing you can be sure

of—if Leyna Milan doesn't want someone around, she'll tell them."

"Don't I know it." Jay sighed and polished off the last of his beer.

* * *

The busy week called for a girls' night out, so Leyna and Emily found themselves nestled in a booth at Rosalia's, enjoying mojitos while a blues band entertained the growing crowd.

"Can you believe him? I mean, who the hell does he think he is, offering to suggest pairings for *my* menu?"

Emily polished off her second mojito, pushed the empty glass to the edge of the table, and signaled to Randy that they were ready for another round. She'd had a rough week, too, and the effects of the alcohol were already elevating her voice.

"This partnership may not be as crazy as you think. You and Jay both bring unique factors to the table, if the two of you can leave the past where it belongs. You did the right thing, though, blowing him off when he showed up unannounced. I wish I'd seen it myself. It would have been a pleasant distraction from the doughnut shop of doom."

Emily had taken the news of the doughnut shop hard, too, afraid the hype would take away business from Tesoro.

Randy delivered two more mojitos and placed some breadsticks and a bowl of marinara in the middle of the table between them. "Are you two planning to order any food, to counteract these drinks?"

"This is food." Emily scooped up some marinara and smiled at Randy. "But thank you for looking out for us."

"If you say so," he replied before disappearing.

Emily launched into a story about seeing Jay and Tim chatting earlier at the marina. "Can you believe it?" she rolled her eyes. "Jay is back in town, what, a few weeks, and he and Tim are already attached at the hip again? It's so predictable."

Emily had a thing for Tim that had come and gone since the eighth grade. Between his cluelessness and her insecurities, she'd never acted on it, and her spot in the friend zone had been cemented by high school. Leyna treaded lightly. "Is Tim still with Melissa?" They'd broken up a few times, so who could keep track?

"I think so." Emily sighed. "Those blue eyes... The guy improves with age. You know, like Bradley Cooper?"

"Jay does, too," Leyna admitted, cocking her eyebrow and scowling. Blame the drinks for voicing her inner thoughts.

Laughter erupted out of Emily and her drink sloshed over the side of the glass. She wiped up her spill with a napkin. "Leyna Milan, was that a half-assed compliment you just paid Jay Wynter?"

"Well, don't get me wrong, his looks don't excuse the rest of his behavior, but even I could never deny the guy is good-looking." She lowered her voice and leaned across the table in secrecy. "He kissed me."

Emily's hand flew to her mouth and her words came out like a yelp. "Are you serious? When?"

"After the gallery opening," she added. "I pushed him away, of course."

"Obviously. How am I just hearing about this now?"

"I debated not telling anyone *ever*, but I needed to get it off my chest so I can stop thinking about it. And now he's everywhere I turn," Leyna continued. "He must go for a boat ride every damn night. I can't even sit on my deck in the evening anymore without seeing him drive by."

Emily bit her lip, trying to conceal a smile. "Well, don't look now, but the two of them just walked through the door."

Leyna turned in the booth while Jay and Tim took a seat at the bar. Tim waved while Jay nodded, avoiding eye contact.

She hadn't expected him to darken her doorstep again already. "Looks like someone is still licking his wounds after the big face-off. You're right about Tim, though, Em, he looks great. Definitely working out."

"He jogs." Emily applied a fresh coat of lip gloss and gave her teeth a quick glance in her compact mirror. "Every morning at six a.m."

Leyna's drink sprayed out of her mouth as laughter forced its way up her throat. "Wow, Em." She wiped her chin with her sleeve. "Do you set your alarm for the occasion, or what?"

"No, but we live in the same building, so I notice these things when I'm picking up the newspaper." She bobbed her shoulders, feigning innocence. "I happen to see him sometimes on his way out."

"You happen to." Leyna grabbed Emily's compact to

check her own reflection. "Like in high school when you happened to jog by his house while he shot hoops in his driveway without his shirt on, even though you were both dating other people?"

Emily scowled at her friend. "Ancient history. I believe *your* exact words were 'a lifetime ago.' "

"Well, it must be a hell of a way to start the day."

They evaluated Tim from a distance. He was already tanned from the endless hours he spent at the marina, and his shaggy blond hair and Hawaiian print shirt matched his free spirit.

Tim wasn't her type, so Leyna didn't bother to fight her gaze as it moved on to study Jay. The sleeves of his shirt were rolled up to the elbow, and he wore a pair of faded jeans. He drummed his fingers on the bar to the beat of the music, but his set jaw radiated tension all the way across the room.

When he glanced her way she was captured by his knowing eyes, like the night he kissed her. For a split second she could read him, catching a glimpse of sadness, guilt, and something else. Regret? The weight of his stare was crippling. Was it possible that leaving had actually hurt him, too?

Leyna blinked and looked down into her drink.

"Whoa, that was some moment." Emily made a show of waving her arms to snap Leyna out of her trance. "I don't care how much you protest. You and Jay have unfinished business."

Her eyes burned from the lock he had on them, and for some reason, the wall she took so much care to build cracked a little. How could she let that happen after only a handful of encounters with the guy? Guilt over Stefan? Leyna sucked up the last of her drink. "I've buried memories of Jay for a long time. It's exhausting. Maybe someday we'll be able to salvage some sort of a tolerance for each other, you know? Let bygones be bygones after all these years."

"That would be major progress." Emily lifted her chin. "Why hang on to negative emotions? It isn't good for anybody."

Leyna slapped her hand on the table. "Let's talk about something else. Did you make up your mind about town council?"

Emily rubbed her hands together. "Actually, yes. I think I have a lot to offer, so I'm going for it, and I think you should run, too, so we can revamp the town together. There are six spots besides Fuzzy."

"No way in hell. Life is hectic enough, and we haven't even broken ground on the second restaurant yet." Leyna shook her head and her earrings swayed. "There's no way I'd have time."

Randy brought them each another drink. "I wasn't supposed to say anything, but since you're the boss and I witnessed the cat fight last week, I feel obligated to inform you that these drinks are from the two gentlemen at the bar. And also, I think you two should order some food. Whenever. Just eat something. You know, at some point." He heaved a defeated sigh before walking away.

Leyna and Emily gave each other a knowing look before a smile spread across Emily's face.

"Looks like we still got it. They're coming over. Leyna Milan, if you screw this up, our friendship is over."

"He has a girlfriend."

"Being friendly never hurt anyone," Emily whispered.

Leyna bit back a groan as Jay and Tim approached the table.

Tim leaned over the back of their booth and cocked a boyish smile. "Ladies, would you mind if we joined you?"

The wailing strings of a broken-hearted guitar solo filled the entire room as Jay, Emily, and Tim all waited for Leyna's response. Emily looked ready to claw Leyna's eyes out if she said no.

Every ounce of common sense, every bit of progress she made toward moving on over the years flew out the window as she eyed Jay and slid further into the booth. "Why not? Have a seat, guys."

"I'll be damned." Jay lowered onto the bench beside Leyna and draped his arm across the back of the booth. "Hell appears to have frozen over."

Leyna's eyes narrowed on upturned lips. "Maybe. But I wouldn't lace up my skates quite yet if I were you."

* * *

Another round of drinks and an appetizer platter later, the lights were dimmed, and the band kicked it up a notch. Most tables were full, and the bartenders poured drinks at a steady pace.

Leyna was enjoying herself, given the circumstances.

It turned out that Tim was interested in running for a spot on town council, too, so he and Emily dominated the conversation, which helped. When they went to the bar for another round of drinks, her impulse was to escape to her office to check messages, but she forced herself to face Jay.

"So the weather has been really nice, huh?" Lame, but farmer types always talked about the weather. Considering their last conversation all but required a referee, it seemed like a safe topic.

He pushed a hand through his hair and sent it into rather sexy disarray. "You don't have to break the ice with conversation about weather. This is us. But I do want to say something. What you've done with Rosalia's is incredible, and I'm not the only one who thinks so. I saw the review in *The Post*."

"Oh, that's nothing." She rushed to downplay it, because his words pulled at some ancient strings she'd believed were long lost. "A friend of a friend knows the columnist..."

"So you still can't take a compliment." He chuckled. "That's fine, but it's really something to see what you've created with the renovations and the live music." His eyes scanned her face and his voice softened. "Joe would be so proud."

A fist clawed through her chest and squeezed her heart until every one of those strings snapped and vibrated. Why did something countless other people complimented her on knock the wind out of her when it came from Jay? The threat of tears stung her eyes, but she fought them off. "I could say the same for you, too, stepping up for Stefan."

"Thanks, that actually means a lot." He toyed with a beer cap, bending it between his thumb and index finger. "I'm sorry about Joe," he said, stealing another glance at her. "I should've said that sooner. Hell, I should have been here for Pop. They were tight."

"Thick as thieves," she agreed. "I think Stefan misses him a lot."

"Yeah, he talks about him all the time. He told me they took a trip to Toronto for a hockey game a couple of years ago."

"I heard some talk of that, but I still lived in the city then, so I never got the whole story."

Jay tossed the beer cap onto their empty plates. "They hired a driver and made the trip the night before Joe's eightieth birthday. Imagine, a couple of old coots on a whirlwind trip because neither of them could stand to be away from home for more than five minutes." His shoulders started to shake with laughter.

Because she could picture the whole scene, she shared in the humor. "They must've spent the entire trip arguing over their teams."

"The only thing they disagreed on." Jay's laughter trailed off.

Instinct nearly made her reach out to touch his hand, but she caught herself. "Look, Jay. I know I've been sort of impossible since you got back."

"You?" he laughed into his beer. "To be expected, I suppose. And God knows I deserve it. Leyna, I want you to know I'll never forgive myself for the way—"

"Don't," she interrupted, with a raised hand. Discussing their breakup would do nothing for the small slice of progress they'd made in the last hour and a half. "I think we should leave the past in the past and try to salvage some sort of..." She searched her brain for the appropriate word. "Acquaintanceship, if we're both going to live in this town. Especially if we're going to work together."

"Acquaintanceship," he repeated with a hint of disappointment in his voice. "I guess that's a start. But do you think that's all we'll ever be? I mean, can't we aim for friends?"

Friends. So her broken heart could be water under a very shaky bridge? "I think it'd be wise to take it one day at a time, given our history."

He held eye contact. "Last time we spoke you said you were going to look at all your options. I took that to mean you were searching for a loophole, a way out of the restaurant deal."

She blew out a breath and relaxed her shoulders. "I came to the realization there's no point in splitting hairs, looking for a way out. It's a done deal, and everyone knows it. What about you—it's no secret you're against this restaurant, too. Have you accepted it?"

Jay sighed and fumbled with his hands. "It's not so much that I'm against it. There is a need for a restaurant. He's not wrong about that. It's just the timing and the choice of partners."

Her eyes narrowed. "Are you suggesting Rosalia's isn't good enough for Wynter Estate?" Here they were again, only this time her restaurant was inadequate.

"No, of course not." He set his drink aside and shifted to face her straight on. "But of all the restaurants in Sapphire Springs my grandfather could have chosen, he'd settle for nothing but the one run by my most significant ex."

Leyna leaned back into the corner of the booth, taken aback by the words *most significant ex*, since she'd thought of him the same way. Surely he'd had serious relationships besides her. Best to breeze past it and ask the more pressing question. "Are you back to stay?"

He grew quiet a moment, and then explained a compromise he made with Stefan to commit to the growing season. "It's not so much that I don't want to stay. My whole life I've wanted to do right by Pop. The thought of letting him down kills me, but I'm just not wired to run a company, not to mention the pressure of it being his life's work at stake. I guess you're no stranger to that."

She could relate, but she'd never considered any alternative. "It is a lot of pressure, and some days I seriously doubt myself, but it's rewarding, too, honoring Gramp's vision and finding a balance with my own. It means the world to me to carry on his legacy and keep his memory alive. I gave him my word I wouldn't let him down. I don't take that lightly." Her gaze fell on the brick wall, where large black-and-white photos of her grandparents in the early days of the restaurant hung gallery style. What the heck was taking Emily and Tim so long?

"Can I assume the sold sign on the Blackhorse means you bought the building?"

How did he know about that?

"I saw your logo designs in the conference room."

Right. When they had crawled under the table, so close that his breath warmed her bare skin. She cleared her throat. "Yeah, no. I lost out on it. Doughnuts. Something else will come along."

"Doughnuts?"

She explained the franchise moving in, and then heaved a sigh. "Aside from that, being back in Sapphire Springs has been great. I always wanted to come back home. Sure, Gramp getting sick wasn't in the plan, and it certainly fast-tracked things. I came home last year—a couple of months before he passed away—to sort of help him transition out of the restaurant. I was relieved in a way, to leave the chaos of the city behind. I'm close to my parents now, and Rob is nearby, just on the outskirts of Buffalo. I spent years not seeing them enough."

Jay stared down into his lap. "Your family must be thrilled to have you back. Unlike mine. I think with the exception of Pop, I'm nothing but a thorn in everyone's side. A threat to my mom and Cass's plans."

The pieces of their bizarre predicament began to morph together. Unlike Leyna, Jay had planned to stay away. He'd been just as blindsided by Stefan's decision to retire as she was. But he did care about Wynter Estate. Otherwise, he wouldn't worry about the pressure or his grandfather's legacy. Despite his flaws, his loyalty to Stefan couldn't be questioned, and his heart was in the right place.

"If there's a hope in hell of this working, the three of us need to sit down and have a meeting where we can be open and honest. You, me, and Stefan, I mean. Don't show up in a T-shirt and grass-stained jeans, and keep your hands to yourself."

Humor flickered in his eyes, and he smirked over the lip of his beer bottle. "Were my jeans grass-stained? I didn't even notice."

"The Sip and Savor Festival is less than a month away. I have your solstice tasting on my radar. Why don't we see how that goes, and in the meantime we'll sit down with Stefan and figure out the rest."

# Chapter Seven

Jay pulled off the gravel road and parked his truck near the edge of the chardonnay plot before the sun crept over the horizon. He liked being the first one on site each day—he savored the peace and quiet and the alone time with the vines before the rest of the crew rolled in and teased him over the way he nurtured and fussed over them.

Things were looking up. The weather had behaved—hot daytime temperatures, with enough rain to keep things moving. Stefan's therapists had made a lot of progress on his speech. He still refused to rest, but the doctors could only do so much.

Whistling, he made his way to the rows of chardonnay, and as he approached, a grin spread over his face.

"Flowers," he whispered. A little early, but then again, the entire cycle was happening faster than he had ever seen it happen before. He squatted down to get a closer look at the blossoms, so delicate you could almost blow them away like a cloud of dust off an old book. A surge of excitement rose through his chest.

"Flowers!" He yelled it as loud as he could, turning on his heel, fisting his hands in the air, and spinning around in a circle. As his voice echoed over the tranquil vineyard, the sun poked over the trees, rising to check out all the fuss. He jogged down the row to check out some of the other vines, pleased the blooming was consistent.

A distant tractor honked a congratulatory horn, causing Jay's grin to spread into an all-out laugh. The tractor belonged to Norman, the vineyard manager at a neighboring winery, who probably was enjoying the same thrill.

Amazing that something as natural as a bud blooming into a flower still managed to excite him every season. It served as proof they were doing something right, he supposed, and that the frost scare last month had left no lasting damage. Pulling his phone out of his pocket, he snapped a picture and texted it to a crew member, with the caption "Wakey, wakey."

Jay stuffed the phone into his pocket and went back to studying the tiny white flowers dotting the tips of the shoots, breathing in their mild scent. Every single flower had the potential to become a berry and, in turn, would determine their yield. If the weather took a turn and they got hammered with wind and rain, the fragile little blossoms could be jeopardized, but if the warm stretch held, they'd have a nice even berry formation in a couple of weeks.

So many factors conspired to take that vine from dormancy to harvest. He and the crew would monitor things, adjust trellis wires to keep up with the growth spurts, and manage the canopy so the sun could reach the grapes, but most of the job was up to nature.

Patience, along with knowing when to leave well enough alone and let nature take its course, was crucial—a valuable lesson his grandfather had taught him when he was still a child.

Speaking of letting nature take its course, an image of Leyna next to him in the booth last week surfaced in his mind. It seemed she'd had a change of heart or, at the very least, made an effort to close the door on the past. He'd banked on it taking much more persistence.

She could be so unpredictable sometimes, but damn if it didn't somehow add to her allure.

Jay mulled over the restaurant idea. He had to hand it to his grandfather: When he was right, he was right.

They'd keep things simple: local food, a seasonal menu, maybe a space where groups could dine in the cellar on special occasions. To mirror the live music aspect of Rosalia's, they could have a quaint area in the courtyard for afternoon or weekend entertainment, and a nice tapas menu to pair with the wines. Someday, maybe they'd branch out into larger-scale events.

Though he hadn't mentioned it to Stefan yet, he considered offering a plot of land for a garden, so the restaurant could grow its own vegetables and herbs for both locations. If he had to give up his syrah plot, he might as well go all-in. The ideas flooded him faster than he could process them. He could already see it, and that's what excited him most.

Maybe this stint in Sapphire Springs wasn't such a bad thing. Those years away had been an amazing experience, but tough at the same time. He missed Stefan and his friends. Not a lot had changed in his hometown, but once upon a time, he'd been happy here. Was it crazy to imagine he could be again?

Something Leyna had said struck a chord, and it had echoed with him ever since: *Honoring her grandfather's vision, and finding a balance with her own.* Could it be done? Leyna's family tree didn't include Cass and Danielle Nixon, circling overhead like eagles about to sink their talons into blissfully unsuspecting prey. He hadn't spoken to them since the morning of the meeting. Cass had business in Boston, which was as good a place for them as any.

Tires crunched over gravel, pulling him out of his daydream. A white car inched up behind his truck, and Emily surfaced from the vehicle, dark sunglasses the size of coasters hiding her face. She toed through the wet grass in heels that boosted her up to average height.

Jay hurried over to meet her halfway. "Are you lost?"

She yanked her leg up, pulling out the spiky heel that was sinking halfway down into the earth. "No, I'm not lost, although I have to say I could never survive in your world. Who starts their day before the coffee house opens?"

Extending a hand, he guided her back across the rugged slope toward their vehicles, where she'd have easier footing. "You know they invented these things a few years back called coffee makers. You can brew it right in your own kitchen. It's quite advanced."

"Good one." She removed her sunglasses and propped them on her head. "I've been mulling something over. We need to talk."

He attempted to keep the mood light. "For a baker, you're not much of a morning person."

"You're right about that. It's a good thing I only have to stumble downstairs to get to work. I'm not accustomed to driving across town this early, but I figured it'd be the best time of the day to pin you down."

"Hold that thought." He crossed over to the truck and grabbed his thermos out of the cup holder. "Since you've come all this way at such an ungodly hour, I'll share my coffee. You can drink out of the cap."

Her eyes narrowed. "Does it have cream and sugar?"

"Some."

"Sweet Jesus, hit me up."

He divided the coffee and passed her the cap. "Is this where you tell me to back off Leyna?"

She sipped, gripping it with both hands. "Yes, but not for the reasons you probably expect."

"Which are?"

"Oh, let me see." Her eyes darted to the side while she pretended to compile a list. "The fact that you stomped all over her heart, told her not to wait for you because you were never in love with her in the first place—"

"Okay, okay, I get it." Jay lowered his gaze to the water droplets clinging to the grass. Emily had no idea it had all been a lie crafted to help Leyna move on, to spare her the guilt when she inevitably met someone better at college and outgrew him, as his mother had constantly reminded him was what his father had done to her. Danielle insisted Leyna would eventually leave him in the dust.

The seed had been planted, and the closer they got to Leyna going off to school, the less worthy he felt of her. Jay remembered the mix of pride and heartbreak he felt when she crossed the stage in her cap and gown at graduation, collecting the countless awards and scholarships. She'd worked her ass off to impress her parents, to prove she could achieve the kind of marks Rob had pulled off effortlessly.

In that moment, all his mother's warnings rang true. Leyna was going places. Sure, she said she wanted to run the family restaurant someday, but things changed. Maybe once she got a taste of life elsewhere, she'd never want to settle down in Sapphire Springs. Plenty of guys would make her realize what Jay had known since their first exchange of eye contact—she was out of his league, and he wasn't even close to being good enough for her.

He folded his arms. "She can't hold a grudge forever. We have businesses to run, and as luck would have it, those businesses appear to need each other. Besides, we were kids when I left."

"I wouldn't say she's holding a grudge," Emily said, "but can you blame her for being hesitant to go into business with somebody who flies across the globe the first time the going gets tough?"

That was some track record he'd established with Emily and Leyna by leaving town when he was twenty years old. He found the lingering judgment unfair, but he also knew better than to argue with either one of them about it. "No, I can't blame her for that. But this restaurant was news to me. It's not like I asked for it. But I'm sure you guessed that anyway."

"Yes. I also know the three of you are meeting to discuss things in more detail."

Jay shifted his weight to one side, settling into the conversation now that Emily's back no longer arched like an angry cat. "Things hit a snag when I became part of the equation, but she's agreed to look past it."

Emily toyed with the ends of the silk scarf looped over her light denim jacket. "Be that as it may, Leyna's got some trouble. Financially."

"Financially," he repeated slowly.

Emily's nod confirmed he'd heard correctly.

"But the place is thriving. The reno is phenomenal, she has kickass entertainment, a top-notch chef...She planned to buy the Blackhorse."

"All of those things came with a price, and she would've needed a miracle to buy that building. Mark Toner tried to sway her into letting him invest."

Jay studied her through the steam curling out of his thermos. Something wasn't adding up. If Leyna was broke, she did a bang-up job of faking it. "Did she put you up to this?"

Emily threw back the rest of her coffee and passed him the empty thermos cap. "The hope is that summer will bring business. She lost a lot of the tourism boost last year being closed for renovations. If Leyna knew I told you any of this, she'd kill me, but I figured maybe you could convince your grandfather to back off a little, maybe renegotiate the terms or give her some time."

Jay followed her toward her car, distracted by his burning questions. "I don't know what to make of all this."

"Just keep the information to yourself." Emily lowered into the driver seat.

"Em." He caught the door before it closed. "Thanks for telling me."

She lowered her sunglasses. "Don't make me wish I hadn't."

As she drove away, Jay reached into the back pocket of his jeans and pulled out his phone.

Stefan answered on the first ring.

"Hey, Pop, we've got flowers."

After a pause, Stefan laughed. "Happy day."

"Yeah. Nice and even, too. Look, about the meeting with Leyna—"

"Yes?"

"Something's been brought to my attention. Something about Leyna we weren't aware of before."

Annoyance coated Stefan's tone. "Yes?"

Maybe he should've gone to Stefan in person to give him the details. Jay squinted up at the sun. "She's been having financial trouble since taking over Rosalia's. Apparently the business took a big hit being closed last summer for the renovations, and it's proven harder to bounce back than she anticipated."

Stefan remained quiet for what seemed like forever.

"That's impossible."

Jay bit back the groan trying to force its way out. He

should have known Stefan would contest the information. "Emily is a pretty good source here, Pop. If anybody would know Leyna's private matters, it's her."

"It's not possible," Stefan insisted. "Joe Leone saved every cent he ever made. He never changed a thing over the years, never so much as replaced a tablecloth, for God's sake. He left her everything. There's no possible way she could have burned through all that money, short of tearing down the building and starting over from the ground up."

"Well, I can't see Emily making it up."

Jay could hear a pen tapping on the desk while Stefan tried to wrap his mind around the new information. Finally, he spoke.

"If she's in trouble financially, there's more to the story—some debts she had to pay off or some other explanation, because I know what Joe had saved, and it was more than enough to update the old restaurant and cover their share of the startup costs for the second location."

"She's not the type to blow through thousands of dollars, Pop. The restaurant means too much to her family, and there's no way in hell she would be careless with the money. There's got to be more to the story, because that is not the Leyna I know."

"It's not the Leyna I know, either." Stefan sounded distant. "Leave it with me. Perhaps we can work around these financial issues."

"Are you saying we would front the money for the new restaurant?"

Stefan considered. "It might be the only way. Set up the meeting with her and leave the rest with me." With that, Stefan hung up.

Jay stared at the phone, torn between finding out the whole story and the fact that he struggled to make sense of something Leyna probably didn't want him to have any part of. Emily knew Leyna's situation, there was no doubt about that, but nobody knew Joe better than Stefan. So why didn't the stories match up? Where did the whole thing go off the rails?

# Chapter Eight

The first week of the Sip and Savor Festival was productive but grueling, with the longer hours and extra tourists in town. Leyna decided that working late every night called for a good meal and a much-needed glass of wine. Maybe she'd even treat herself to a hot bubble bath and start the new paperback she picked up at Boundless Books that afternoon when she'd strolled down the street after lunch.

Jay and Stefan came to Rosalia's three days ago to sort out plans for the restaurant, which, she had to admit, were growing on her. She wasn't without her reservations, but they all agreed to proceed with caution for now. The summer solstice event would be a trial run of sorts, and longer term, Wynter Estate would partner with Rosalia's for cross promotions like vineyard tours and tastings and winemaker's dinners. Jay had suggested some pairings for many of their most popular menu options, and Leyna agreed to sell the entire Wynter product line.

What caught her off guard was Stefan offering to invest the money to get Rosalia's second location up and running. That couldn't have been his plan all along, or he'd have mentioned it before now. In any case, it alleviated some pressure and allowed a glimmer of excitement to take root and bloom.

In the nights since, she'd lain awake, pondering ideas into the early hours of the morning, tossing and turning, as daybreak began to swallow the dark sky.

The practical side of her pointed out all the reasons a partnership with Wynter Estate was risky. Between the stress of keeping the restaurant afloat while also opening a second location and her messy past with Jay, it had red flags all over it.

Why was she warming up to the idea so much then?

Her belly flopped when she pulled into her driveway to find Jay tying his boat to the dock in front of the cottage. If you'd asked her a month ago, she'd have said he'd be long gone by now, but here he was, still showing up everywhere she turned.

She climbed out of the car. "What are you doing here?"

The warm breeze danced in his chestnut hair, lifting it off his forehead as he made his way up the hill. Dark sunglasses shielded his eyes from the rich early evening sunlight, and the shadow of stubble tracing his jawline glinted with silver, reminding Leyna how many years had passed since he'd been a part of her life.

He removed the sunglasses when he reached her car,

squinting against the vivid rays of the sun. "I tried to call you at work, but they said I just missed you, and then you didn't answer your cell."

Leyna popped the trunk open and began lifting grocery bags out. "I left it in the car when I stopped by the market." She passed him a couple of the heavier bags. "Since you're here, you might as well give me a hand bringing these inside."

"Haven't we come a long way?" He peeked at the contents of the wine bag. "You even picked up a bottle of Wynter. I'm flattered."

Not liking him proved impossible. Whether you wanted to or not, he just had this way of making people warm up to him. She unlocked the cottage door, and he followed her inside, which unnerved her a bit. Had she left a mess this morning, frantic to get out the door on time?

Turned out the place was presentable, except for her French press on the counter, still full of coffee she'd forgotten to drink.

"I bought some Wynter, yes, and Thai takeout." She stuck a bottle of carbonated water into the fridge.

He wandered past the kitchen to check out the rest of the main floor.

"Make yourself at home," she quipped, though he was out of earshot.

After a few minutes he circled back to the kitchen and leaned against the side of the refrigerator while she unpacked groceries. "This place suits you."

Spoken like he gave his seal of approval.

"Yeah? How so?"

"Well, for starters, I can tell some of the art is your own work."

He remembered she painted. That seemed like a lifetime ago.

"And the place has an eclectic vibe... Kind of like you."

Before she could come up with a response, he did a double-take at one of the photos stuck to the refrigerator door.

"Who are the two little girls at the beach?" He tapped the door with his knuckle.

Leyna smiled at the picture taken last summer, thankful for the distraction from Jay hanging out in her personal space. "Those are my nieces. They're Rob's kids."

He leaned a little closer to the picture. "I can see the resemblance. Man, I still can't believe Rob's got kids."

"Me either, sometimes. No matter how old he is, or how successful he becomes, Rob will always be Rob, you know? My doofus brother." She sliced up a watermelon wedge she had picked up at the grocery store and passed Jay a piece. "The girls can be a handful, but they're good kids most of the time. Everyone says Carly looks like me."

"She does. She looks just like you when you were a kid." He took his time inspecting the rest of the candid shots, pausing in front of Rob and Issey's family picture. "So Rob's married off, huh?" He sunk his teeth into the watermelon. "What's his wife like?"

Jay and Rob had once been like brothers. In all the years they'd been out of touch, she'd never considered that Jay probably missed her brother. She'd been too wrapped up in wondering if he ever thought of her. But the care he took to study the photos and the tight line of his lips told her there was a void there. She considered before answering. "I never thought I'd say this about my brother, but sometimes I think he deserves better."

Jay's eyebrows shot upward. "Really?"

"Don't get me wrong. Rob isn't perfect, contrary to popular belief, and I know firsthand he's not easy to live with, but Issey is a total workaholic. I don't think she's ever put Rob or the kids first. She's a slave to her cell phone and constantly works late, and there's always a meeting she has to get to. She expects Rob to roll with it, like he's got nothing going on in his own life. I'm sure you've seen the type."

"Selfish, in other words." Jay chucked the watermelon rind into the compost bin and wiped his wet hands on his jeans.

"I never actually labeled it, but yeah. Selfish is how I would describe her. We were all surprised they chose to have kids. Rob took paternity leave both times, because she wanted to get back to work. She doesn't have much patience for them, and her maternal instinct seems to be lacking." She paused, dismissing Rob's personal life. "Anyway, they make it work."

"Speaking of work, how was the rest of your week?" Jay crossed his ankles and leaned back against the counter before helping himself to another slice of watermelon.

The trail of juice that ran from his lip down to his chin distracted her a fraction of a second too long, and when she tore her gaze away from his lips, he watched her. Something inside her stirred.

With a quick swipe of the back of his hand, he wiped away the juice, so carefree, like he belonged in her kitchen. Alarm bells went off in her head. She had to get rid of him before she started imagining him in other parts of her house. She cleared her throat. "Things have been a little crazy, but I guess tourist season is officially here. I'd hoped to leave it all there for the weekend and have a me night, so at the risk of sounding rude, you're sort of crashing it."

Yes, best to get rid of him before she did something catastrophic, like lick the juice off his lips.

He snorted back a surge of laughter before speaking. "Relax. I have plans, so I won't be crashing your night for long."

Plans? Right, he had a life outside of this partnership. A date probably, because that's what single people did on Friday nights, they went on dates, and hooked up, and had no-strings relationships. Everyone except her, apparently. She opened the refrigerator and grabbed a carbonated water.

"I thought we should get together tomorrow to go over some stuff, and I could give you a tour of the vineyard," he said. "You can learn a little more about the product, get a feel for the whole process."

Because meeting one on one with him made her heart flutter, she crafted an excuse. "That sounds like work, and I need a break." She twisted the cap off the bottle of water. Before she could process what was happening, the liquid surged and gushed toward the opening, spraying all over herself and the rest of the kitchen.

Jay grabbed the bottle out of her hands and lunged toward the sink to contain the overflow, giving in to a fit of laughter.

Leyna stood frozen in the middle of the kitchen, blinking rapidly while lime fizzy water dripped from her forehead and down her arms and soaked into her thin shirt.

"Smooth." Jay grinned over his shoulder while he controlled the erupting mess.

She grabbed the dish towel hanging on the stove and joined him at the counter, wiping up the liquid smeared all over the fronts of the cabinets. "Ugh."

The fizzing subsided, and he set the bottle down into the sink, shaking water off of his hands. "You were saying?"

Laughing, she wiped at her forehead and cheeks. "Just that I had a long first week of the festival and that week two will be even busier with the solstice tasting. You must be swamped too." She passed him the towel.

"I am." He dried his hands and tossed the towel. His brown eyes sobered, searching her face. He stepped closer, tracing his fingertip across her bare shoulder, to wipe lingering water droplets away. He trailed his fingers down her bare skin, thumb settling in the soft spot in the crook of her arm, fingertips curling around to graze her elbow, in a warm gentle hold.

Her gaze fell on his lips, soft in contrast to his five o'clock shadow and still coated with a sheen from the watermelon juice. On instinct, she leaned forward. He shifted closer, tightening his clasp on her arm, guiding her toward him, until his warm breath swept over her face. His nose brushed the side of hers, tripping her heart rate. Their lips were dangerously close, and God, what was happening?

Leyna stepped backward and diverted her attention back to the groceries. An imaginary needle dragged across an imaginary record.

Jay shoved his hands in his pockets and paced around the kitchen. He cleared his throat before continuing on. "Here's a better idea. Why don't you let me cook you dinner? Next weekend—Saturday—after the solstice event is over and the festival wraps up. Being sort of like work doesn't mean it has to be a total drag. You can come over to my place, and I'll cook something to go with the wine. I have people covering the tasting room the last day of the festival, so I can take the day off. We can kick back with the knowledge that the solstice tasting will be behind us. It'll be good for you to relax and let someone cater to you for a change. You look tired. You've been working too hard."

Did he just ask her out? Great, she was starting to sweat.

He scooped up Felix, who had been worming himself through both of their legs, curious if anything in the bags of groceries was for him.

It was as though she was in some kind of battle to keep Jay at arm's length. On the one hand, he was the boy who broke her heart, the boy she spent years getting over, but let's face it, she'd have to have the libido of a rock to not be attracted to the man he'd become. Despite her best efforts, she wavered, wanting to pursue things and get to know him again.

She made a conscious effort to remind herself that while they were great together eighteen years ago, their lives between the day he left town and now contained huge gaps. Not to mention he'd hurt her more than anyone else ever had. He'd broken her when he left—ruined any chance of her having a trusting relationship ever again. Years of counseling hadn't made her forget or mended the hole in her heart. Could she ever completely let that go?

"You're one to talk," she countered, determined to keep her head on straight. "And anyway, *that* almost sounds like it could be misinterpreted as a date." She leaned against the counter. "We've seen enough of each other lately, don't you think? Acquaintanceship, remember?"

"There you go, overanalyzing it." Felix had his paws planted on Jay's shoulder, and he rubbed Jay's face with his own in some sort of welcome gesture. "Is there some cap on the number of times we're allowed to run into each other in the span of a week, because this is a pretty small town, so that's a little unrealistic, don't you think?"

Leyna rubbed at the building ache in the back of her neck, racking her brain for an excuse.

"Since when do you turn down food, anyway?"

Valid.

"Trust me, it's not going to be like work. It's not going to be like a date, it's not going to be *like* anything. Just come over. I'll pull out an older bottle from Burgundy. I'd like you to try it so you can see the difference between Old World and New World, and also in a wine that's been aged. Besides, I can't possibly drink the whole bottle myself." He smirked.

He ignored her muffled laugh. “Seriously, will it kill you to let me cook you one meal?”

Realistically, they were fast becoming business partners, so she couldn’t avoid meetings with him forever. If seeing him made her squirm, she’d have to address those feelings. Later.

She uttered an overdramatic sigh. He could be pretty persistent when he wanted to be. Felix didn’t seem to mind him, either, which wasn’t typical. Besides, who was she kidding? His offer intrigued her. Damn it, was she slipping down the shaky slope of Jay Wynter all over again? “I guess it won’t kill me. It is important, after all.”

Who strung together these words that poured out of her?

“Yeah?”

“Are you staying at the guesthouse or the main house?” She couldn’t be sure he was listening, because he made some kind of noise in the back of his throat that Felix seemed convinced was purring and the two of them seemed to be communicating through this weird language.

“I like your cat.” Jay’s attention remained focused on Felix. “What’s his name?”

“Felix. And judging by the looks of things, I’d say he likes you, too.”

“Felix... He looks like a Felix.” As an afterthought, he answered her question, tearing his attention away from the cat and wiping at the fur clinging to his facial stubble. “The guesthouse. That’s where I’m living.”

*Living.* A subtle correction to her choice of words, or coincidence?

He set Felix on the armchair as carefully as he would a newborn baby. "How about seven o'clock?"

"Fine. Can I bring anything? Takeout from Rosalia's perhaps?"

"Just yourself." He started out the door, ignoring the insult to his culinary skills, and then turned back. "You know, if this is acquaintanceship, it's not so bad after all."

"Go," she warned. "You're walking a very fine line."

He flashed a grin over his shoulder. "Luckily, I have great balance."

# CHAPTER NINE

Jay had to park two blocks from Rosalia's. A few weeks ago he'd had to be dragged there, and now it seemed like the only place worth grabbing a beer and some dinner before meeting Tim to check out a boxing match on the big screen at Piper's Pub. Apparently half the town had the same idea.

Noisy chatter and a frantic waitstaff confronted him when he pulled open the heavy glass door. There didn't appear to be an empty table in the entire place. He approached the bar, where Leyna filled drink orders. Rather than her usual dress clothes, she wore faded jeans, and her hair was pulled up in a loose ponytail.

He admired her quick, methodical bartending skills from a distance until the drink orders slackened off a little. "So much for your night to yourself," he yelled across the bar as he hoisted himself on the only empty stool.

"Tell me about it," she shouted back over the buzz of the music and the clatter of the kitchen. "I had to hightail it back here in the middle of a bubble bath. One of the bartenders was a no-show for his shift, and the chef is off tonight. With the kitchen being short-staffed, they couldn't keep up. I should know by now there's no such thing as going home for the weekend to forget about work when you own a restaurant. Stella?"

Jay ignored her offer of a beer, distracted by the damp tendrils of hair curling at the nape of her neck and the way her skin flushed, dewy from her bath. "Looks like the place still is getting slammed." He nodded back toward the kitchen. "You say you're understaffed back there?"

She blew a strand of hair out of her eyes that had escaped her ponytail while pulling the cork from a wine bottle. "Yeah, the chef had something with his kids, a couple of people quit, and I didn't want to start the new guy on a Friday night, because... Well, I didn't want him to see this fiasco and get scared off. Did I mention that for some reason there are lemon slices all over the floor back here, and my shoes keep sticking every time I lift my feet?"

Jay rolled up his sleeves. "I'll help out back in the kitchen. I'll do whatever I can."

"Jay, no, that's sweet of you to offer, but we're fine. The dinner rush will be over soon. Besides, you said you had plans."

"I do, but not for at least another hour. I came in for a beer and some food. I don't mind. Besides, we're business partners now. It's the least I can do." He handed her his cell phone, sunglasses, and car keys to keep behind the bar for him, and before Leyna could stop him, he headed to the kitchen.

* * *

Once the dinner crowd had thinned out, people began to trickle in for the rock band booked in from Niagara Falls.

Jay helped out in the kitchen for a while to get the line back on track and now bussed tables to make room for the next flow of customers. Leyna's staff was capable enough with the right supervision. He'd had a lot of fun helping out.

"Jay," Leyna sang out, stepping around the bar.

"Hey." He balanced empty glasses on a round tray. "Looks like things are getting back under control, huh?"

"Yeah, and my server finally showed up for his shift. I'm undecided as to whether or not it should be his last. Look, thanks for coming to my rescue. I don't know what you did back there, but the moment you entered the kitchen, the rest of the restaurant started running smoother. I appreciate it."

Because he couldn't resist, he brushed a stray tendril of hair behind her ear. It took every bit of strength he could muster to resist tracing his finger down the curve of her neck to rub away all her tension.

"I'm glad to help." He kept his voice soft despite the volume level of the band, using it as an excuse to lean in close enough to catch a trace of her citrus-scented lotion.

"I think they'll be okay back there now that the dinner rush is over."

She nodded and held his gaze. "Let me buy you dinner."

Taken aback by the offer, he lifted a brow.

"It's the least I can do, considering dinner is the reason you came in here tonight to begin with. You can order anything you want, on the house."

Dinner with Leyna, huh? Damn, that was the most intriguing offer he'd had in years. There was one problem. Tim would already be wondering where he was. Then again, he was an hour late anyway. Once he explained, Tim would understand. "One condition. You sit down and eat with me, because I know you weren't home long enough to eat that Thai feast."

Her lips pulled back into a smile. "Now that you mention it, I *am* starving..."

Jay grabbed his phone from behind the bar and shot Tim an apology text while Leyna poured them each a beer. She filled three more drink orders before handing over the reins to join him on the other side of the bar. Jay was pretty sure she had no idea that every time she leaned over he caught a glimpse of her pink lacy bra. Not that he was complaining.

As their food was served, she grilled him about his kitchen skills.

"Okay, I guess it's time I came clean." Jay drizzled house dressing over his side salad. "When I first went to Europe, the work was only seasonal. I worked in the bottling plants in the winters, but I needed money, so I picked up some shifts in winery restaurants, too. The more I got exposed to different kitchens and different types of foods, the more I got into cooking. So I started apprenticing part time, and eventually I ended up getting my chef certification. It was never my calling or anything, but I realized I loved to cook, and so it became this hobby that went hand in hand with wine."

Leyna's jaw couldn't have come closer to hitting the floor if he'd told her he walked on the moon. "You're not serious," she managed.

"Shocker, huh?" Surely his points as a business partner just shot up.

Her fork fell to her plate with a clatter. "To put it mildly. This from a guy whose idea of a gourmet meal used to be Hamburger Helper with shredded cheese on top."

Laughter surged, making him spit his beer across the bar.

"Admit it, you're laughing because you know how accurate my memory is," she added, tossing him a napkin.

"Believe me, nobody was more surprised by it than me, but it helped me understand wine even more, and taught me quite a bit about pairing wine with food, too."

"Well, I didn't see that one coming. I peeked into the kitchen a couple of times and was in awe of the way you led my crew with such a Gordon Ramsay level of authority."

"Albeit with fewer F-bombs," he put in.

*"Slightly."* She grinned before her glass covered her mouth. "It all makes a bit more sense now."

After they finished their meals, the conversation came to a lull while they listened to the band. One by one the kitchen staff trickled out to sit at the bar, having changed into their regular clothes. Their night was just beginning. With Jay on his third beer and Leyna on her second, they'd both be cabbing home.

The band had announced their last set about half an hour ago. Jay assumed they were wrapping up when the first few notes of "Brown Eyed Girl" floated over the room.

Leyna's head whipped around to the band, then to Jay.

His breath caught in his throat. Back in high school he, Rob, and Tim had formed a band called Wounded Pride. "Brown Eyed Girl" was a faithful cover. The first time he ever sang it at a talent show, he announced to the entire school who his brown eyed girl was. The tribute embarrassed the hell out of her, but in time, the song became a kind of ode that they played at every show.

Leyna blinked rather frantically and opened her mouth to speak, but nothing came out.

For eighteen years, he'd been guilty of switching the station any time that or any of a handful of other songs came on the radio. Some memories had the ability to knock you flat on your ass. He had a sudden urge to spare her any more hurt than he'd already unleashed in this lifetime. He swallowed. "You wanna get out of here? Maybe share a cab?"

She glanced at the band one last time before her eyes met Jay's and held there. "After this song."

The long look had him reaching for a drink. Gradually, the tension in Jay's shoulders melted so much that when the crowd around them chimed in on the last chorus, he couldn't help but sing along. Leyna's eyes glistened, but she smiled.

Happy tears. He could handle that.

They left through the back exit into the cool, quiet night and followed the brick pedestrian alley out to town square.

"Well, look at this, just like old times."

Mark Toner swayed back and forth, scowling at them through squinted eyes.

For Christ's sake, did the guy even own a pair of jeans? Jay eyed Mark's disheveled suit. It looked a little snug on his massive arms. He placed a protective arm around Leyna's waist.

"Isn't this cozy," Mark slurred. "I shouldn't be surprised to see the two of you out and about together. What are you commiserating over how to run your hand-me-down businesses?" He erupted in laughter and slapped his leg, pleased with his own insight.

"Mark, this isn't the time," Leyna warned.

"I'm sorry, Leyna. That was rude. You, of course, are capable of running your family's business should you decide to make the right choices, but Old Man Wynter must have lost his mind to be putting this guy in charge. Everyone knows that to run a successful company, you need to be able to read."

A low blow. Just the kind of insult Mark would have tossed at him back in high school. Jay took a step forward, forcing himself to remain calm in Leyna's presence. "I'm only going to say this once, Mark. Shut your mouth about my grandfather, or you'll be waking up tomorrow morning in one of those dumpsters in the back alley, and you won't even remember why."

Mark ignored Jay's threat and narrowed his glassy eyes. "It looks like you two are making up for lost time. I thought it would take much longer for you to settle in here again and worm your way back into Leyna's life. What's it been, not much more than a month, right? To think if you hadn't turned up back in town, she'd still be stringing me along."

"You bastard," Jay said through clenched teeth. "Say what you want about me, but I'd advise you to never speak about her like that again, you hear me? You don't know a damn thing about Leyna and me."

"Jay, stop." She glared at Mark. "He's not worth it."

Jay took a step backward. "You couldn't be more right."

Mark balled up his fist and lunged forward, but before it could connect with Jay's face he tripped over a crack in the pavement. He tumbled, breaking his fall with outstretched hands.

The back seam of his pants gave way with a loud rip, exposing a glaring pair of tighty-whities, Mark's jaw dropped in horror.

Leyna's hand covered her mouth, and she bent over with laughter.

Just then Mark's cab pulled up to the curb, and relief spread across his face. Clenching his butt cheeks, he hobbled to the back passenger door and got in without a word.

As the cab's taillights disappeared around the corner, Jay gave in to his own laughter.

"I'm sorry." He panted, leaning over and resting his

hands on his knees as he tried to catch his breath. "Before he split his pants, I actually thought that scene might escalate."

Leyna dabbed at the corner of her eye. "Why should you be sorry? He made a fool of himself, and karma's a bitch. Besides, I'm the one that should be sorry I didn't see through his compassionate act, sorry I ever considered an investment from that disrespectful, arrogant—"

He stepped forward, and before he could think it through, his mouth took hers. He led with urgency, fisting her hair, pulling her toward him, to savor the taste of her before she pushed him away again. Instead, she clutched his loose shirt, her chest colliding with his. His heart hammered, and he drank her in like he'd been wandering through the desert for eighteen years, dying of thirst. He wanted to devour every inch of her.

*Slow down. Take your time with her.* He forced himself to soften the kiss.

When he backed up, she bit her lip. "I have to admit, after the near-kiss in my kitchen earlier, I wondered when you'd get up the nerve to try again."

Nope. Nothing predictable about Leyna Milan. He loosened the grip he had on her hair and turned on his playful charm. "Were you hoping to take advantage of me, Milan?"

She stifled a grin. "I'm not even going to answer that. You want to try to find a cab to share?"

"Sure." They started walking, and when she rubbed her hands over her arms, he put his arm around her shoulders. They fell into an easy stride.

"You know I never liked that guy."

"Who, Mark?" She snorted. "I had no idea."

Jay ignored her sarcasm. "He made fun of the Wynters for being farmers when his dad was some hotshot lawyer. I think he thrived on mocking my dyslexia, too. He's held a grudge against me for as long as I can remember."

"Remember how mad he got when he asked me to the Valentine's dance and I was already going with you?"

Jay stopped walking. "No. I never knew that." Huh. The grudge gained validity. "I guess he was jealous I got you first."

The smirk spread to a smile, and she glanced away, lacing her fingers together.

"You'd chopped your hair off all shaggy," he went on, enjoying the detour down memory lane, hoping to lure her into it. "It was sexy as hell."

She elbowed him. "Stop."

Though she still avoided eye contact, the gleam in her eye revealed the reminiscing sucked her in, so he went on. "Rob's little sister was suddenly putting me at a loss for words. I didn't know what to make of that."

"You got all weird," she added, finally looking at him. "Suddenly you stopped stealing the remote and mocking me for watching *My So-Called Life* reruns every day after school."

"I had to stop making fun of you for that. Rob watched it, too. He had a thing for the redhead, or at least that was his excuse."

"Even your harsh reviews on my nights to cook supper came to a halt."

"Because I couldn't string together a reasonable sentence in your presence," he admitted, laughing.

"I was so suspicious when you asked me out. I thought for sure Rob was hiding outside my bedroom door and the whole thing was a cruel prank. That is until I realized how nervous you were. And then you said you'd asked for Rob's *permission*." She erupted in laughter, unable to go on.

"A true gentleman," Jay joked, taking a sidelong glance at her.

"You still are." She held his gaze and the humorous tone faded. "Sticking up for me like that with Mark..."

He kicked a rock across the cobblestone sidewalk and watched it roll into the street before turning the corner. "What pisses me off the most is the way he tried to degrade what we had, you know? The guy couldn't possibly understand what we meant to each other."

"You were right about his hair. It's definitely thinning."

Jay snorted.

Leyna stopped walking and turned to face him. "Look, there's something I need to tell you. Something I should have told you and Stefan both."

"You don't have to explain anything—"

"I have pretty much zero inheritance or savings left."

Jay took her hand and led her across the street to the nearest iron bench in town square. "I know."

"It's a long story," she began, "But... Wait a second. What do you mean, you know?"

Wishing he could backpedal, he chose his words carefully, regretting the fact that there was no way to avoid throwing Emily under the bus. "I heard you've been having some financial difficulties since taking over the restaurant."

She crossed her arms and narrowed her eyes. They looked black as the sky. Even in the dark, he could tell by the rise and fall of her chest that her temper was already escalating.

"You heard... And where by chance did you hear that?"

"Emily told me."

"Of course she did," Leyna said, with a shake of her head.

"Don't be mad at her. She hoped I could convince Pop to back off a little."

The faint trickle of water could be heard from the fountain in front of town hall while Leyna processed what he'd said, probably making her own conclusions about the meeting the three of them had.

"I see."

"Look," he began, resting his arm across the back of the bench. "The first few years are hard on any business. Ten years ago, after the ice storm, we had to replant a huge portion of our vines. We couldn't harvest those grapes for almost five years. That's practically a death sentence, but we pulled through somehow, and look at us now. You're doing an amazing job, and I'm sure things will turn around now that it's summer and tourists are starting to pour in the door."

Pulling her feet up onto the bench, she hugged her knees. "It's not so much the lack of business. We're busy enough, most days. To be honest, there was a lot less money than I expected, when all was said and done. My grandfather racked up a small fortune in lawyer fees for meetings and consultations. The firm waived a big portion, but ultimately, I spent too much on the renovations. With these old buildings, you always run into issues that aren't in the budget." She craned her neck upward, gazing at the row of brick and stone heritage buildings standing before them, then glanced at Rosalia's across the square. "The contingency plan my grandfather had in place before he died wasn't enough when we discovered all of the stuff that had to be brought up to code."

A cab drifted by, but neither of them made any attempt to hail it down. Stealing a glance at her, he played devil's advocate. "I still think we can make it work." Turning to face her, he went on. "Think about it. You're already hitting the town tourists, the window shoppers, the ladies who lunch, the locals. With a small second location at Wynter, you'll hit a totally different clientele—the younger couples, the men, the wine country bus tours...It's guaranteed to be a success, because there's no other restaurant within a twenty-minute drive. With two locations, you'd be hitting every single person who comes to Sapphire Springs, and one restaurant will always be promoting the other."

She stared at him, no doubt questioning his sanity. "Aren't you the least bit nervous this whole thing could backfire and I won't be able to pay back Stefan?"

"No. Not in the least. Stop doubting yourself all the time." He nudged her with his elbow. "You've got this."

That got a laugh out of her, and she obviously felt no need to offer a rebuttal.

"I'm serious. Stefan is willing to put forth the investment on good faith. The way I see it, you can't afford not to do this."

"Okay, now you're starting to sound ridiculous. You clearly need some sleep."

When she stood up and started walking again, he followed suit. "At least admit I have a valid point."

"Fine, you have a valid point."

Satisfied, he dropped the subject and fell into step beside her. Mark's insults from the night at the gallery still nagged at him, and he chanced bringing up their breakup again. "Leyna?"

"Hmm?"

"How were things... after I left?"

She stopped again and shrugged, avoiding eye contact. "U2 went disco. It was a weird alternate universe."

He had to laugh. "But they bounced back from that. Quite righteously, I might add."

"Yeah, well, so did I," she murmured, meeting his gaze and then starting to walk again.

"Okay." That was all he needed to hear. They continued on, their shoulders bumping under the glow of the lampposts as they combed the narrow little streets in search of a cab.

# CHAPTER TEN

The chaos that had disrupted Wynter Estate in the days leading up to the summer solstice tasting transformed into serene elegance by Friday evening. Jay folded his tasting notes for his wine flights and tucked them into the inside pocket of his charcoal sport coat. As the jazz trio finished their sound check, a server moved past him with the first tray of appetizers, leaving the scent of fresh basil trailing in its wake.

Everyone had worked tirelessly setting up tables and lights while the kitchen crew prepped food. There were times during the planning when the trivial details nearly ate him alive, but the end result made it all worthwhile.

He had to hand it to Leyna. The woman knew how to throw a function. Wynter Estate had never embodied such a level of swank, at least not in his memory. The crisp white linens and chair covers she'd spent hours steaming were pristine, and the single lily standing in a skinny glass vase in the center of each table added a feminine vibe without appearing too fussy. Even the damn twinkle lights were perfect, reflecting off the groupings of empty wineglasses at each place setting, throwing just the right amount of light to fill the tent with a warm peachy glow.

"Incredible, isn't it?" Stefan stood a few feet away, hands clasped together while his wide eyes darted around the tent, like a child at Christmas.

It really was. He owed Leyna an apology for how difficult he'd been during the early stages of the preparations, for his resistance to all her ideas. "The place has never looked better." And by God, the descending sun promised a spectacular view, just as Leyna had insisted.

"Leyna has impeccable taste. The two of you make quite a team when you set your differences aside," Stefan remarked, his lips pulling back into a smug smile.

At least he hadn't uttered the actual words *I told you so*. Not out loud, anyway. But who was Pop kidding with the teamwork comment? He couldn't take credit for any of this. Leading the tasting would be easy compared to the effort Leyna had put in.

Speaking of Leyna, she marched into the tent, hands waving orders to whoever was unfortunate enough to be on the other end of her cell phone. Gone were the worn jeans and tight black tank top she'd worked in all afternoon. A pale purple cocktail dress hugged her curves, and strappy silver heels accentuated her lean calves. The ponytail she'd hauled her hair back into was gone now, too, leaving her dark hair flowing in long loose waves down her back.

Which version was more gorgeous, he couldn't say.

"Stefan!" She rushed over to greet him with a warm embrace. "You look so handsome all dressed up." She adjusted his tie, and Pop kissed her hand and spun her around to look at her. Such adoration on both their parts. His grandfather always treated Leyna like the granddaughter he'd never had.

Stefan hugged her again, and then held her back to look at her. "My old ticker can't cope with this. Leyna, you are stunning—the image of your grandmother. Jason, isn't she stunning?"

"Yeah." Jay nodded, digging his fists into his pockets. Did the word *stunning* even scratch the surface? He swallowed hard, meeting Leyna's sultry gaze. "She's beautiful." Tense, though, he realized as she wrung her hands together. She did an alright job of hiding it from his grandfather, but Jay knew her too well.

"I thought the three of us should kick off the evening with a toast before guests arrive." Pop raised a hand to a server, who appeared with a bottle of Dom Pérignon in hand. "Open the Champagne, Jason, we've all earned it."

Leave it to Pop to think of everything. Jay twisted the wire casing and eased the cork out of the bottle with a hollow pop, releasing a whirl of fog and a minor rush of fizz.

"This was an exceptional vintage." The year they'd fallen in love, coincidentally. He ran a thumb over the label, catching Leyna's eye and holding her gaze, daring her to remember the way they couldn't get enough of each other.

She reciprocated with a warning glare, albeit with a twinkle in her eye.

Stefan raised his glass, the bubbly gold liquid rapidly rising to devour the frothy white foam. "To Rosalia's and Wynter Estate—a fine pairing, indeed. Wouldn't old Joe love to get a load of this?"

A few beats to the snare drum counted the jazz trio into full swing.

With his Champagne in hand, Stefan hurried away to greet a few early arrivals. Something told Jay he hadn't been referring to business in that toast. He reached for the pitcher of water on the nearest table, but before he could pour a glass, Leyna grabbed his arm.

"What are you doing?"

"I need some water."

"Well you can't drink water from the tables, it's for the guests," she hissed. "There's bottled water behind the podium for you and Stefan."

Because her fingers still gripped his bicep, he raised his other hand in surrender, and set the water pitcher back down, careful not to slosh it onto the tablecloth. "Okay, sorry."

She let go and took a step back, tucking her hair behind her ear and releasing a sigh.

All nerves, he realized, as she paced the small area between tables. She hadn't touched her Champagne. Jay clasped his hand under her elbow and pulled her closer. "Are you okay?"

Letting out another deep breath, she leaned forward, so she could speak without being overheard. "I'm terrified. There's been so much hype over this event, and with the announcement of the new restaurant and Stefan's retirement, it's like we're under a microscope. I've got this feeling of dread, like something is going to go wrong."

He knew the feeling. The local media and industry reps were all over him being tentatively named Stefan's successor, and the more questions that got hurled at him, the less confident he became that he could fill those shoes. He glanced around to gauge if anyone paid them any attention, and when he was satisfied they didn't, he grabbed the bottle of Dom and led her away from the guests that had begun to trickle in, winding them through tables until they reached the far edge of the tent. "Have some Champagne to take the edge off."

"I don't drink when I'm working, as a rule," she said, eyeing the glass he held out with a look of longing.

Jay moved the glass under his nose, enjoying the burst of honey, lime, and apricot. "That's a shame." He took a sip from the glass before extending it to her again. "Because you're wound so tight you're going to snap." He'd like to do a lot more than pour her a glass of Champagne for that, but for tonight it would have to do.

"Oh, screw it," she muttered, stepping forward and plucking the glass from his hand. She tipped it back and drank the entire thing in one long gulp.

By the time she handed the empty glass back to him, and wiped her mouth, Jay's shoulders were shaking with laughter. "Do you feel better? You just chugged the equivalent of about fifty dollars."

Leyna smoothed the front of her dress. "Ask me after it kicks in. And thanks. I've got to go check on the servers."

Before she could turn away, he reached for her hand. Her expectant look had his mouth going dry again, and he regretted that she'd downed the entire glass. "The place looks incredible. Everything does. You knocked the ball out of the park tonight."

She smiled and kept her hand in his. "*We* knocked it out of the park."

"Oh no." He shook his head, unable to stop his thumb from stroking the silky underside of her wrist. "You did this. All I did was give you a hard time at every single turn."

She took a step closer. "That's not entirely true. Look at this stunning backdrop." She turned to gaze beyond the tent at the slopes of lush vines, their tips ablaze with the gleam of the setting sun. "You did *that*."

Pride swelled inside Jay's chest. He had no response, because he wasn't certain he could speak over the lump growing in his throat. Their fingers drifted apart, and as Leyna disappeared into the buzz of activity, he turned back to the vineyard. Maybe he was getting caught up in the romantic atmosphere and the allure of Leyna, but for the first time since he'd returned to Sapphire Springs, Jay's feet were firmly planted, and there was nowhere else he'd rather be.

* * *

Hours passed before Leyna had a moment to collect her thoughts. Since they'd long reached the point in the night where they could officially call the event a colossal success, she kicked off her heels to run her tired feet through the cool, soft grass. And because no one was looking, she sat in the grass behind a nearby table at the edge of the tent to massage her aching feet for a minute and absorb the events of the night.

Stefan made an appearance early in the evening and officially opened the event with a toast to the next vintage. He described the summer solstice as being a time for renewal, love, and growth. A time to honor the earth and celebrate the potential for a good harvest.

Jay led the tasting from there, talking the guests through their flights of wine, and Leyna had to admit, he was a great host. She hadn't planned on staying this late, but before she knew it, the sun had descended and a white slice of moonlight glowed over the vineyard. The magic of the evening left Leyna envisioning the partnership with more optimism than she ever thought possible back before Jay did things like show up at Rosalia's to lend a hand, give her pep talks about her financial woes, and surrender his land for her restaurant.

It seemed he surprised her at every turn.

Footsteps approached, and Jay crouched down to her level, holding a bottle and two empty glasses. He'd lost the sport coat and rolled up the sleeves of his white shirt. "Busted. The sexy shoes lying in the grass blew your cover." His lips parted into a grin, and he rocked back on his heels. "We have got to stop meeting like this."

A wave of heat crept up her neck. "I needed a timeout. Between the prep earlier today and the hustle and bustle of the evening, my head is spinning."

Jay settled onto the ground beside her and poured them each a glass of wine. "I can relate." He passed her a glass and tapped his own against it with a cheerful ring. At the far end of the tent, the trio broke into a rendition of "Feelin' Good." "Congratulations, Milan. We pulled off a hell of an event."

Nothing could have stopped the victorious smile from spreading across her face. She adjusted her dress so she could face him while she sipped her wine. "Wasn't it amazing? The chitchat among guests was all positive."

"Everyone raved about the food," he put in.

"And the wine," she added. "You led that tasting like a pro." She'd enjoyed seeing him in his element. There had been lots of talk of his success as a vintner, but educating and entertaining the guests with such charisma was a side of him she hadn't witnessed before.

Jay didn't offer any response, just simply watched her.

His eyes had a weight that tapped into her self-conscious side. "What, no smart comeback?"

"All I could think about during the tasting was how right you were about the location of the tent. The view of the sunset was priceless." He snuck a look at her before balancing his glass on the grass and shifting his position a little closer. "Master artists couldn't have painted a better backdrop."

He brushed the hair away from her shoulder and let his fingertips linger. Awareness left her nerve endings tingling. She'd been aching to kiss him again since that night in town square. As her heart began to pound, she licked her lips.

He met her halfway, brushing his soft lips against hers with light feathery strokes. The tension she'd carried earlier disappeared with every flick of his tongue. Hot tamales, he was a good kisser. She could get used to this. Her eyes fluttered open at the warm whisper of his breath on her lips. The event wrapping up on the other side of the table was the only thing stopping her from inviting him back to her place. Unfortunately, her little timeout was only supposed to be a mini break. Her staff probably wondered where she'd disappeared to.

"I should probably get back," she said, resting her hand on his chest, pleased to feel the warmth through his shirt and the drumming of his heart against her palm.

"Yeah. Me too." He traced his fingertip along her cheekbone and then offered his hand to pull her up to her feet.

Leyna slipped her shoes back on and set her wineglass on the table to brush a few pieces of stray grass off her dress. Jay gave his pants the same going over as his mother and stepfather approached.

"Jason, we've been looking for you for twenty minutes." Danielle squeezed herself between them. Her voice was elevated, like she'd had too much to drink. "Mr. Murphy, from *The Post*, requested an interview, and where do we find you but crawling around on the ground."

His jaw set, Jay gripped his glass. "Mom, Cass, you remember Leyna."

Danielle barely offered a nod in Leyna's direction. Not surprising. She couldn't be bothered to acknowledge Leyna even when she sat across from her in the boardroom, so why expect any different at a social function? Cass, at least, offered a fake smile and a measly handshake.

Cass placed a hand on his wife's shoulder. "Your mother and I went ahead and gave the reporter his interview."

"*Somebody* had to," Danielle added, with a defiant lift of her chin. Yep, she had definitely overindulged.

Jay stepped toward Cass and Danielle with his finger pointed at them. Because he spoke through clenched teeth, Leyna had to strain to hear him over the clanking of cutlery and dinnerware being stacked and the slamming of tables being dismantled.

"The two of you knew how much media hassle I've been getting these last few days. You had no right to speak on my behalf."

"Hassle you didn't want," Danielle shot back, sending the stack of bangle bracelets dancing up her arm. "We did you a favor."

"That's not the point. It isn't your place. Pop and I planned what we wanted to say to the media."

Danielle pointed a diamond-clad finger. "Well, maybe you shouldn't have been drinking wine behind a table with your ex-girlfriend during a major event. Talk about unprofessional."

Leyna moved closer to Jay's side. "We worked our asses off on this event. God forbid we take a breather."

Amusement danced across Danielle's burgundy-stained lips as she evaluated Leyna with a catty once-over. "A breather, hmm? Is that what they're calling it these days?"

The cow hadn't approved when she and Jay dated, but she had no reason to be so disrespectful now. Adrenaline propelled her forward, eye to eye with Danielle. "The two of you have no right to show up here and accuse anybody of not having what it takes. You think you can sit in on a few staff meetings and start passing judgment? Jay is better for this company than the two of you put together." A month ago she'd never have believed she'd be defending Jay to anyone.

"Oh, darling." Danielle feigned sympathy, but her tone was coated in ice. "I hope you realize my son is not the settling down type. This little stint is nothing but a passing notion."

"That's enough." Jay placed an arm around Leyna's waist and guided her back a step. "Antagonize all you like. It's not going to make either of you CEO of this company."

A server approached them, waving to get Leyna's attention. "Lane, Chef is looking for you."

Hesitant to leave him to fight the battle alone, Leyna turned to Jay, unsure of what to say. He offered a silent nod that assured her he had it under control.

He'd been at odds with his mother and stepfather for years, so he could handle it, she was certain. Still, as she made her way across the tent, she glanced over her shoulder, wishing she could go back and stand in his corner.

# Chapter Eleven

The heated confrontation at yesterday's solstice tasting left Jay's head reeling. By the time he got a word in to tell his side, Cass and his mother had already tried to paint him as lazy and indifferent, and they waxed poetic about their loyalty to Wynter Estate and drive to carry on the family business. Fortunately, his grandfather saw through the self-righteous act and straight to the dollar signs in their eyes. They were clearly trying to undermine things, and Stefan was no fool.

With a few choice words, Pop put them in their places, which resulted in his mother's tear-filled confession that Cass's investments had taken a dive and they wanted to become more involved in the family business to secure a solid future. A damn pity party was what it had turned into. Still, they'd crossed the line, speaking to the media on behalf of the company, claiming the partnership was nothing more than a passing thought between two senile old friends. His grandfather seethed when he read the interview. Lies or not, their comments successfully cast a shadow of doubt over the new direction of Rosalia's and Wynter Estate, and acted as a glaring reminder of why he'd dismissed the idea of any commitments involving them.

Thankful for the opportunity to make it up to Leyna, Jay spent the rest of the day prepping for their date. Or non-date—whatever she labeled it. He'd taken great care in deciding what to cook for dinner and which wines would best complement each course. This was, after all, supposed to be about work.

Tidying up the house had also been a must. It wouldn't do to have Leyna thinking he lived like some college guy. He wanted her to see him as the grown-up he'd evolved into over the years. She'd surely written him off as fickle and irresponsible because of the way he left her all those years ago. More than ever, he wanted to prove he wasn't that reckless teenager he once was.

For years after he left Sapphire Springs, Jay had buried his feelings for Leyna. He thought about her, sure, but he never tried to contact her, never owned up to the lie he told about not loving her. Living with the choices he made became a penance of sorts. But that didn't stop memories from surfacing once in a while when the breeze rustled the honeysuckle vines or a certain song came on the radio.

His own personal purgatory.

*Focus.* He'd claimed the night was about work. After

all, they had the fate of their grandfathers' companies in their hands, and the whole thing could still go horribly wrong, especially if they blurred the lines and slipped into old habits and ended up getting hurt.

He was getting ahead of himself with Leyna. Sure, they'd shared a few great—okay, knee-buckling—kisses, but she had every reason not to trust him. And yet he knew without a doubt that she would not be easy to walk away from a second time. Which raised the question, should he just agree to stay and step up as Pop's successor? Could he accept that the deal basically made him nothing more than a puppet, with his grandfather guiding the strings?

In France he wasn't the boss's grandson. He'd earned his way with grit and determination. Nothing had been handed to him, and that mattered. But Wynter Estate held his heart. Leyna held his heart, and damn it if that didn't make things a whole lot more complicated. Hurting her again wasn't an option, which put him at a crossroads.

He needed to keep a clear head, and the only way he could do that was to focus on the food. Though Leyna had been a vegetarian way back when, he pieced together that she was an everything-in-moderation kind of girl these days, so he settled on pork tenderloin. Wild mushrooms hit the pan with a satisfying sizzle, and he drizzled wine over them for flavor.

He leaned over the steaming pan, inhaled, and by God, the buttery, earthy aroma practically made his eyes roll back into his head. The pinot noir he'd pulled from the cellar would be a fine pairing.

Those words, uttered by Stefan just yesterday, brought

him back to Leyna, as it seemed everything did these days. A soft knock had him turning off the burner and heading for the door.

"Hey," he greeted, motioning for her to come in. "Welcome." She looked incredible in jeans and a low-cut white top, vibrant against her olive skin. Her hair was piled high on her head. As she passed him in the doorway, he caught the faintest trace of vanilla and citrus from her perfume. Christ, give him strength.

"I hope I'm not late. Things were so hectic last night. I took a moment to appreciate the view."

"No worries. I catch myself doing the same thing all the time. How about we take that walk through the vineyard before we eat?" He grabbed a gray hooded sweater out of the closet before leading her out the back door.

They made their way to the edge of the vineyard and meandered through the rows. Jay pointed out different grape varietals and explained the various conditions in which each thrived, waiting for an opportune moment to launch into the apology on behalf of his parents, which he had mulled over all day.

As the sun began to lower, a warm palate of golds bled into oranges and pinks, casting long shadows across the lush fields. Her silence had him turning around to face her. "Look, about last night. I'm really sorry you had to witness the blowout with my mother. As you can probably tell, not much has changed here on the family front." He dug his fists into the pockets of his jeans and glared toward the main house. "Suddenly they've taken an interest in Wynter Estate, like it's Mom's birthright or something. The fact that Pop wants me in charge has her foaming at the mouth."

"You don't need to apologize." Leyna folded her arms. "Especially not for your parents. Besides, the interview could have been worse."

"She and Cass let the reporter believe they planned the entire event. And did you read the part about Rosalia's? They called it a one-time deal, nothing more than a catering job. A charity gesture for the town's little *underdog* restaurant." Because his temper rose all over again, he spun on his heel and kicked the nearest post. "I made some calls in the morning, but it was too late. It had already gone to print."

"They did this to get under your skin." She moved closer, placing a warm hand on his shoulder. "Sure, they took advantage of the situation, but keep in mind that it's only one interview. By tomorrow's paper everyone will have forgotten about it. Besides, they can tell the media whatever they want. The restaurant is happening. Speaking of which, what did Stefan have to say about it all?"

They circled back toward the house, and Jay let them inside. "I think he's torn because of a sob story they gave about Cass's investments collapsing. He seemed genuinely concerned, but he also said they overstepped, and that they overreacted about my disappearing when the paper was looking for an interview. I caught the slightest trace of satisfaction on his face when my mom told him I was under a table with you and a bottle of estate reserve."

Color rose in Leyna's cheeks, and she bit her lip,

surely to ward off the smirk threatening to play across her mouth.

They got a start on dinner, eating in silence for a few moments before Leyna put down her fork to take a drink of wine. "So, besides being an unbelievable cook, what other surprises do you have hiding from the past eighteen years?"

Jay leaned back from the table. "That's basically all the surprises. I immersed myself in vineyard work to soak up everything I could possibly learn. Pop would come and visit fairly regularly, and I came home to help out here when I got the chance. The truth is those trips home were way too few and far between."

If she held that detail against him like half the other people he knew, she didn't show it.

"You must've had time for a little fun."

Jay's lips curved upward. "Naturally. What about you? You must have done something in the past eighteen years that would shock me."

She remained quiet a few moments, considering. "I studied business after high school, as per my grand plan. I wanted to take over the restaurant more than anything, so I needed to make sure I could pull it off when the time came. Jury's still out on that," she added, shaking her head.

He stroked the back of her hand. "You're doing an amazing job with Rosalia's. I wish you could see that through all the turmoil."

She shrugged. "I do appreciate you saying that. It's just hard when you're in the thick of it, I guess. There's a lot of pressure, combined with knowing the only reason I've even been entrusted with the restaurant is because Rob didn't want it."

She trailed off, but Jay could read what she couldn't admit—that even now, as a grown woman, a small part of her still lived in Rob's shadow. Christ, after all these years, did her family really still underestimate her? He kept his hand there, and she turned hers over to lace their fingers together before continuing.

"I moved to New York after college for a taste of the big city and stayed there until last year—right before my grandfather died. I worked in some high-end restaurants, and for a while had a part-time gig at an event-planning firm."

"Is that where you met the guy you were engaged to?" Jay asked, sitting back.

Her eyes darted away, and she let go of his hand to tuck a strand of hair behind her ear. "You knew about that?"

Jay raked his fingers through his hair. "I might've heard something about it at the time."

Leyna stiffened, clearly wishing she hadn't brought it up.

"You can tell me about it. I won't say a word, I promise."

She kept it light, explaining that Richard had been a sort of mentor at first—a restaurateur himself, using his contacts in the industry to help her gain experience. Eventually it led to more. "For some reason, I couldn't give up my independence. He'd get frustrated, point out he was ten years older than I was, and we'd fight about where the relationship was going. He always sent flowers a few days later with an invitation to go away for the weekend, and eventually I'd cave.

"When he proposed, he had our entire future figured out. If I married him, we'd hire somebody to manage Rosalia's when the time came, so I could stay in New York and focus on his family's restaurants, since they were so much more profitable."

Jay set down his glass before it could slip from his hands. His stomach took a ghastly turn.

"Initially I said yes, but the more wedding plans we made, the more I remember thinking, is this really it? I just couldn't bring myself to completely trust him, and how could I marry someone I didn't trust? Not to mention my grandfather would've been rolling over in his grave right now if after all the convincing it took to trust me with the restaurant, I turned around and hired somebody else to run it."

Jay offered an understanding nod but, staying true to his word, uttered no comment.

She finished the story about how she broke off the engagement three months after Richard proposed, and then caught him with his assistant the very next day. She stopped talking long enough to take a sip of wine. "I didn't even bother to interrupt. When I wasn't particularly surprised or heartbroken, I realized I couldn't have been in love with him in the first place and considered myself lucky to have dodged a marriage to a man who'd likely been cheating the entire time. I vowed to make it on my own from there on out."

Jay lifted his glass with an unsteady hand. While he was living in France, burying his head in the sand, Leyna could have married this sleazy rich guy and been living happily ever after by the time he bothered to come back to Sapphire Springs. Relief that she wasn't, and that the wedding never saw the light of day, was the only thing that made him able to regain some composure. "I don't know what to say. I'm sorry." He leaned his elbow on the table and rested his chin in the palm of his hand.

"I'm not sorry it didn't work out, but the whole thing did make me question my judgment, considering I was engaged to somebody it didn't even really hurt all that much to walk away from."

Unlike when he'd broken her heart, he suspected she was thinking when she fell silent. Berating himself, Jay made a move to clear their dishes from the table. Suddenly his long-ago departure from Sapphire Springs weighed heavy on his chest. Maybe the time had come for them to finally discuss their past.

* * *

The house was decorated with a masculine touch—earthy colors, clean lines, and minimal clutter. With the exception of Jay's guitar on the brown leather armchair and his laptop sitting on the coffee table, providing the background music, nothing was out of place.

Why had he gone and mentioned Richard? Hello, awkward, discussing an ex when having dinner with a man, who come to think of it, was also an ex. Why didn't she just list them all? Yeeesh. And then admit the ex's cheating didn't even break her heart, because let's face it, she had no heart, because nothing compared to the unbearable heartache when Jay had left Sapphire Springs—the helpless abandonment, the tragic loneliness, the self-deprecation…It pained her to remember the way her friends had to rally around her and how her parents took her to counseling to try to pull her up out of her depression.

No, nothing in her life had ever hurt quite like that.

Leyna wandered around the living room while he fussed in the kitchen, pausing to linger in front of a grouping of framed photos of Jay and Stefan taken in the vineyard over the years. That he would have such a personal display on the wall surprised her, seeing how the place had never been more than a spot to lay his head for a few weeks here and there.

In the oldest photo, Jay was no more than two, reaching for the trellis, while Stefan held him on his hip. There was one from about the mid-nineties, she guessed, of the two of them in town square, hoisting up the trophy they won in the barrel-rolling contest at the Ice Wine Festival. Another more recent picture was of the two of them standing in a field of what appeared to be little sticks, but she knew they were vines, because Jay's foot was propped on a post with a sign that read PINOT NOIR. Stefan's head was tipped back in a barreling laugh you could practically hear, given the glow of his white teeth and the creases around his eyes. The most recent photo must have been taken in the past couple of weeks. Jay was so tall compared to feeble Stefan, leaning on his cane, surrounded by what would be their next vintage. Leyna's heart swelled at the touching display.

All these years she'd accused him of having no loyalty, but that was clearly not the case. Jay might not have been present in Sapphire Springs for every pruning and harvest, but his heart had been here all along. The proof was on the wall, and it caused the axis on which her entire world rotated to shift a little in that moment. She'd grossly misjudged him.

She crossed her arms, hugging herself. Every single relationship since Jay had been doomed by an inner voice that told her nobody stayed, devotion didn't exist anymore, and now…not only was he back, but his presence pried open a part of her that she'd kept locked tight for half her life.

Unnerved, she moved on to gaze out the window. Being here, on this property with him after so much time had passed, felt like coming full circle. His bedroom window at the main house was in plain sight, which made the days they spent there doing homework and listening to music practically within reach.

Jay breezed through the doorway, the stems of two wineglasses propped in one hand and a book of matches in the other. "Sorry for taking so long." He set down the glasses. "I gave up searching for a lighter." Striking a match, he lit a candle on the coffee table before pouring them each a glass of the pinot noir that he had decanted earlier in the evening. "Cheers." He tipped his glass to hers. I hope you enjoy."

Swirling it around the glass, he breathed in the scent and sipped, closing his eyes.

She took a seat next to him and sampled her own. Since the solstice event last night, she'd been considering the unique scents and flavors of wine. This one was like silk in a glass. "What's the deal with pinot noir?"

His eyes opened, and he blinked a few times. "What do you mean?"

"The heartbreak grape?" She shifted, angling toward him and tucking her feet under her. "I read the magazine article, like everyone else in Sapphire Springs. You clearly have a thing for pinot noir. Why was it so important to you to grow?"

"Ah yes, the interview. Pop practically demanded Fuzzy start carrying the magazine at the coffee house when he heard about the two-page spread." Jay turned to face her and draped an arm across the back of the couch. "The attraction to pinot is that it can be... impossible. The vines are temperamental, high maintenance, and they require constant monitoring and persistence. The grape itself is one of the most vulnerable because it's thin-skinned, so too much sunlight and the grapes will overripen... Too much rain and they'll rot. In the early stages of spring, if you get hit with a heavy frost like we almost did this year, it's over. Pinot is always a gamble, and the odds are almost never in your favor, but the risk is part of the fascination."

He leaned a little closer before going on. "For a grape grower, the perfect pinot noir is always slightly out of reach. It can take a lifetime to figure it out, and it'll still throw you a curve ball every time. And that's all before the grapes even make it to the vats." He grinned, tipping his glass again toward the candle so slivers of pink reflected on the table.

Listening to him lead the solstice tasting had left her with an appreciation for the way he put words to wine, almost like putting words to a melody. "How about the wine itself? What makes it special?"

Light music drifted from his laptop, and he paused for a few beats before going on. "The color is like a ruby that's been tucked away in a chest for years. It's got this seductive scent of berries and earth that gets you all turned around inside, even if you just catch a hint of it. Silky, sensual body, soft and elegant on the mouth, yet explosive at the same time."

Their eyes met and Leyna's heart rate picked up. Hot tamales, there was no way out of this one. She licked her lips.

"A young pinot is fresh and delicate, but as it matures it becomes much more complex... exotic, even. It's got a finish that won't let go, and once you've had a taste of it, it's unforgettable. The challenge to achieve something that good can be enough to drive a grower insane. But if you can actually manage to get it right, it's like... finding the love of your life after years of searching."

Eyes locked on hers, he gently set down his glass. "Completely worth the wait."

Leyna exhaled a shaky breath and looked down into her glass. She cleared her throat and forced herself to stand up and stray away from the couch, put some space between them so she could think clearly. "Jay, we need to be careful about the direction we're headed. I'm back in Sapphire Springs, and I'm all-in with Rosalia's, for better or worse." Richer or poorer might have been a better analogy at the moment. She stopped pacing, hands on her hips. "I planted a garden. Do you know how much commitment that is?"

He reached for her hand and stroked his callused thumb over the back of it. "I've got a pretty good idea, yeah."

Right. Of course he did. She lowered to the cushions again, his warm touch encouraging her to be honest with him. "When you left Sapphire Springs, I was broken, and I say that meaning more than just my heart. I retreated from everything. It was...it was bad."

His brows drew in, and he took her hand in his and brought it to his soft lips. "I'm so sorry I hurt you, Lane." He paused, pressing his lips together and then taking a deep breath. "I think we should talk about what happened."

She waved her hand. "Like I said before, it's the past, and we should leave it there."

"No, I really need to get this off my chest. I'm not saying it'll make up for everything, but it might give you some perspective."

Did she really need the gory details after all this time? It wouldn't change anything, would it? But he looked so intent, his dark eyes pleading to open the door to the past. She bit her lip and tasted the lingering trace of wine. "Okay, go on."

He pushed off the couch and paced to the window. For

a couple of minutes, he said nothing, just stared toward the main house. "I didn't leave Sapphire Springs because I wasn't in love with you. I always hoped deep down you realized the opposite was true," he said, turning around, his eyes weighted with sadness. "There were things going on here with my family, obviously, but all of that aside, I wanted everything we talked about. I wanted to marry you, Leyna."

He lifted his hands and then shoved them into his pockets. "Crazy, I know. I was twenty and you were eighteen, but I was so in love with you I couldn't see straight."

A pang stabbed her chest and a weight of dread moved in.

Jay rubbed a hand across his face and came back to the couch to rest his elbows on his knees. "But we were too young...I was scared it would never work out. You had the whole world ahead of you, and I could almost feel you slipping through my fingers. I grasped at ways to hang on to you." With eyes unfocused, he nodded. "I see that now. Hell, I knew it, even then."

A ball of fire caught in Leyna's throat, and she turned her head away to blink back the tears that threatened to flood her eyes. Her whole life might have been different... "But you said—"

"I know what I said." He swallowed, meeting her gaze. "Because I thought it'd be easier if you hated me."

She squeezed her eyes shut, but the tears came anyway. She swiped the back of her hand across her cheek. Her throat closed in and her breath hitched. She couldn't seem to catch it.

Jay rubbed the edge of his hand across her other cheek, and his voice softened. "I'm only telling you this so you understand my reasons. I was a kid, with no college education. I didn't have two nickels to make a dime. At best, I had a rocky future at Wynter Estate."

"The decision wasn't only yours to make." The words came out of her in a hollow whisper—all she could manage with her throat so raw.

Jay's bottom lip quivered a little before he drew it into a tight smile. "Maybe not, but we went our separate ways and lived our lives. We got educations and saw the world. I'm not saying that if I had it to do over, I'd break your heart like that again, but I can't possibly regret it anymore when after all these years and all the ways we've evolved, we're here, together, in this moment."

She couldn't entertain regrets right now, either. Leyna pressed a trembling hand to the center of her chest. "Jay, you haven't even committed to staying on after harvest. The more time I spend with you, the more time I want, and I'm afraid to fall for you, because I can't watch you walk away again." She sighed out a long breath and tucked a strand of hair behind her ear. "I'm scared I can't handle it. I didn't even think I was the relationship type anymore, but with you it's different."

Jay cradled her hand between his warm, rough fingers. "I don't know what is going to happen at the end of the season. I want to be what Wynter needs, and you make me believe I can be, but I have... *limitations* that I've got to be realistic about. Pair that with Pop refusing to relinquish control and my mom and Cass sniffing around, trying to stake a claim, and I've got a lot to consider."

Tears stung Leyna's eyes again, but she blinked to ward them off. "Some of the most successful people in the world have dyslexia, Jay."

He sighed. "I know."

"I don't want to add pressure by laying down expectations." That was partly what sent him packing the first time around. At least that's what she'd always believed.

He brought her hands to his mouth and kissed her fingers. "All I know is that every woman I have ever met I've compared to you. And every time I came home I had no choice but to leave again, because being here and not being with you proved too much to bear. But if you want me to take a step back, I will, Leyna. I can respect that."

There wasn't a man since Jay that she'd completely let in, not even Richard. She wasn't naive enough to think she and Jay could ever be *just* friends, but maybe she could keep a clear head this time around and not lose herself in those expectations. One thing was inevitable: She was sleeping with Jay tonight. "I don't want you to…step back."

"Then you're just gonna have to trust me."

Before she could say another word, he pulled her toward him, lips hot and urgent. Nerve endings came to life under the brush of his fingertips. Leyna's breath caught when her body clenched in all the right places. Every instance she imagined being with him again culminated in this moment. Her body practically screamed *It's about time*.

They were on the couch, though. That might put a damper on the situation. It could get awkward. Could they maybe kick some of the cushions away so they weren't so cramped for space?

"Come upstairs with me."

Oh thank God, he'd been thinking the same thing. Heart pounding, she held his hand as he blew out the candle. She followed him upstairs, and they stumbled into his room. They found the bed under the white glow of moonlight streaming in the window. Pausing at the foot of the bed, Jay squeezed the clip holding her hair, so it tumbled down around her back. When her eyes adjusted to the light, they held each other's gaze.

Gentle hands eased her top over her head. He took his time, skimming his fingertips down her bra strap and along the lacy edge of the cup. He scooped her hair up in his fist, and trailed kisses across her collarbone that left her shivering.

When she tugged his T-shirt over his head, her eyes narrowed on the tattoo on his right shoulder. Welling up, she trailed her fingertips over the dark ink adorning the curve of his warm tight muscle. "A Celtic knot," she whispered. Identical to a pendant he'd given her years before, on another moonlit summer night. The interlacing lines stood for no beginning and no ending, the continuity of everlasting love and the intertwining of two souls. The double lines represented the love between two people who, even if separated, would always remain connected.

"You're still the one," he whispered on a shaky breath.

A tear rolled down her cheek. The side of his nose brushed hers, and his warm breath lingered on her lips as he whispered her name. Intoxicated by his husky voice, she tilted her head to catch his bottom lip and melded to him the moment their tongues brushed together. The scrape of his scruff against her face sent a shudder through her core, and strong hands lowered her backward onto the bed. Was she floating? It certainly felt that way.

Leyna practically writhed with the need to touch him and be touched. The room spun into a blur as she surrendered to his hands and his lips. He found the little hollow below her ear that practically turned her legs to mush, and spent some time there, working his way up to her earlobe. His hot breath and the graze of his teeth against her ear had her blood pumping fluid, like lava flowing through her veins.

Time hadn't clouded his memory. Jay Wynter still knew every inch of her and exactly where she wanted him to linger. He came to an abrupt stop, backed up a little, and brushed some hair and the remainder of the tear from her cheek.

His voice was low. "Are you sure about this?"

How could she not be sure? Jay was here. They were together, against all the odds. A lost piece of her had finally been found. Leyna swallowed and nodded. "I'm sure."

And that was the last clear thought she had the rest of the night.

* * *

Leyna snuggled into the curve of Jay's warm body. "Is this a dream?"

"It's not a dream." His warm breath made her ear tingle.

She turned to face him in the dim morning light. "We should take this slow," she began.

Jay brushed his fingers through her hair, lifting it away from her face. "Any regrets?"

"Not a single one. But we have a lot going on. Let's just try not to get in over our heads."

"I promise we won't get in over our heads, but Lane, you're the only girl for me. There's nobody else I'm even remotely interested in."

"So then... will we be seeing more of each other?" she asked, without looking up.

"If you'll allow it, with all your damn rules, then yeah, nothing would make me happier," he said, squeezing her hand. "But I'll leave the ball in your court, because I don't want to pressure you. That way you can make the next move."

"Let me cook you dinner this week." Zero hesitation. She couldn't remember the last time that happened.

A smile formed at the corners of his mouth. "Leyna Milan, are you asking me out?"

His husky morning voice was so sexy. She grinned, running her fingers through his messy hair. "I am. So what do you say?"

"Well, I don't know." He furrowed his brow and stretched back against the pillows, hands behind his head. "You're seeing me right now, so would cooking me dinner this week be too soon? Because, you know, that would mean we'd be seeing each other twice in one week, which is kind of a lot, don't you think? Not to mention, your cooking might kill me." He couldn't go on for laughing and had to dodge her playful punch to his arm.

"I'm serious. What do you think?"

"Come on, Leyna, what do you think I think?" He tipped her chin up and brushed his lips over hers. "I thought you'd never ask."

# Chapter Twelve

Leyna spent the morning combing through resumes. Business at Rosalia's had picked up enough she could justify hiring another part-time server. She posted the job online and updated the restaurant's Facebook page with the night's dinner special. A quick knock sounded at the door.

Before she could respond, Mark nudged open the door and entered her office. "Leyna," he began, adjusting his paisley tie. "Do you have a minute?"

Despite the vision of his tighty-whities practically glowing under the lamppost in town square, she narrowed her eyes. "Why should I have five seconds after the disrespectful way you treated me the last time I saw you?" She stepped into the shoes she'd kicked off and rose from her chair.

"Can I sit?" He motioned toward the chair on the other

side of her desk. "I want to apologize and leave things on better terms. Please?"

Reluctantly, she sat and closed her laptop. She'd let him say his piece. It wouldn't hurt to clear the air. They were adults, after all.

Mark offered an appreciative smile. "First of all, I really am sorry for whatever I said to you the night I ran into you on the street. I don't even remember most of it. I'd been out with the guys and we were all drinking—a lot."

Not off to a strong start. Blaming alcohol for misjudgment seemed a bit juvenile.

"Anyway, I'm not trying to make excuses," he continued as Leyna cocked an eyebrow. "I didn't mean the things I said. I would never dream of treating you with any kind of disrespect. I wanted to lash out at someone, and I took it out on you, when Jay is the person I have the problem with."

Leyna crossed her arms. "What is your problem with Jay anyway, Mark?"

"My problem with him is he used you back when you were too young to know any better. From what I hear, he left you damaged and heartbroken when he took off without so much as a backward glance, and then he drifts back to town when things are getting good between us, and in no time, has you wrapped around his finger all over again."

Apparently, she'd totally missed the part where things between them were getting good. "Allow me to point out the fact that you weren't even there when Jay and I were together or when we broke up, so your source of information you seem to carry so much faith in, is nothing but town gossip," Leyna shot back.

Mark pounded his fist on her desk. "I don't want to see you get hurt again, Leyna, but you seem to have this thing for Jay where you lose all common sense the moment he looks at you, and it's not fair to you that he plays on some childhood infatuation. You deserve someone who would never hurt you. You know I would never hurt you, don't you?"

His hang-ups on Jay were becoming a bit unnerving. "First of all, I've made it clear I'm not interested in any kind of relationship. Second, my personal life is not up for discussion."

Mark inched forward in the chair. "All I want to do is help you. Are you sure this partnership with Wynter Estate is what you want, because I'm sure we can find a loophole. It is not your only option. I'm still more than willing to invest in Rosalia's so you're not so financially strapped. We'll find another building for you. It's actually one of the reasons I came here to clear the air."

Leyna stood and opened the door. "I appreciate the apology, but if you'll excuse me, I have work to do."

Mark's heels barely cleared the threshold before she slammed the door.

She put a hand up to her aching forehead, closed her eyes, and leaned back against the door. Seconds later, another sharp knock nearly had Leyna jumping out of her skin.

"What now?" she barked, whipping the door open. A deliveryman balancing an orchid on top of a clipboard shrank away from the door.

He held out the potted flower. "Are you Leyna Milan?"

"Do I have to be?"

"You might be glad you are when you see the delivery I've got for you." The man was dressed in a navy uniform, and his jacket had KEN stitched on the pocket. "I'll need you to sign here." He pointed a stubby finger at a line on the bottom of the invoice.

She grabbed the pen dangling from the clipboard by a piece of white string and scrawled her signature on the delivery form as Ken turned and waved to the front of the restaurant. Orchids were carried in from a white van parked outside, through the restaurant, and toward her office, while an astonished-looking Mark and the rest of the patrons gawked.

There were so many orchids her staff helped carry them in. They passed her in the doorway, setting pots on her desk, the windowsill, the bookcase, and even the floor when there was no more space. They were all different types of orchids, in an array of colors. She'd never seen anything more beautiful.

"What's going on?" she finally managed to ask Ken before he followed the delivery crew back outside.

"Oh, I almost forgot the card." Ken pulled an envelope out of his jacket pocket. "This should explain things a bit. You have a good day now, Miss Milan."

"Thanks" was her dazed response as she took the card and glanced around the room. She caught sight of Mark storming out onto the street and the rest of the restaurant's customers watching her in her doorway. She shrugged her shoulders, closed the door, and ripped open the envelope;

hands trembling as she opened the plain ivory card and stared at the message.

*This doesn't even begin to make up for lost time,*
*But how about one for every year we've been apart?*
*Jay*

She raised her head and gazed at the potted orchids taking over her tiny office. There were indeed eighteen of them. She blew out a breath as her cell phone rang to life.

"Leyna Milan."

"Surprise," Jay replied.

His sexy morning voice. Now that she'd been in his bedroom, she couldn't help but picture his chiseled V-shaped torso ending with bedsheets draped dangerously low on his hips. Damn, she had one vivid imagination. "Jay, the orchids are beautiful, but you shouldn't have done this. It must have cost a fortune."

"You're welcome." He chuckled. "I can't stop thinking about you. I know we planned dinner in a few days, but I can't wait that long to see you. What do you say I pick you up when you finish work, and we take my boat on the lake, maybe watch the sunset together?"

Sleeping with him had been unavoidable. She'd known since the first kiss in the parking lot that no matter how much she resisted, he would pry open her shell. A sane person would proceed with no strings attached, but who was she kidding? She and Jay had more strings than the

New York Philharmonic, and she was falling for him again fast.

Her toes curled inside her shoes, and her belly took a flop. "I'd love that." She took stock of the collection of orchids cluttering her office, and her heart swelled. "Jay," she said before she hung up. "I love the orchids, but no more grand gestures, okay?"

He chuckled. "Leyna, when someone matters to me, I show it. You might as well get used to it. See you later, beautiful."

She put down her phone, gave into the squeal of anticipation rising within her, and did a happy dance all around her office.

Seconds later her phone chimed again, this time with a text from Emily.

> WTF is going on with all the flowers?
>
> Get over here and fill me in. I can't leave. I have macarons in the oven.

Leyna grabbed the nearest orchid and left Rosalia's through the back door. She cut across the square and sailed through the door of Tesoro.

Emily glanced up from a cupcake she was frosting. She stood her piping bag in a tall jar, licked the pastel-pink goop off her finger, and smeared the rest of it on her apron. "Spill it, sister. Who bought out the flower shop to impress you?"

"Jay." Leyna could barely say his name without heat flaring in her cheeks. She set the orchid on the glass case that displayed decorative treats. "I figured I could spare one, since there are *eighteen*."

Emily's mouth flew open. "Eighteen orchids? What the hell?"

"One for every year we've been apart."

Emily's jaw dropped even lower, and her eyelids fluttered. "Are you freaking kidding me?" Then she gasped, and her hand covered her mouth. "You slept together." The words flew out in a loud whisper.

Nodding, Leyna closed her eyes and bit her lip to try to stop the smile about to spread across her face and wrap around her entire head.

Emily hopped up and down a few times and then fanned herself with her hand. "Well, I'll be damned. Sit down and give a girl some details." She gestured for Leyna to have a seat with her on the pale blue loveseat by the window. Books containing glossy photos of Emily's work towered on the table in front of them for customers to browse through for ideas. "When? Where? I want to know everything."

A timer went off and Emily glanced over her shoulder. "Wait. My macarons!" She darted back to the kitchen and resurfaced a couple of seconds later. "Okay, we're good. Go on."

"Okay." Leyna began settling back into the cushion. "I'll start from the beginning." She gave Emily a rundown beginning with the solstice event, and then all about the dinner at Wynter Estate, and how one thing led to another.

Emily's eyes sparkled. "I am so beyond happy for

you." She folded her arms and stuck out her chin with an air of *I told you so*.

"Oh, don't look so smug." Leyna scrambled to finish the story before Emily boiled over with excitement. "We're going to take it really slow."

"Well, it was inevitable," Emily replied. "But we have more important things to discuss at the moment, like how was it?"

Leyna gave Emily a knowing look. "Seriously, you're asking me how the sex with Jay was?"

At Emily's impatient glare Leyna gave in. "Amazing." She curled forward, resting her head on her white linen pants, because reliving it practically made her knees buckle.

Emily clapped her hands together. "So now what?"

Leyna sat back up and forced herself to focus. "We're seeing each other again tonight and I'm cooking him dinner this week."

Emily's expression turned serious. "*You're* cooking?"

Okay, ouch. She was a really bad cook, but still. "Probably ordering in, now that I actually think it through."

"If you cook, go with pasta of some kind. It's next to impossible to burn boiling water. You can handle it." Emily straightened the stacks of books on the glass table.

Could she, though? Leyna nodded, considering the list of ways boiling water could possibly go wrong. "Maybe I can convince Marcel to whip me up a nice carbonara sauce, some grilled chicken...Oooh, I could pick up a baguette and pretend I baked it myself."

Emily burst into laughter. "Yeah, do that and see if he

believes you. But you don't need to try so hard. Jay loves you the way you are."

The wave crashed against her heart again. *Jay loves you.* Of course Emily hadn't meant the expression in the literal sense. But the words made Leyna's cheeks hurt from smiling.

"It's great to see you so relaxed and back to your old self again. The decision to date Jay is really agreeing with you. It's been a long time since you've actually been excited to be going on a date with someone."

Leyna gave Emily a sidelong glance. "Lying to myself about the feelings I have for him was senseless. Life is too short."

"Exactly." Emily held up her hand in an offer of high-five. "You have no idea how glad I am to hear you say those words."

A rush of guilt washed over her as she slapped Emily's hand. Had she really become one of those friends? The ones people hated being around because all they ever did was complain? "I guess I started to sound like a broken record, huh?"

"I did consider billing you for all the times I had to lend an ear, but it was worth it. Besides, you've seen me through more breakups than I care to count. That's what friends are for."

* * *

Friday evening brought little relief to the stifling day. Soft breezes teased the leaves on the trees, but it didn't make up for the sweltering humidity.

Jay knocked on Leyna's door, holding a bouquet of lilies and a bottle of pinot grigio.

"Come on in," Leyna called. "It's open."

He found her in the kitchen. "Hey." He passed her the flowers and eyed her black dress. "You look incredible."

She smiled, maybe blushed a little, but then again, it could have been the heat. "Thanks. You look great, too...really tanned. You're obviously spending a lot of time in the vineyard."

A tap to a remote unleashed soft jazz music, and she paused at the table and struck a match to light the candles.

"You can put the wine in the fridge if you want," she said. "These flowers are gorgeous. I'm going to get them into some water."

She cut the stems of the flowers and pawed through the cupboard for a vase.

Jay rubbed his fingers across his damp forehead and forced himself to tear his gaze away from the dress clinging to her curves and dipping low in the neckline. *Put your eyes back in your head before she catches you gawking, Wynter.* He cleared his throat. "Dinner smells fantastic. Do I detect the scent of baking bread?"

"Good nose, I'm warming it up. I actually considered trying to pass it off as my own baking."

Eyeing her as she moved around the kitchen, he recalled the quick, methodical way she worked behind the bar at Rosalia's. She moved nothing like that tonight. She was off her game, worried about her cooking, no doubt, which somehow put him at ease.

Crossing the kitchen, he took the flowers out of her hand and stuck them in the vase so she'd stop fussing. He set the vase on the table between two glowing candles. "You don't look like someone who baked bread all day," he said, his voice husky.

She turned to face him, her back against the counter. "Oh yeah? How do I look?"

"Sensational…but tired."

"I haven't been sleeping."

"Me either."

"I haven't been able to concentrate on work…anything."

"Me either."

"I can't stop thinking about us."

"Me either." He put a hand on her hip and pulled her toward him, engulfing her mouth. With a soft moan, her lips parted and she met his with equal urgency. She tasted like freshly picked berries, and he could probably live off them and nothing else.

"That's some way to start a date," Leyna managed, when their lips finally parted.

"I think you better offer me a cold drink before I clear off this table and skip dinner altogether."

She tore herself away from him and pulled open the refrigerator door. "How about a Corona?"

He accepted the beer and bottle opener she passed him, and then grabbed a lime wedge off the counter and shoved it inside the bottle. Taking a long thirsty gulp, he wandered toward the window to take in the view of the sunset blazing over the lake. He spoke without turning around. "So what are we having besides burnt bread?"

"Shit!" Leyna bolted to the oven and hurled open the door as black smoke curled out, clouding the kitchen with a dense fog. The smoke detector began to shrill. "Damn it!" She grabbed the black wreckage with oven mitts and tossed it outside onto the deck, where it landed like a brick.

Jay waved a dishcloth in front of the smoke detector. When the alarm subsided, he opened all the windows and doors to air the place out. "Now *that*, I would have believed you baked." He gasped and coughed, fighting back laughter.

"So much for our bread." She pouted, but laughter took over. "You want to eat before I ruin the rest of dinner?"

"Might not be a bad idea," he teased, grabbing the corkscrew and opening the wine.

They plated their salads and pasta and took a seat at the table. Jay poured them both a glass of wine.

He tasted the carbonara, impressed with how she'd nailed the balance of all the rich flavors. "I must say I like this domestic side of you. Your cooking has definitely improved since Leyna Wednesdays at the Milan house."

The term made her grin. "I do recall force-feeding my family some vegetarian culinary experiments gone wrong over the years. But I guess it's confession time. Marcel made it."

"Aha. The truth comes out."

She grinned. "How was your week?"

The days between seeing her were consumed by anticipation. He sipped his wine. "I spent a lot of time thinking about you. I almost called last night, but I didn't want to come on too strong." After all, she'd said she wanted to take it slow.

"I almost called, too," Leyna admitted, drizzling vinaigrette over her salad. "I could have been sixteen again, staring at the phone, willing it to ring or willing myself to have the nerve to call you. I guess I'm glad I didn't though, in hindsight. Seeing you tonight after some distance this week is thrilling. Like butterflies, you know?"

"Yeah, I know exactly what you mean. When I came here tonight, it could have been high school and our first date all over again. The only difference was I didn't have to worry about your parents or Rob grilling me over my intentions."

He reached across the table to stroke the back of her hand with his thumb, and they carried on with their meals until Leyna got up and produced a box from the fridge.

"Emily made us some chocolate-covered strawberries. Why don't we have dessert outside on the porch swing? It's a beautiful evening."

How sexy. He'd have to thank Emily for her contribution next time he saw her. "I'll grab the wine." Dusk approached, so Jay grabbed one of the candles from the table, and Leyna plugged in the little white patio lights.

He poured each of them a glass of wine and raised his glass, trying to devise the perfect toast, something meaningful and monumental, that looked toward the future, but signified all they'd overcome. After all, he'd waited eighteen years for this night. The best he could come up with was "To new beginnings."

"I like that. New beginnings," Leyna repeated, biting into a strawberry. "Oh my…you have to try this." She reached up to feed Jay a berry.

"I'm in heaven." Jay sighed, tasting the sweet berry mixed with the milky chocolate. He draped his arm around Leyna's shoulders, gliding the swing slowly to the rhythm of the melodic bamboo wind chimes. "I could stay right here in this moment, forever."

"Me too," she agreed, curling into his side. "It's absolutely perfect."

"Ten years ago, when I was home for the replant, we were all so stressed out. So I went for drives in the evenings to escape. The first night home I got into the truck with no destination in mind, just drove. Before I knew it, I found myself here, talking to Joe.

"He said all these really insightful things, told me Wynter would get through it and bounce back. I guess he was right."

The story made Leyna smile. "He was always right. Kind of like Stefan."

Her smile didn't quite reach her eyes, so he gave her a nudge. "Everything okay?"

"Yeah, everything is fine. Just thinking about Rosalia's. I can only hope for the same fate. That I get through this financial rough patch and bounce back." She looked down into her wine.

Most of the time she hid her worries well. That she trusted him enough to show her vulnerable side struck him as a major step in their relationship. Smoothing the hair away from her face, he kissed her forehead. "You will. I know it." They'd get through it together. He'd make sure of it.

Leyna closed her eyes and lowered her head onto Jay's chest. He tightened his hold around her shoulders.

"Are you getting chilly?" he whispered.

"A little," she admitted. "It's such a perfect evening, though. I don't want to go inside yet.

"I'll go get us a blanket." He grabbed the little afghan off the couch, returned to the swing, and draped the blanket over Leyna's legs.

"What's on the agenda tomorrow? Does the restaurant need you?"

Leyna curled into his side. "I intended to go in, but if you've got a better idea, I could be persuaded to change my plans."

God, he loved the feel of her cheek resting on his chest, the warmth radiating through the thin fabric of his shirt. "We could rent a couple of kayaks from Tim and spend the day paddling. Maybe pack lunch if you want to make a day of it."

He held her in his arms as the sky darkened, and they made loose plans as the first few stars began to twinkle. "Maybe we should go to bed early." He took her hand and pulled her off the swing. "You know, to get a good night's sleep."

She grinned, rising up on her toes to kiss him. "I get the feeling we won't be getting much sleep."

He wrapped his arms around her and breathed in the smell of oranges from her hair. "Whatever. Sleep is highly overrated."

# Chapter Thirteen

Town square buzzed with activity despite it only being eight o'clock in the morning. The holiday weekend kicked off later in the day with activities for the kids, followed by a street closure that evening for the annual Fourth of July street dance. The next day's schedule began with a breakfast at town hall, followed by a maple syrup contest. Local bands were slated to play sets of live music in town square all afternoon, segueing into the parade of lights and fireworks down on the harbor beginning at dusk.

Leyna had hired extra staff for the weekend and would probably spend a good portion of it at the restaurant if they needed her. Working her pace up to a brisk jog, she turned the corner, leaving the honking horns in town square behind and heading for the marina.

There was a time in her life when she avoided the harbor whenever possible. The dappling reflections of lights on the water only served to remind her of the nights she'd spent down there with Jay as a teen. Especially the night they'd shared their first kiss. That giddy nervousness, his soft lips against hers, the way the wind teased the hair around her face, and the sound of the rippling water lapping against the boats in the marina.

Now, with the morning's warm sunlight bouncing off the water to envelop her, she basked in those memories, welcoming them for the first time in years and letting them transport her to another time, rather than burying or belittling them. How far she and Jay had come since their paths had crossed again. They shared a connection neither of them could deny, and despite all those years apart, they just…fit.

Life seemed dangerously perfect these days. She and Jay found excuses to see one another almost every day, not to mention the phone calls and texts.

Consequences nagged at her, when she allowed them to. Would she end up with a broken heart again? If Jay went back to Burgundy, where did that leave things on a professional level? What if he left and for the rest of her life she never felt the way she did when she was with him? Still, Jay was worth the risk. If he did leave, at least she'd always know they tried. She owed it to herself to give it a shot, and so she put those fears aside and chose to trust. Besides, he barely mentioned his life in France lately. It didn't seem to be a factor at all anymore.

She'd just upped the volume on her music when she spotted her mother exiting Tim's Boat Shop. Crap. Her parents were likely wondering why she was so scarce lately. She wasn't prepared for that conversation just yet, so she changed course quickly, heading toward the gallery.

"Leyna," Mom yelled, waving a stack of papers.

Double crap. With a sigh, she removed her earbuds and switched to a slower jog on the spot. "Hey, Mom. What brings you downtown?"

Nina propped her sunglasses into her freshly set brown hair, the tortoiseshell frames nearly getting lost in her caramel highlights. "We're doing a promotional package with Tim—discounted boat rentals for B&B guests. I dropped off the contract. Are you running early to beat the heat?"

Leyna pulled her long ponytail to the side and fanned the back of her neck with her hand. "I am. It's going to be a hectic weekend, so this is the last run I'll squeeze in, I'm sure."

"We're booked solid," her mother said, admiring a sailboat gliding across the lake. "Tim said the Nightingale Inn is booked up, too. Rob wants to come for the long weekend, but we've got nowhere to put him."

"They could stay at my place," Leyna offered. She wasn't sure where that left her, considering she only had one guest room, but it might be a perfect excuse to have a sleepover with Jay. The idea had goosebumps rising to the surface of her skin, despite the rising temperature.

Tapping a French manicured nail to her chin, Nina considered. "Actually he's coming alone, so you would have room. I hadn't thought of your place as an option. I'll call him when I get to the car."

Visions of playing house with Jay for the weekend slowly evaporated. "Why's he coming alone?"

Nina hoisted her purse onto her shoulder. "They were supposed to be going to Issey's parents' place, but something came up, and Issey ended up having to work on a special project. Her parents had their hearts set on having Carly and Sarah for the weekend, so Rob decided they could still go, and it would give him a chance to come here for the weekend and see Jay. The two of them have a lot of catching up to do now that it seems you and Jay are... an *item* again," she added, pursing her lips.

Exhibit A in why she'd been avoiding her mother. If she were talking to Emily, she could gush on and on about the fairy-tale couple of weeks she'd had with Jay, but what exactly were you supposed to tell your mom? Leyna feigned shock at the statement, but her act was no competition for the smile creeping across her face. "I'm not sure I'd use the term *item*."

"The two of you have practically been inseparable for days. It's not as though your father and I don't see his truck parked at your house. Are we getting the wrong impression?"

"No..." Leyna shook her head, focusing on the wooden planks of the boardwalk. "Things are going really well. Better than I could have imagined, but I hesitate to label it at this point. It's early, you know?"

Nina's mouth formed a tight line when she tilted her head to the side, swinging her gold hoop earrings. "Take your time with him. You never know when he might decide to go back to France, and I can't bear to see you heartbroken again."

Leyna nodded, shifting her weight from one foot to the other, causing the wharf to dip under her weight. It shouldn't have surprised her that they would be reluctant to accept Jay back into their lives after the way he'd hurt her. "Jay's changed a lot. He's grown up, you know? I think he'll surprise you when you see how committed he is to Wynter Estate."

Nina smiled, reaching out to squeeze Leyna's arm before putting her sunglasses back on. "A parent always worries, especially about their little girl. But your father and I have been mulling it over, and if you can forgive Jay and move forward, then so can we. In fact, why don't we all have dinner after the holiday? The guests will have all checked out, so your father and I can host."

"Thanks, Mom," Leyna said, relaxing a little at the mention of forgiveness. Her parents' acceptance of a relationship between her and Jay took a lot of the pressure off. Her family and Jay gathering under one roof was bound to happen eventually, especially with the family businesses working together, and the way things were going with them on a personal level. The longer they put it off, the more awkward it might be.

"I appreciate the two of you making an effort. I know Jay will, too."

* * *

The humidity cast a thick haze on the horizon, blurring

the view of the skyline. Jay's crew complained so much all afternoon about the heat, he invited everybody back to the warehouse for a cold beer before sending them home early for the holiday weekend.

He let himself inside his house, appreciating the blast of air-conditioning that met him as he stepped into the foyer. His plans included a cold shower and texting Leyna to see if she could sneak away from work early enough to join him for the steaks marinating in the refrigerator. Hopefully he could entice her to spend the night, too. His cooking seemed to work some sort of magic spell on her. Maybe good food really was a prelude to sex.

Jay relished the spray of cool water, welcome after the hot, dusty day spent outside. Only a couple of weeks had passed since he and Leyna crossed the line to lovers again, but he was already getting accustomed to rolling over in the night and wrapping her in his arms to draw her close. Each night they spent together, Jay fell asleep combing his fingers through her silky hair, quietly amazed she was really there.

Something had shifted since they'd spoken openly and honestly about their fears, and a new understanding had been reached, leaving him wondering...Could it really all be within reach? Leyna *and* Wynter Estate? Had the timing simply been wrong up until now?

Maybe some things really were worth the wait.

Recharged after his shower, he bumped down the stairs to get a start on dinner. Still no text from Leyna. They were probably getting slammed with the influx of tourists in town. He debated going down and giving her a hand, at least until the dinner rush ended, but his back and shoulders throbbed from the day's work.

A knock took priority, and Jay flung the door open. "Rob?"

Framed by hanging flowerpots, Leyna's brother stood on the welcome mat with his finger hovering over the doorbell. He hadn't changed at all, other than a few creases around his dark eyes and some extra cushioning around the midsection. "My God, what's it been, eighteen years?"

"About that, yeah." Rob took a step forward and grabbed Jay in a hug, slapping him on the back. "Good to see you, man."

Leyna insisted Rob was cool with whatever was going on between them, but a man-to-man talk was no doubt the purpose of this surprise visit. Jay invited him into the kitchen and grabbed a beer for each of them while Rob parked himself on a stool at the butcher block island.

Rob accepted the beer Jay handed him. "So. You're back."

Yep. The riot act was about to be read. Not that he blamed Rob. Any self-respecting older brother would be skeptical of his sister's ex coming back on the scene. He lowered onto the other stool. "I'm back. Cue the lightning bolt."

Rob swiveled to study Jay with a furrowed brow, and then leaned closer to inspect his hair. "Are those a few grays coming in around your temples, Wynter?"

The jab broke the tension, and Jay touched the hair in question. "Maybe a few here and there—all of which are a result of moving back to Sapphire Springs, I'm sure. What about that spare tire you're sporting? Drinking too much beer?"

Rob shot Jay a glare. "It's called sympathy weight. You'll know all about it someday when you've got a pregnant wife craving Ben and Jerry's at all hours of the night."

The useless banter was refreshing, but they were stalling. "How is the family? I heard you got married, spawned a couple of rug rats."

Rob smiled at the mention of his kids, and Jay detected a tenderness he'd never known his friend to have.

"They're great. They didn't come with me this time. They're spending the weekend with their other grandparents."

Rob was a dad. Jay still had a hard time believing it. "You must have your hands full, and you're outnumbered by females, too."

"Tell me about it. I've got Guinness, though, our chocolate lab. He's my best friend."

The term *best friend* hung in the air, amplified by the ticking of the hall clock. Jay took a swig of beer before broaching the elephant in the room. "Look, Rob, I know we're both thinking it, so I might as well bring it up so it's out of the way. I broke your sister's heart when I left Sapphire Springs. Just so you know, I've never forgiven myself."

Rob bit his lip and leaned an elbow on the island. "Man, you guys were something else. I couldn't believe you wanted to date Leyna—wasn't entirely sure I should let you," he added, side-eyeing Jay. "My little sister suddenly became a girl guys our age talked about in the locker room. Any one of them would have tried to get with her if I wouldn't have killed them with my bare hands, but you had the class to ask my permission. To promise me you'd be careful with her."

The memory, and all it implied, reduced Jay to dirt. His stomach twisted, and he picked at the callus on the palm of his hand to avoid looking at Rob, who continued to lay it on.

"Dad always said your charm and chivalry were a result of being raised by an old man. I took one look at you the night of your first date, and I knew I could trust you with her because your feelings for her were written all over your face. I wouldn't have had that kind of faith in any other guy."

"And then two amazing years later I threw it all away." Jay stared into his empty bottle. Amazing, how fast you could knock back a drink when your head rested on the chopping block. If the goal of Rob's reminiscing was to make him hate himself even more, he did a bang-up job.

"But it broke your heart, too," Rob countered, with a lift of his shoulders. "Anyone could see that. You looked like you'd been dragged behind a train."

"It felt that way," Jay admitted, rising to fetch them each another beer.

Rob twisted off the cap but set the bottle to the side without taking a drink. "I understood why you broke up with Leyna. The two of you were too young to settle down, and you were at a crossroads with your family. Better to end it than to grow apart and fizzle into nothing. I also realize you hurt her in the best way you knew how, so that she'd hate you instead of love you. But what I never could figure out is why you thought you had to sever ties with me, too."

Rob's words were a sucker punch to the gut. Jay swallowed hard. "I didn't deserve your friendship after the way I hurt Leyna. And to be honest, I assumed you wanted my head on a platter."

Rob gave a knowing nod, and a smile teased his lips. "Maybe I did have it in for you at first, but mostly I was pissed because of what your leaving meant for the band." He turned serious again as he went on. "I'm not going to get all overprotective, because Leyna can handle herself, but I need to know if you plan on sticking around this time, because if you hurt her again, I will have to break both your legs."

The hint of humor in his voice suggested Rob was probably exaggerating with the remark about breaking both his legs, but he did have the Milan temper, which meant anything was possible. Jay rubbed the heel of his hand over his three days' growth. "Leyna has good reasons for keeping her guard up. I want Wynter Estate, but I don't know if I've got it in me to deal with the family drama here. The only thing I *do* know is I've never stopped loving Leyna, and I'm tired of trying to fill a void with women who don't measure up. I want to work things out with her more than I ever realized."

Rob gave his silent nod again, but this time he picked up the beer and drank. "I hear the two of you are poised to be business partners if you decide to stay."

Jay grinned, despite the serious nature of the conversation. "I know what you're thinking, and trust me, I thought Stefan was batshit crazy too at first, but the more I think about it...Man, we could make a hell of a team."

"Leyna's got some stuff to figure out."

Jay debated bringing up the finance issues for all of about ten seconds. "I know about the money problems with the restaurant, and to be honest with you, it doesn't add up to me."

Rob scratched his head. "I'm surprised she put her pride aside long enough to admit any kind of weakness, especially to you, but I'm not sure I understand what you think doesn't add up."

Maybe he should have quit while he was ahead. After all, the financial state of the Milan family restaurant was hardly any of his business, but so far Rob hadn't told him to go to hell, so Jay deemed the visit a success. Unfortunately, the can of worms was open, so he pressed on, explaining how Stefan claimed to know the details of Joe's will and how much money he left Leyna.

"I don't doubt Stefan was privy to the details," Rob said with an absent wave of his hand. "Nothing against either one of our grandfathers, but they may not have understood just how much Leyna's vision for the place would cost, especially when you factor in the age of the building and her plans for a concert venue. She's got big ambitions and very expensive taste."

"But does it make sense that Joe would owe so much in lawyer fees?"

Rob tipped back his bottle before going on. "Gramp

settled on the decision to leave Leyna the restaurant about two months before he died. Apparently he had numerous meetings to hammer out all the details so it'd be a smooth transition for Leyna. She wasn't aware of the meetings until they were all broken down on the invoice. Mark even waived some of the fees as a favor, because he felt bad that she got hit with bills she wasn't prepared for."

Jay's stomach took a turn. "Mark?"

"Well, yeah," Rob said, meeting Jay's gaze. "Toner's is the only estate law firm in Sapphire Springs."

"Which puts Mark front and center in this puzzle." Heat rose up the back of Jay's neck and his jaw hardened. "If he's got a role in this, then the plot just thickened."

Rob sat up straighter and pulled his stool closer to the island, scraping the legs against the ceramic tile floor. "Are you suggesting Mark's firm took my family for a ride?"

There was the Milan temper, on the verge of flaring up. If they jumped to conclusions, it may not end well. Jay held up his hands. "I don't know the specifics of any of it. I'm just saying Mark's involvement might be an angle that deserves some consideration."

Tapping a finger to his chin, Rob blew out a long breath. "Alright. I'll ask Leyna to let me review the paperwork from the law firm, and if I find anything sketchy, he's got a lawsuit on his hands. For now, let's put it out of our minds.

Jay's phone vibrated with a text. "It's Tim."

"What's he got going on these days? It's been a while since I saw him."

Jay craned his neck to check the grandfather clock in the hall. "Probably just leaving the shop. Melissa is arriving tomorrow. He's itching to check out the street dance in town square tonight."

Rob rubbed his hands together. "Great idea. You got any more beer in that fridge?"

"Among other things," Jay said, a mischievous smile playing on his lips.

Rob pushed off the stool and opened the refrigerator. "Good. I'm without my kids on a Friday night for the first time in months, and it's about time us guys caught up. Nice steaks in here, too," he said, rummaging. "Let's get your grill fired up."

Though he'd imagined a quiet night with Leyna, damn, he'd missed Rob. The tension from earlier melted, and Jay couldn't have been more relieved. He reached for the phone to text Tim, but paused to look at Rob.

"What?"

"I just thought of something. If your youngest kid is a year and a half old, how come you haven't lost that sympathy weight yet?"

Rob rolled his eyes before breaking into a bellowing laugh. "Screw you."

# Chapter Fourteen

Nobody made it to the breakfast at town hall Saturday morning.

Sunlight filled Leyna's bedroom with a hazy glow. She stretched lazily, basking in the warmth of it on her face, and rolled into the warm spot where Jay had slept. Her eyelids fluttered open as she registered voices and the scent of coffee and bacon wafting up the stairs.

Rob was staying at her house, and he and Jay were downstairs cooking breakfast.

No need to be alarmed. When she had gotten Rob up to speed with everything going on with Jay, he'd promised not to be an ass. If last night's street dance shenanigans were any indication, her brother and Jay had worked out their differences, and the bursts of laughter coming from downstairs confirmed their truce crossed over into sobriety.

She'd had no intention of going to the street dance when she got off work the night before, but several texts from Emily and Jay wore her down. Drinks were being had at Jay's place beforehand, and by the time she arrived, the guys had pulled out the guitar and were brushing up on a handful of songs their band used to play at the coffee house.

When the cab dropped them amid a mob of people in town square, the dance was well underway. A bunch of girls from the salon belted out the chorus of "Here for a Good Time," beer sloshing over the sides of their cups, while Fuzzy nudged his way through the crowd handing out schedules for Saturday's events.

Near the end of the night, when "Wonderful Tonight" trickled through the swaying couples in the square, Jay wrapped his arms around her and whispered, "Come home with me?"

They'd compromised on her place, since Rob had to get home, too, and it would be easier to find a cab if they were all going the same way.

She stretched contentedly and then made her way down to find the guys.

Shoulder to shoulder at the kitchen counter, Jay and Rob diced up the makings of an omelet and buttered toast. Funny how Rob was the one who could cook, but she'd wanted the restaurant.

"Morning."

Both of them spun around, and Jay crossed the kitchen to kiss her. "Morning, beautiful."

Rob passed her a cup of coffee, bless him.

"What did I tell you two about PDA last night in the cab?"

Jay winked and let go of her hand to tend to the sizzling bacon. "Sorry, dude, I couldn't help myself."

"You two haven't changed at all." Leyna settled at the table with her coffee. "Are you going to be able to stomach maple syrup a couple of hours from now?"

Slowly, they turned to look at each other. Recollection in the form of panic flashed across their faces.

Rob planted his face in his palm. "Right...How'd we get roped into judging a maple syrup contest again?"

"Fuzzy Collins wouldn't take no for an answer," Jay offered. "And Leyna and Emily were right there with him like a couple of cheerleaders."

The egg mixture Rob poured sputtered in the hot pan. "After a night of drinking, what could possibly be more appetizing than tasting countless types of maple syrup?"

"The sugar headache is coming on at the very thought," Jay added.

"Sugar headache, right...It's got nothing to do with the alcohol last night." Leyna's phone chimed with a text. "Em says she can't wait to see the two of you in action."

Jay placed a plate of toast on the table and took the seat opposite her. "I thought she'd be busy campaigning for the election today."

"Or wallowing because Melissa is coming to town." With a few twists of the grinder, Rob added pepper to his bubbling concoction. "I can't believe she's still hung up on Tim twenty years later."

Leyna's head snapped up from her phone fast enough to trigger whiplash. "What did you say?"

"Did you really think nobody noticed the hair tossing and longing gazes?" With a flick of his hand, Jay did a pathetic impression.

Oh, this was not good. "Does Tim know?"

"Please." Rob flipped the omelet with a quick jerk of the pan. "Tim is so oblivious, he's probably the only person in Sapphire Springs who *doesn't* know."

She shrugged it off to save face. "She'll be fine. It's not like she's in love with the guy." Leyna wasn't willing to admit that to Tim's two oldest friends, anyway. Before they could discuss it further, she took the plate Rob passed her and changed the subject. "I saw Mom down at the harbor yesterday morning, and she invited us to dinner on Monday."

Jay's fork froze inches from his mouth. "Us?" A glob of egg slipped off the fork and landed on his dish with a plop.

"Yes, *us*. And Rob, too, because you'll still be here, right?" She looked to her brother for reassurance and gave him a little kick under the table.

"Yeah, I'll be there," he managed through a mouthful of toast, too absorbed by his food to pick up on her hint to help downplay the significance of the dinner.

Jay's eyes darted left. "Um…"

"It'll be fine." Leyna reached across the table and squeezed his hand. "They don't hold a grudge."

His shoulders settled. "Okay, sure, if you think they're alright with me."

"None of us held a grudge as long as Leyna, trust me." Rob grinned and topped up everyone's coffee. "In fact, I'd like to propose a toast. To Jay. It's been far too long. I've missed you. And to Leyna, for having the courage to believe in second chances. The two of you look beyond happy, and I want you to know, without getting all weird, that you have my blessing. If you care…"

Rob's blessing did matter, though she'd probably never tell him as much. Leyna's heart swelled, despite the knot in her stomach as a flash of uncertainty crossed Jay's face.

He cleared his throat. "And to *you*." Jay tipped his mug toward Rob. "For being the brother I never had."

"Hear! Hear!" Rob raised his mug and tapped it against theirs.

Whatever trace of hesitancy she'd picked up on vanished when he clasped hands with her and flashed that irresistible smile, taking all her reservations away. As usual, she was probably jumping to conclusions, already preparing herself for the bottom to drop out of her good fortune, since that was what she'd grown accustomed to. But she and Jay were making progress, and she needed to stop reading something into every questionable expression on his face.

Still, as the morning wore on, he grew quiet, and Leyna couldn't shake the notion that Rob's words added weight to an already delicate situation. She didn't say anything, though, because she didn't want to pressure him. They got serious really fast the first time around—too fast. It would be stupid to repeat mistakes.

Thankfully, the festivities in town square were a perfect

distraction. Fuzzy nabbed Rob and Jay the moment they arrived, ushering them off to the tent where the maple syrup contest was happening.

Leyna wormed her way through the park toward Tesoro, stepping around blankets spread on the grass. Emily had a table set up on the sidewalk where she handed out flyers encouraging people to vote and complimentary cupcakes decorated in fluffy white frosting. "Those look downright heavenly, but it's a bit too early for dessert."

"Tell me about it." Emily tipped back a large bottle of water and chugged. "I'm trying to hydrate. What do you think of my outfit? Is it too childish?"

Red-and-white-checked seersucker with a little ruffle of lace around the neckline—definitively summery. "It's adorable."

Emily fiddled with the ruffle around the hem of the shorts. "I found it in the kids' section, but I started second-guessing. You're sure it's not too cutesy?"

Cutesy, sure, but in the best possible way. "You're the picture of summer. I so envy the fact that you can shop in the kids section—much more selection, and so much cheaper." Leyna glanced down at her white capris and simple black tank. "I'm boring next to you."

"Stop." Emily elbowed her. "You've never been accused of being boring in your life." An elderly lady paused in front of the table long enough to snap up two cupcakes. Emily smiled and passed her a flyer. "Where're Jay and Rob?"

"The maple syrup tent, much to Mr. Mayor's delight."

"He's in love with them," Emily said, grinning.

Leyna took the lawn chair Emily handed her and opened it up so she could take a load off. "Jay and Rob seem to be in a good place. It's like they picked up right where they left off."

"And *you* and Jay are definitely in a good place." Emily's eyebrows popped above the frames of her dark sunglasses.

Like every time anyone mentioned Jay, Leyna gave in to the knee-jerk smile. "So good. I'm still a little scared to believe it though, you know? This summer's brought back feelings I haven't allowed myself to have in years. I am in so much trouble. What am I gonna do, Em?"

"I have one point to make." Emily cocked her head to the side, sending her blond ponytail swinging over her shoulder. "Not so long ago you told me you didn't want to settle, you wanted sparks. So if you've never felt about anyone the way you feel about Jay, then why does that have to spell trouble?" She removed her sunglasses and pointed them at Leyna. "Do you realize some people never get a shot at the kind of love you're tiptoeing around? And now you're on the verge of a second chance with him. For the life of me, I can't figure out why you have to worry so damn much about it."

Clearly Emily had never been dumped and left to try to put her life back together with half the pieces missing. "What if it doesn't work?" Leyna sank back in the lawn chair. "We're different people now then we were back then. I don't think I could handle it if I fell in love with him all over again and then had to lose him a second time."

"What if it's even better?" Emily challenged her. "Of

course you're both different. You've both had nearly two decades of growing up to do."

Leyna tore her gaze away from the three-tiered tray of cupcakes and rubbed her fingers over her temples. "I'm trying to be a grown-up about this. There's still a chance he could leave after the harvest. I don't want to jump back into things with Jay because I'm in love with what we had. I want to take my time and get to know him as an adult, like I would with any other man I was potentially starting a relationship with. Is that so wrong?"

Emily's tone softened and she returned the sunglasses to her face. "Of course not."

"Ladies." Tim's suave voice trickled through the crowd before he surfaced in front of the table, dragging Melissa by the hand. "Mel, you remember Leyna Milan and Emily Holland?"

Melissa offered a meek smile and clutched her Coach purse.

"Emily's running for council, too. I'm rooting for us both to win seats so we've got each other for moral support." Tim sank his teeth into a cupcake, then licked white frosting off his bottom lip. His eyes rolled back. "Oh my God, babe, you have got to try one of these."

Melissa wrinkled her nose and pulled her long dark hair over to one side, revealing an immaculately toned shoulder. "No, thank you. I quit sugar, remember?"

"Right." He offered Leyna and Emily a wink. "Well, there's nothing here we can feed you then. We'll mosey on." He grabbed another cupcake and turned to Emily. "You've got serious skills, Shorty."

Emily's large sunglasses hid her face well, but Leyna knew her smile didn't reach her eyes. "I'm sorry," Leyna whispered when they finally wandered away, Tim's hand resting on the small of Melissa's back.

Emily removed her sunglasses momentarily to wipe sweat from the bridge of her nose. "I didn't realize I was so transparent. With everybody hanging out again lately, the age-old crush seems to have resurfaced. It shouldn't be hard, seeing him with her. I've seen him with countless women over the years, but it's easy to forget she's in the picture when she doesn't live in Sapphire Springs. I keep holding out hope that someday he'll see me as more than one of the guys and I'll be the girl on his arm, but the older we get, the more unlikely it becomes. I'm such a loser."

"Hey. That's my best friend you're talking about." Leyna angled her chair to better face Emily. "You can't help how you feel. Tim is a great guy, plus he's caring and funny." Albeit a bit clueless.

"And so, so beautiful," Emily added wistfully.

"I just wish he realized that an amazing woman is right under his nose. You shouldn't beat yourself up over being attracted to him. It's fine to appreciate those broad shoulders from a distance, but he is off the market. You've got to trust that the perfect guy for you is out there. When you find him, all those wonderful feelings will be reciprocated." Listen to her, giving advice as though she were some relationship expert, after two weeks of doing it with her ex.

If only there was something more useful Leyna could

say. With Jay all those years ago, the moment they connected on a different level, they both knew it, leaving her unsure of how to relate.

"Maybe it's time I focused on meeting someone. Really gave it a chance. God knows I could use the distraction." Emily tore her gaze away from the direction of town hall, where Tim and Melissa were taking a selfie. Despite the stifling heat, she paled. She reached under the table into the red cooler and passed Leyna a bottle of water dripping with condensation.

Leyna immediately pressed it against her cheek, berating herself for not cluing in sooner to how hung up on Tim Emily actually was. All Emily had ever done was be there for her, and while she'd been spending every second with Jay and worrying about money and details of the merger, her best friend had been silently hurting.

Some friend she was.

Emily sighed and twisted the top off her water. "I just need to accept the fact that Melissa is everything I'm not. She's tall, curvy, and drop-dead gorgeous in a J.Lo kind of way. Probably super nice, too, once you get to know her. She's the fancy doughnut franchise to my mom-and-pop shop."

Leyna rubbed Emily's shoulder. "You know the problem with doughnut franchises? They're a dime a dozen, and the quality is mediocre."

The analogy brought a small lift to Emily's frown. "Thanks, Lane."

* * *

Maple syrup had a time and place. Drizzled over a large stack of pancakes was best, but occasionally it served as a nice twist on coffee sweetener or a unique addition to curry dishes. If Jay never tasted the sweet sap again in his life, it'd be too soon. In return for judging the contest, he and Rob each received the biggest bottle of syrup he'd ever seen, a month of free coffee from Jolt Café, and a handful of passes for the lake cruise during the evening fireworks display.

As the day wore on, town square became cluttered with people. A local band kicked off the afternoon festivities. Bouncy castles and snow cones kept the kids happy and cool, and food vendors lined the whole harbor front. A slight rain shower dampened the parade, which everybody joked was typical, and the sun came out again before evening.

As darkness crept in, people lined up in front of the yacht club for the cruise. Tim led the tour, and Melissa didn't stray far from his side. She was different, that Melissa—quiet compared to the eternally jovial Tim. She radiated boredom. Sapphire Springs was no New York City, for sure, but something told Jay that Tim's girlfriend wasn't overly enthused to be visiting. It was none of his business, though.

"Does Tim ever stop fussing over that princess?" Rob worked on his second sausage, his excuse being that he had to rid his taste buds of all things maple. "It's pathetic."

Since Melissa arrived that morning, Tim had constantly asked if she needed anything and if she was having a good time. "Surely if she's thirsty she can handle asking one of the half dozen food vendors if they sell water," Jay agreed. Emily's usual bubbly nature had evaporated faster than her supply of cupcakes since Tim and Melissa arrived. "Something tells me Leyna is making an effort to distract Emily so she doesn't dwell on the happy couple."

Rob took a FaceTime call from his kids, which gave Jay time to consider the upcoming dinner with the Milans. He'd run into them at the gallery opening, and they'd genuinely seemed happy to see him, so at least any pressure over the initial face-to-face had been lifted.

Still, since the chat with Rob the night before, Jay had been struggling with conflicting feelings about the future. Should he stay? Should he go? What about Leyna? Actually there was no *What about Leyna*. Never in his wildest dreams had he imagined she'd ever take him back, and to still click with her after all those years apart? He'd be a fool to throw that away a second time.

Whatever happened with Wynter Estate, he and Leyna would make things work.

The simple solution was calling Frank and officially quitting his job in Burgundy to move back to Sapphire Springs permanently. It would certainly make his grandfather happy, but what complications would the CEO of Wynter Estate title come with? Add to it the possibility of his ruthless parents being involved, and he was frantically searching for an exit strategy.

Jay had to be realistic. He did have very valid limitations. Mark wasn't too far off the mark when he taunted him about his difficulty reading. Sure, he'd gotten through school with therapy and the help of tutors, but his dyslexia was a lifelong battle. So how could anyone expect him to decipher reports and run a company? Not only would his grandfather and Leyna be depending on him, but the fate of every Wynter Estate employee would be at stake.

Pop might be cornered into pairing him with his parents to utilize Cass's business strengths to counteract Jay's…*weaknesses*. The problem was, Jay didn't trust Cass as far as he could throw him, and the future of Wynter Estate was too important to place in the hands of somebody motivated purely by dollar signs.

Shoving his phone into his pocket, Rob stepped back into line. "The girls are doing great. Their grandparents are spoiling them rotten."

Margo Montgomery, the owner of the antiques store, and her husband were behind them in line, and they struck up a conversation with Rob that turned into an all-out history lesson about downtown Sapphire Springs, with Rob promising to stop into their store on his next visit.

Leyna chatted up Hazel, the hippie lady Jay couldn't believe still owned the yoga studio, trying to convince her to start a hot yoga class.

"That trendy stuff is not my thing," Hazel said, rolling her eyes. "Just a fad."

Emily was somewhere ahead of them in line with a guy Jay recognized from the local police force. He'd been patrolling on foot throughout the afternoon and must've hooked up with her after his shift. It was dark enough that she blended into the rest of the bodies, but her flirty laugh filtered back through the murmurs of people waiting to board.

Leyna moved to his side and he caught a whiff of her citrus-scented shampoo. “Hazel is so set in her ways,” she whispered. “People are going to resort to taking classes out of town if she can’t keep up.”

He put an arm around her to guide her onto the boat and nuzzled her ear so he wouldn’t be overheard. “You don’t need hot yoga, you’re hot enough already.”

Her lips curved upward, and the boat began to glide across the deep quiet water.

Tim introduced himself as the host and launched into a candid spiel about the town’s history and landmarks to entertain the crowd.

Jay and Leyna found a spot by the railing to take in the fireworks. When bright stars began to dot the rich velvety sky, the first one fired off with a loud bang.

Beyond the rails, the skyline was illuminated with each blast echoing through the night.

Jay was already wrapping his arms around Leyna’s shoulders and pulling her back against him. They’d been here before, on another hot summer night.

She leaned into him and squeezed his forearm. “Did I mention I’m happy you judged the contest and snagged these tickets?”

“This view was worth it.” Jay rested his chin on her shoulder, enjoying her warm cheek pressed against his. The sky lit up the lake with a different color with each and every burst.

Leyna looked over her shoulder, and their eyes met. “The view from here is pretty great, too.”

He turned her around to face him. "Yeah. The view from here is perfect."

She leaned against the railing. "I'm getting tired. I might need you to take me home after this."

His lips clung to hers and they swayed with the current below the boat, losing themselves a little with each passing second, until the cluster of people on board around them ceased to exist.

"I think the show is over." Leyna sighed when their lips parted.

There were people all around them, but Jay didn't care. "Very funny." He smiled slowly before tracing his tongue across her bottom lip. "But I'm just getting started."

The crowd applauding the fireworks brought him back to earth. Gray smoke curled in the sky, masking the glow of a nearly full moon. "I guess you're right. The show's over."

When they arrived back at the marina, Rob hailed a cab back to Leyna's and Jay and Leyna found his truck parked behind Rosalia's. Déjà vu prickled Jay as they bumped along Lake Road, sitting close in the cab of his truck, the radio tuned to the oldies hour. He turned to look at her, and she took his hand. Her voice was soft. "Remember when we used to throw sleeping bags in the back of the truck and drive up to the springs?"

Away from the lights of downtown, so they could lie under the blanket of the clear starry sky. Sapphire Springs had brighter stars than anywhere else in the world, they'd say. He'd dreamed of those nights over the years. Nights with just enough chill to wrap up in a sleeping bag, when the air was so pure, so fresh you could nearly get high off it. Through the open windows, peepers grew louder the farther they got from downtown. Wind teased the hair around Leyna's face that had slipped out of her elastic.

An ache crawled through Jay's chest. "If we still had those sleeping bags, I'd take you there right now."

She licked her lips, her gaze dreamy under heavy lashes. He could turn down any one of the old farming roads and pull her on top of him, but he wanted her in his arms and in his bed, where he could appreciate every single inch of her.

Back at his house, he took her hand and led her inside, directly up the stairs.

As the bedroom door clicked shut, he turned to her, eyes locked on hers. He traced his fingertips over her brow bones, then her cheekbones, and gave her lips a delicate brush with his thumb. He wound his fingers around the hem of her thin cotton top and grazed his hands up the sides of her torso as he lifted it over her head. His arms circled her back and his hands roamed down to the hips of her denim pants. In one quick motion he lifted her, and with a little yelp of excitement, she wrapped her legs around his waist.

They crossed the room, and though his focus was on teasing the side of her neck up to her earlobe, he managed to get them to the bed and eased her down onto it. He took his time undressing her, recommitting every inch of her body to memory. If someone told him a year ago—hell, two months ago—that he'd get another chance with the love of his life, he'd have said it would never happen. Too good to be true.

But here they were.

* * *

Hours later, when she lay sleeping in his arms, his phone vibrated from somewhere on the floor. He had no intention of checking to see who texted at such an early hour, until it vibrated two more times.

*Pop.* He threw back the sheets, and Leyna rolled over into his spot without waking. In his jeans pocket, his phone vibrated again. The string of texts was from his boss Frank, in Burgundy.

> We won the award!!!
> All thanks to your crew
> Well done!
> Can you talk?
> Where are you?

Jay glanced away from the texts toward Leyna, her dark hair spilling across the white sheets, her chest rising and falling peacefully. In the dark, he pulled on his jeans and ducked out onto the terrace, where a breeze rustled the trees and daylight bloomed on the horizon. He hit dial on Frank's number and waited two rings before his boss's voice came over the line.

"Jay. I know it's early on your side of the world, but I've got good news. The job is yours. When can you be back?"

# Chapter Fifteen

Bed and breakfasts were to the Niagara region what luxury hotels were to Las Vegas. One thing John and Nina Milan had perfected in their years in the hospitality business was how to entertain. They pulled out all the stops, even for a family dinner.

Leyna arranged her mother's best silverware over the linen napkins that flanked each place setting. So much for keeping it casual. In a few short days the menu had gone from ribs and salads to salmon and filet mignon. Her mother had even draped Nona's lace tablecloth over the wooden table under the pergola and then topped it with a clear plastic one in case anyone spilled wine. An elegant touch, perhaps, if it didn't rattle like a plastic bag caught on a tree every time the breeze picked up.

Why did Mom go to so much trouble? Even before she dated Jay, he stayed for dinner almost every night when he and Rob used to jam in the garage after school. The concept wasn't new.

She filled glasses with ice water and placed the pitcher in the middle of the table next to a bouquet of fresh daisies. Everything was set. At the end of the deck, overlooking her mother's rose bushes, Dad and Rob manned the grill and discussed options for renovations to the bed and breakfast. Through the open window where she tossed salad, Mom hummed the song "Summer Breeze." How appropriate.

Dad's gaze flickered from the grill to Mom in the window, and they shared a tender smile.

"How were the fireworks last night, honey?" Nina asked through the screen.

Leyna recalled the bright blasts of light mirrored on the surface of the lake and Jay's arms around her. "Really nice. We ended up on the cruise Tim hosted for the yacht club. The view was amazing."

And then she and Jay made some fireworks of their own. Heat crept into her cheeks, along with paranoia that her most inner thoughts were written all over her face. She was flat on her face in love with Jay. Again. It made her giddy, but anxious. Afraid to hope.

Jay would be showing up any minute, and Leyna couldn't think of a single thing to do to distract herself in the meantime. She stepped into the kitchen, where Mom dressed coleslaw. "What can I do to help?"

"I put the white wine in the freezer to chill, and nearly forgot about it," Mom said, wiping the rim of the bowl clean. "Would you mind taking it out?"

The blast of cold from the freezer raised goosebumps on her arms, and she clasped her hands together to warm them. Why was she nervous? She had nothing to prove to her parents.

A soft knock startled her. "That's Jay. I'll get it." He was already poking his head inside when she reached the door.

"Hey." Juggling a bouquet of pink gerbera daisies and a bottle of Scotch, he leaned forward to brush his lips against hers. "You look beautiful."

She glanced down at her carefully chosen pink sundress, then at his khaki pants and crisp white shirt. Okay, more like the tanned forearms below his rolled-up cuffs. He was clean-shaven, which meant he was trying to make a good impression. Some of her nerves subsided. "You look great, too. Come on in, so we can get those flowers in water."

"Jay, it's so good to see you." Nina tossed her tea towel on the counter and crossed the kitchen to hug him and kiss his cheek.

"Thanks for inviting me. These flowers are for you, and the Scotch is for John."

"Oh, you shouldn't have." She beamed. "They're just perfect. I'll get a vase before they wilt in this heat." She turned away to rummage through the upper cabinets. "Leyna, where are your manners? Get the man a beer, for goodness' sake."

Right. As she opened the refrigerator, she caught Jay's eye. "Bet you never thought you'd hear her say that." He grinned but didn't offer one of his smart-ass replies. No doubt playing it safe with the wisecracks, at least for now. "Dad and Rob are out at the grill. Let's get them a refill, and you can give Dad that bottle."

Jay sipped his beer and followed her, glancing at the family photos on their way down the hall. "The place looks great."

Leyna slid the back door open. "They've done a bit of work over the years, but they're actually considering a major renovation." In the late afternoon sun, the smoky scent of barbecue curled out of the grill, a casual contrast to the fussiness in the kitchen.

"Hey, man, perfect timing." Rob crossed the deck in his bare feet. "Dinner's almost ready."

Jay set his drink on the deck railing and held the bottle out to her father. "It's great to see you, John. I hope you still collect Scotch."

In his ridiculous lobster apron, John inspected the bottle of single malt. "I sure do. That's a dandy," he said, peering up at Jay. "Thank you, son. Maybe we can celebrate with it, once you officially step into Stefan's shoes."

"For sure," Jay said, nodding, before tipping back his bottle.

How could anyone take her dad seriously in that apron? Still, sweat dampened Jay's brow. Hopefully the temperature was to blame, and not his nerves. Throughout dinner, she studied his reactions to comments, his answers to questions. The memory of Rob's toast from breakfast the day before surfaced, the flash of hesitance on Jay's face, similar to his reaction to John's mention of him taking over Wynter Estate.

Every time she got involved with someone she over-analyzed every detail to the point where she convinced herself they were doomed to fail. Well, not this time. She would not allow herself to sabotage another relationship by putting her guard up. This thing with Jay could work. It *would* work. She rested her hand on the leg he bounced under the table, bringing the motion to a halt.

Mom passed dishes around the table. "I hope everyone likes the maple glaze I made for the salmon."

Jay and Rob exchanged a quick glance across the table, but neither of them commented.

"It's so strange being here without the kids." Rob loaded up on everything but the salmon. "I can relax and actually enjoy my food while it's hot."

John eyed Rob's heaping plate. "Take it easy. There's enough to go around."

"Sorry, I'm just used to having to shovel my food in as fast as I can, you know? It's the only way I've managed to eat a full meal in three years."

Jay cleared his throat, and her hand slipped off his lap when he rubbed his palms on his pant leg. "Will you be bringing them to Sapphire Springs over the summer?"

"Oh yeah," Rob replied. "Next time, they'll be with me for sure."

"How come no one's eating the salmon?" Mom pouted and squeezed a piece onto Rob's plate.

Rob speared another piece with his fork and dropped it onto Jay's plate. "Hey, you forgot to take salmon, too, man," he said, flashing his teeth.

Jay's eyes narrowed, and he bit his bottom lip, looking

like he was trying to stop a grin from spreading across his face. "Thanks for the reminder."

A lull fell over the conversation, and the clanking of cutlery on stoneware cut through the silence. A breeze picked up, stirring the blown glass wind chime hanging above Rob's head, but its melodic hymn was quickly drowned out by the rat-a-tat-tat of the plastic tablecloth.

John put down his knife and fork. "So tell us more about the restaurant and Stefan's retirement. When is it all going to be official?"

What was Dad's freaking preoccupation with business today? Why not just ask when the two of them were getting married? On a scale of freedom to commitment, they were practically the same thing, anyway. She snuck a sidelong glance at Jay. His mouth gaped open, and his expectant eyes begged her to take the lead.

"There's a big meeting with Stefan later this week regarding the timeline and how he envisions everything happening," Leyna explained. "It's such a busy time of year for both businesses with tourists and all the festivals that the details have sort of taken a back burner."

Thankfully, Jay found his wits and jumped in to elaborate. "Yeah, we'll have a better idea after the meeting. I'm guessing it'll be after the harvest, though, before anything major happens."

John picked his utensils back up and cut into his steak. "What an exciting time for both businesses. A new chapter."

"That's right," Mom chimed in. "Stefan and Dad had been talking about the possibility of this for a long time.

They put a lot of thought into it. Stefan must be thrilled everything is finally falling into place."

"He is." Jay flashed a smile at Leyna and stretched his arm across the back of her chair. "He couldn't be happier."

Jay's charming grin might've fooled everyone else at the table, but it didn't reach his eyes. For the sake of dinner, Leyna forced herself to relax against his arm and pushed aside the nagging worry that he was having second thoughts.

* * *

It was a little-known fact that wines reacted to the trauma of being bottled by temporarily closing up—a condition known as bottle shock. They took on strange characteristics, turning flat and muted, tasting more like alcohol, and losing their original fruitiness. The effects of bottle shock wore off eventually, and as the wines aged, they regained composure, adjusting to life on the shelf.

Pinot noir in particular was known to take longer than any other wine to recover from bottle shock, which was just another one of its quirks. Not that it made up for the previous vintage Jay squirted into his tasting glass. Flabby. Too young yet. He tossed the remaining juice into a bucket and set the empty tasting glass aside to make some notes.

"Must be bad if you're pouring it out."

Pop was a dark silhouette, standing in the open doorway of the wine cellar. "Not *bad* so much as unbalanced,"

Jay clarified, moving away from the table. "The potential is there, but the sugars and alcohols need to mellow."

Stefan shifted his feet and leaned on the door jamb. "It'll come."

Frank's offer was eating Jay alive. Just having it on his mind felt like a betrayal of everyone he loved. He forced himself to face his grandfather head-on. "It needs more time."

Nodding, Pop shuffled across the stone floor of the dim room, took a seat on one of the stools, and laid the pruning shears he carried on the solid oak table. His oversize wool sweater was heavy for early July. How was the man not overheating?

Stefan trailed his stubby finger along the tabletop, tracing the grain in the wood. "I haven't seen much of you since the solstice event. You've been spending time with Leyna, I suspect?"

Jay bit back a groan, bracing for the business and pleasure lecture he'd been anticipating ever since his mother ratted him out for fooling around with Leyna during the event. "I have spent some time with her," he confirmed, taking the stool opposite Stefan. "And before you start cautioning me about all the ways this could backfire, let me say one thing. Leyna and I... We fit. Always have."

Stefan peered at Jay through tired eyes. "I know you do. I also suspect you've never loved anyone else."

Did that make him pathetic or fortunate? Jay leaned into the palm of his hand, struggling to decide. Things with Leyna had gone from slow motion to fast-forward. Like history repeating itself.

Leave it to Frank to finally offer him the job he'd been vying for for nearly two years on the same weekend Rob gave his blessing and John and Nina welcomed him with open arms. John had even called him *son*, as if the past eighteen years had never happened. Unlike his mother and Cass, the Milans were the ideal family—a mom and a dad who adored their daughter and son. They'd included Jay in things like baseball games and trips to Niagara Falls. When he was with them, he believed he could belong.

He was stuck in a cruel predicament. Add to it that he hadn't breathed a word to anyone about Frank's offer, and Jay Wynter was a walking mess. He'd been given a week to make a decision, and the fact that he was even considering anything other than turning it down was a crippling load to bear. The only thing he knew for sure was that he didn't want to lose Leyna.

After a few moments of nothing but the voices in his head and the hum of tractors outside, Pop broke the silence. "Jason, when you and Leyna were kids falling in love, it worried me. It concerned John and Nina, and your mother, too, which I suspect was why she made everything so difficult. I don't think she ever disapproved of Leyna, personally. She resented that while she was off finding herself, you found other people to lean on, and by the time she tried to make up for the time she'd missed, you weren't her little boy anymore."

Pop had always made excuses for her.

"What was happening between you two wasn't some kind of puppy love, but…*more*. But the two of you were becoming too dependent on one another," he continued, twisting the simple gold wedding band he still wore, three decades after Gram's death. "Kids your age were too young for feelings like that. I knew moving to France would tear the two of you apart, and the last thing I wanted was for either of you to be heartbroken. But if the two of you were meant to be together, then someday you would be. That apprenticeship was a wonderful opportunity, and you were too young to settle down. I hope you don't resent me for encouraging you to go."

"No, of course not." At least not anymore. At the time, when he was at odds with the entire family, he might've been slightly resentful. "You're absolutely right. I had no idea how to deal with a love like that. I was a kid, and what I felt for her was so immense I thought I could drown in it." It had scared him, too, when he bothered to let himself think about it that way. If he was honest, it still did.

The air in the cellar was thick and stale. Jay pushed off the stool and moved toward the doorway, because reliving his breakup with Leyna always made the walls close in. "When I see the person Leyna's become, the way she's evolved, I'm glad I went. She'd never have become the woman she is today if I'd stuck around here and tied her down. I don't think I could've lived with myself if she'd woken up one day and realized I had held her back."

Nodding, Stefan tented his fingers. "And now, after everything, you're both back here, both unattached, and it's obvious you still care about each other."

"I guess were both still wrapping our minds around the fact that we're on the cusp of a second chance."

"Take your time," Stefan pressed. "Love takes patience, and who in hell is patient if not a grape grower? In the end, it is worth the battle. It's worth everything." He rose and joined Jay at the door, holding it open for him to lead the way. "Besides, life isn't as simple as when you were eighteen." He cast his gaze toward the vineyard, where two crows were having a heated argument. "There's a lot more at stake this time around, with the restaurant and my retirement. Is it safe to say this development with Leyna means you've decided to stay permanently?"

"I want to, yes, and it's a better possibility than a month ago," Jay admitted, putting on his sunglasses to shield the sunlight. "But that fiasco with Mom and Cass and the journalist was a reminder of why I've stayed away." He skipped over the opportunity to come clean about Frank's offer. There was no point in stressing Pop out. He'd probably turn it down, anyway.

They crossed the courtyard and made their way back to the main house. Pop laid his pruning shears on the windowsill of the tool shed before gazing back over the vineyard. "Which brings us to the meeting tomorrow. We'll set some boundaries and solidify decisions. You'll see my email with the agenda, when you bother to check it. It's important that we finalize the details of everything. Cass is pushing for me to make him CEO so he and your mother can run the company and you can focus on vineyard operations."

Funny how Cass and his Mom hadn't given Wynter Estate a passing thought before it achieved some success and Stefan's health began to deteriorate. Now suddenly running a winery was their life goal. They had dollar signs in their eyes, and their transparency was sickening. Every nerve ending in Jay's body coiled into knots. "I don't like the sound of that."

Stefan patted Jay on the shoulder. "They brought it up as an option. I'm not saying it's the answer, but I also can't in good conscience leave them in financial jeopardy. You're going to have to get used to the idea of them being around, and maybe get over your teenage grudges."

With two more taps to Jay's rigid shoulder, Stefan changed the subject. "Now. Has any light been shed on these debts of Leyna's?"

He should have known that question was coming. Actually, his grandfather's patience was commendable, considering the mystery was gnawing at both of them. "No real progress. In fact, after talking to Rob about it, I'm more confused than ever. Apparently Joe was having weekly meetings with the law firm, and they added up to a lot more than Leyna anticipated. You know, she was stuck with all those bills when the chips fell."

"Weekly meetings? What meetings?"

"And guess who that lawyer happens to be?" Jay continued, ignoring Stefan's interruption.

Stefan's deep-set eyes narrowed and he threw his hands in the air. "Don't even say it. I told Joe not to hire him, damn it. Those Toners never could be trusted."

"Pop, calm down." Jay guided him past the kitchen, where Maria was humming over a salad she tossed. If she thought Stefan's blood pressure was on the rise, they'd both be in trouble, so they made a beeline into his office and closed the door.

"Joe and I talked every day. Every single day," Stefan repeated in a harsh whisper. "We knew each other's plans. Every morning we'd meet at the café for a coffee and biscuit. We discussed everything... If there was some kind of weekly meeting, I would've known about it. It's not possible, it's just not."

Stefan's adamancy had Jay going back to questioning the story himself, but right now he needed his grandfather to relax. "I'll tell you what, Pop. I'll ask Leyna about the meetings again, and Rob is going to go through the invoices to make sure they all add up. There's gotta be an explanation."

Coming to a halt, Stefan pointed a crooked finger at Jay. "There. Were. No. Meetings. You *must* get to the bottom of this."

"Okay, okay, I will, I promise." Jay patted Stefan on the arm and was surprised to repeat his grandfather's own words from the last time they'd discussed the issue. "Leave it with me, okay?"

With Pop tucked away in his office, Jay rounded the corner to the main entrance of the house, checked his phone, and calculated the time difference in France. The clock was ticking on his decision for Frank, Pop had actually uttered the words *Cass* and *CEO* in the same sentence, and the most crucial meeting of the summer was getting closer by the hour. Plus he had to make good on his promise to get to the bottom of Mark and his meetings. There was only one solution: Buy some time on the job offer. He was almost certain he'd turn it down, but Frank had been very good to him, and when the time came for that conversation, it should be in person.

Skirting past the rose bushes along the side of the house, he called Frank's number and tapped his fingers against his leg while he waited.

Frank answered on the third ring.

"Jay. What's the word, buddy?"

The scent of Maria's marinara sauce wafted out the kitchen window, churning up a low growl in Jay's stomach. "Frank, I have a lot going on here in Sapphire Springs. Is there any way I can have a few extra days to make up my mind about the job offer?"

There was a pause on Frank's end of the line, and the silence had Jay clenching his back teeth.

Finally Frank spoke. "I've gotta say, Jay, I'm kind of surprised you need so much time to make up your mind. You're the only man for the job, you know that. Have you got other offers to consider or something?"

Jay scanned the pristine backyard to be certain no one was in earshot before continuing in a hushed voice. "My grandfather is retiring, and he wants me to take over. I'm not convinced I'm right for the job, but there's a lot riding on my decision."

A long sigh came from Frank. "Sounds like you've got a lot to deal with. Tell you what. Take a couple of extra days. The board won't meet again until the middle of the month anyway. But by then, we're going to need an answer. You're important to us, don't forget that, okay? Call me back if you want to talk pay or benefits, or anything else that might help make your decision." Jay thanked him and hung up the phone.

He continued across the winding stone path to his own

yard. The offer was good, no doubt, but like Tim pointed out weeks ago, it wasn't Wynter Estate. His name would never be on the label. Those vines, wonderful and deep-rooted as they were, did not represent his grandfather's life work. Wynter Estate was as much a part of Jay as the blood in his veins.

Wynter estate held his heart.

He swung open the gate and dialed Rob.

"Rob Milan."

Jay let himself in the front door and into the air-conditioned foyer and glanced at the stack of mail Maria had left on the table. "It's Jay. Just following up on Leyna's invoices."

There was a muffle and some murmuring before Rob spoke again. "I can't really talk right now. I'm on my way into a meeting, but can I call you back tonight?"

He hadn't even considered Rob would be in the middle of work. "Yeah, of course. No problem."

"Perfect. I'll call you after the kids go to bed. I think you might've been onto something with this Mark theory."

# CHAPTER SIXTEEN

Rainy days called for a caramel macchiato with extra whipped cream. Leyna cupped her hands around the warm turquoise mug that easily could have held a decent size bowl of soup and chose a small table by the window under one of the suspended industrial light fixtures. Heavy winds knocked out the Wi-Fi in the downtown core, which meant the majority of the writer types that normally hung out at Jolt Café were scarce today.

Fuzzy opened the coffee house in the nineties, during what he referred to as his Ethan Hawke phase, except even then, he'd been balding. Heavy rugs used to cover the worn floors, and big comfy couches were the meeting place of many a local art student. Very Central Perk.

Fuzzy's vision had evolved since then. Though he still featured local art on the walls, he was a bit more selective, and he'd turned the back area where Wounded Pride used to jam on Sunday afternoons into a tea bar. Leyna wasn't sure where the teens hung out these days, but Fuzzy's support of an all-ages music venue back then was what had originally prompted her to envision the Blackhorse as a concert hall.

Across the square, past the rain-streaked view of day-care kids splashing in their brightly colored rain slickers and rubber boots, a couple scurried inside Tesoro. Emily had mentioned they'd be sampling cakes for their upcoming fall wedding. Since the fireworks, she'd been hanging out with Todd, the police officer. He seemed nice, and he was cute, and if he distracted Emily from dwelling on Tim, it was win-win, especially since they were both shaping up to be top contenders for the upcoming fall election.

Leyna fetched her day planner from her handbag and flipped the pages. The two o'clock meeting at Wynter Estate was highlighted, and she'd been scrawling down a few points to discuss as they came to her the last few days. Excitement built each time she and Jay discussed ideas. Still, she wished Rob could go to the meeting with her. He'd been her lifeline—her voice of reason during the transition of Rosalia's.

Traffic was heavy and parking spots around the square were few and far between. She watched Jay's truck circle twice before he snagged a spot in front of the health food store and dashed across the square. Whatever he wanted to discuss before the meeting must've been important.

Maybe he'd finally made up his mind about what would happen at the end of the season. Every time she let her mind wander there, nausea set in. It seemed a given that he'd stay, but she couldn't let herself hope and wouldn't allow herself to envision a life with him.

At least not yet.

The door opened with a swoosh. Jay shook the rain off his leather jacket and rubbed his brown boots on the carpet in front of the door. He gave a little wave on his way to place his order, and a flutter danced in her belly. His five o'clock shadow was so sexy. What a shame she'd have to remind him to shave before the meeting.

When he brushed his lips across her forehead, the scrape of his chin sent shivers through her. He settled into the wrought iron chair across from her and set his paper to-go cup on top of a dog-eared copy of yesterday's paper. Droplets of water skipped across the table as he shrugged out of his jacket and hung it on the back of the chair. "Sorry I'm late." He lifted his cup to sip, leaving a soft wet ring encircling Meghan Markle and Prince Harry. "Parking was a nightmare."

"That's okay. It gave me some time to go over my notes for the meeting." With a scrape of iron on hardwood, she pulled her chair closer to the table. "Do you know who will be there besides the three of us and your mom and Cass?"

Jay raked his fingers through his dark hair, sending more water cascading onto the table and his locks into sexy disarray. "I don't know. It's not a full staff meeting, but Pop's lawyer will probably be there."

Leyna dried off the table with the napkin her cup had been resting on. "I've been spending my downtime these last couple of days trying to mentally prepare, but I'm not sure what to expect. There're still a lot of unanswered questions." And they all hinged on Jay. How could they make any solid plans before they knew whether or not he was staying on past harvest? Cass and Danielle had made it clear that Rosalia's was not part of their plans. Even with it written in stone, how could she be expected to open a restaurant somewhere she wasn't wanted?

Jay's eyes followed Fuzzy, rushing by the window, struggling with an umbrella that threatened to pop inside out. When he was out of sight, Jay turned back. "Have you talked to Rob this morning?"

She brushed aside the worries for now. "No, I haven't heard from him since he left."

Jay placed his cup on the table and skidded his chair closer. "He's come up with some pretty interesting information."

Midway through licking whip off the side of her mug, Leyna frowned. "Pertaining to what?"

He leaned forward to be heard over the grinding of beans and the spewing and sputtering of the espresso machine. "Estate law."

Relief dissolved a weight on Leyna's chest, and she drew in an unsteady breath. "Did he find a mistake on the invoice?"

"No, not a mistake, exactly." Jay glanced toward the counter, where a few girls from the salon joked with the cashier about the calorie content of the brownies. Lowering his voice, he went on. "But by the sounds of things, there are some shady deals going on in that line of business." His dark eyes held hers, and his eyebrows shot upward.

A catchy Mumford & Sons riff filtered through the chatter from the counter, filling the lull while Leyna processed what Jay had said. "Go on..."

He glanced over his shoulder again before elaborating. "The will itself is very cut and dried—nothing out of the ordinary there, at least to Rob's untrained eye, but there do seem to be a hell of a lot of meetings for a man who knew exactly what he was doing with his business."

Leyna's shoulders sagged. "I could've told you that."

"But does it make sense that Joe would need to have so many meetings when his plans for Rosalia's have always been to pass it on to someone in the family? He must have known that every minute he spent with Mark would rack up the bill like a meter on a taxi."

That was the very question that had been gnawing at her for months. "The problem is that it's not as though we can just ask him."

Jay leaned his elbows into the small square table so their heads were close. She could smell his woodsy cologne. "Some colleagues of Rob's said sometimes lawyers find little ways to overcharge in these instances, and because their client is dead and gone before anyone sees the bill, it's next to impossible to prove. Apparently it's pretty common in estate law."

Leyna furrowed her brow, unsure she understood. "I'm sorry, are you implying that Mark ripped me off?"

He shrugged and picked her pen off the table to click the end. "It's just a theory."

"It's a pretty serious accusation, Jay." Farfetched, too. Was this why she'd barely heard from him the last few days? Here she'd been questioning every detail of the family dinner, worrying if he was having second thoughts about a relationship with her, when all the while he was playing Hardy Boys with her brother. She uttered a long sigh. "If my grandfather's lawyer were anyone other than Mark, would you be as motivated to dig into this?"

"Yes. Something doesn't add up, and Rob agrees with me. If we're wrong, and the billing is accurate, then we'll let it go, but either way, we're going to get to the bottom of it. Besides, if there's any kind of foul play, I owe it to you to figure it out, Leyna. Hell, I owe it to Joe and your family too. Even Pop."

Aha. Guilt fueled this determination. She should have seen it sooner. He wanted to make amends, rectify the past. What he didn't understand was that having him poke around in her finances was humiliating. "Jay, you don't owe me anything. You don't have to solve some mystery for me to make up for the past. You don't have to fix it for my family because you hurt me, or Stefan because you stayed away too long. It doesn't work that way."

He blew right past what she'd said, still clicking the pen. "Obviously we can't prove anything, but we need to give this consideration."

Mark was a lot of things, but criminal wasn't likely to be one of them. Sure, thousands of dollars was a lot of money to her, but not enough of a payout to be worth risking his career. She shoved her cup away. "I think you're scrounging for something that isn't there."

He narrowed his eyes. "You don't know that, Leyna. We need to consider the possibility."

She snatched the pen from him to put an end to the damn clicking. "He might've been rude to us the night he was drunk, and he's arrogant as all get-out, but he's been super understanding about the payments and even waived fees because he felt bad over how shocked I was at the total. He offered to invest in Rosalia's to ease some of the burden, for crying out loud." Which, if all else failed, she may have no choice but to take him up on, if it meant getting her concert venue. "Why would he rip me off and then offer to invest what would basically be my own money?"

"Because he's twisted," was Jay's gruff response. He rubbed his thumb over the day's growth on his jawline. "I'm thinking out loud here, but he asked you out a few times, right? Is it possible he's hung up on you enough that he wanted you indebted to him in some way? Think about it—he works it so you're financially strapped, your family business you care about more than anything is on the line, and he's there, willing to cut you a break on the bills and invest money into the restaurant. It'd be pretty hard to walk away from him if he saved you like that. You see where I'm going with this?"

She searched his face for signs he'd taken a hallucinogenic drug. "You're grasping at straws."

Jay rolled his eyes. "Why are you so willing to trust him?"

With a huff, Leyna sat back. "I'm not saying I trust Mark, but I'm being realistic. Why are *you* wasting time playing detective right now when we have more important things at hand, like this meeting today or whether or not you're even staying in Sapphire Springs?" That's right, she'd said it. The words were on the table now.

He opened his mouth to speak, but closed it again, clearly thrown by the mention of his future. "Forget about the meeting for five minutes and think about it."

As she tuned out his irrational theory, the pieces began to fall into place. Stefan offered to invest in Rosalia's, which would undoubtedly eat up a lot of their money, so now Jay was suddenly trying to solve her financial crisis, should he back out and Cass and Danielle took over. She tapped the end of the pen on the table. That had to be it. He wasn't committing to Wynter and he wanted to make sure she was covered if Cass and Danielle tried to renege on the investment.

Heat flared in her cheeks. "Maybe I should worry about Rosalia's, and you should worry about Wynter Estate."

"Leyna, you're accepting Mark's version of events at face value without even questioning anything." Jay leaned back in his chair. "Just humor me, okay? Let me help you. Besides, if he's doing this to you, he could be doing it to other clients, too."

She checked the time, stood and hoisted her purse onto her shoulder. "Okay, fine. If you want to spend your time chasing theories, be my guest. I've gotta go. I'll see you at the meeting."

* * *

Jay rapped his knuckles against the door of Mark Toner's condo until they stung. A quick chat with his assistant revealed that Mark had taken the afternoon off, so like a cop on a stakeout, Jay parked his truck on the street outside the high-rise building and waited. Eventually another tenant came along and Jay casually followed him inside the main entrance, because, let's be real, Mark would never buzz him in.

The door flung open and Mark's icy blue eyes narrowed in on him before scanning the rest of the dim hallway.

"Split your pants lately?"

Mark ignored the dig. "What can I do for you, Wynter? I'll go out on a limb and guess you're not seeking legal advice."

Funny, even on a day off the guy still wore perfectly pressed khakis and a golf shirt. Jay followed him inside into the professionally decorated suite, where a commentator on the sports channel ran through highlights from last night's Spain versus France soccer game.

"Nope, not here for legal advice." He paused in front of a dreary painting—one he'd seen at the harbor gallery that reminded him of something a real estate agent would hang for staging. "I know better than to seek legal advice from you. Unfortunately I can't say the same for Joe Leone."

Mark crossed his massive arms and peered at Jay through rapidly blinking lashes, then glanced up at the whooshing ceiling fan momentarily before focusing on Jay again. "I'm sorry, Wynter, I'm confused. You're going to have to fill in a few gaps for me here, starting with how Joe Leone's will is any of your business."

"Maybe the will isn't my business. But Leyna sure as hell is."

"Leave Leyna out of this," Mark barked. Stalking over to the bar, he selected a bottle of the same premium whiskey Cass liked and poured two fingers. "She and I would probably be together by now if you hadn't crawled out from under whatever rock you've been hiding under all these years and taken advantage of some childhood infatuation."

Jay moved closer and caught the scent of good whiskey. "Were you hung up on her before you got yourself in the middle of her inheritance, or did your little crush come afterward?"

Mark took a step backward. *Hit a nerve.*

"I don't know what the hell you mean by that."

Circling the pool table, Jay studied Mark like a detective hot on the case. "Imagine my surprise when I learn the firm that handled Leyna's grandfather's will was yours, and coincidentally, she came out of the whole thing broke."

Mark snorted and set his glass on a coaster on top of the bar. His hand trembled ever so slightly. "So, what, you're implying Leyna's crap inheritance is somehow *my* fault?"

"The thought crossed my mind. It wouldn't be the first time a lawyer screwed somebody over."

"Get a life, Wynter. You don't know what you're talking about. As usual, you're out of your league." He stretched the last word over several seconds.

Trying to make Jay feel small was the only card the guy knew how to play. Jay shrugged and began to wander. "It makes sense. Leyna suddenly owes a bunch of money to your firm, so ever the hero, you offer to waive some fees, maybe invest some cash in Rosalia's to help her out."

Mark rolled his eyes and put on a charade of checking his watch. "Those are some fine detective skills, Sherlock, but in case you didn't notice, I'm not on the clock today, and I don't have any interest in whatever game you're playing. Besides, even if there was any truth to your little theory, you'd never be able to prove it."

Jay stopped moving and was suddenly eye to eye with Mark. "So there is something to prove."

Mark tossed his head back, his deep laugh echoing against the vaulted ceilings. "What are you trying to be, some kind of knight in shining armor?" He pointed a finger and thrust it in Jay's direction. "I don't owe you any explanations, because there's a little thing in my line of work called confidentiality. If Leyna had a problem with my firm's handling of her file, this is the first I'm hearing of it. Now, while I *so* enjoy your company," he drawled as he walked over to the door and whipped it open, "the rain is letting up and tee-off time is soon."

Jay moved past the enormous window, where the gray fog masked what should have been the skyline. The thought of Mark taking advantage of Leyna and her family left a bitter taste in his mouth. So bitter he could spit right there on the Persian rug adorning the gleaming hardwood floor.

He paused in the doorway, inches from Mark's face. "Your luck is running out."

Mark sighed. "I'm terrified, truly."

Jay's heels barely cleared the threshold before the door slammed shut.

# Chapter Seventeen

Wynter Estate's boardroom was icy cold, and not because of the air-conditioning. Cass and Danielle huddled at one end of the long rectangular table, like a couple of tag team wrestlers. It could have been high school all over again, their disapproving glares silently threatening to turn Leyna to stone. She forced a smile in return. Kill them with kindness.

When Leyna was a kid, Jay's mother was somebody she heard about all the time but had never actually met—one of those people you wondered if they actually existed. Until Danielle and Cass breezed into town and set up lodging at Wynter Estate the spring of Leyna's senior year of high school, she'd never fully appreciated why Jay held so much resentment for his mother. Leyna had been seriously dating Jay nearly two years at that point. She'd known him since she was a kid but had only met Danielle and Cass a few times. That said a lot.

Suddenly Danielle was trying to parent an already adult son, meddling in his decisions and inundating him with brochures from colleges that offered nothing he was interested in. Danielle hadn't taken kindly to Jay telling her to go to hell. She made no bones about her irritation over how much time Jay spent at the Milan house, either, and that was the root of the issue.

Leyna crossed her chilly legs and pulled her feet under the chair. Since Stefan had reprimanded Cass and Danielle about their behavior at the solstice tasting, they had been scarce, but being here today solidified what she'd feared all along. They were serious about taking over Wynter Estate, and if that happened she would be bound to a partnership with people who didn't want the new restaurant to succeed, and she would probably be nursing a broken heart, too.

Where was Jay, anyway? Hopefully not confronting Mark. The meeting was already running behind, and he was the only one missing. Since their conversation at Jolt, she'd texted him twice, with no response. Most likely he was in the vineyard, realizing this notion about Mark was ridiculous. Besides, Rosalia's was her problem to figure out, and she would. She'd given her grandfather her word.

Already tired of sitting, she rolled her shoulders and pulled out her phone to bring up her calendar. Might as well do something useful while she waited.

Stefan tapped his pen against the untouched pitcher of

ice water on the table, and Cass picked some lint off his trousers and flung it on the floor.

Danielle drummed perfectly squared acrylic nails on the table, dramatically checked her watch, and shot Stefan a scowl. “Dad, how long do we have to wait? Some of us have other places to be today.”

Stefan heaved a sigh and offered no response.

Leyna pushed her coffee to the center of the table. She couldn’t stomach the bitterness. She shot Jay another text. Where the hell are you? He was going on twenty-five minutes late.

Cass rose from his chair, straightened his navy tie, and strode toward Stefan’s end of the table to sit. “With all due respect, Stefan, it’s difficult to have faith in Jason taking over this company when he can’t be bothered to show up to a meeting where he’s a star player. I know you see him through rose-colored glasses, but let’s face it, he’s as irresponsible as a teenager. If you decide to make him CEO of Wynter Estate, I’m not sure I can bear to stand by and watch, much less be the one who has to pick up the pieces when it all comes crumbling down.”

Stefan’s tapping came to a halt and he glared at Cass. “Who asked you?”

With a sigh, Cass shrugged and took a seat back down at Danielle’s end of the table.

As transparent as Cass was, he was right about one thing—Jay being a no-show for a crucial family meeting was incredibly irresponsible. His behavior lately wasn’t adding up.

Had she convinced herself he was loyal to Wynter

Estate because that's what she desperately wanted to believe? Because he charmed the guests at the solstice tasting with his sexy smile and wisecracks?

Nausea clenched her stomach. Any minute now, he'd rush through the door with an excuse, but everyone around the table knew he had let Stefan down. And he'd let her down, too.

She couldn't work with somebody who didn't take things seriously. Too much was at stake to be so nonchalant. Sure, Wynter Estate had a lot on the line, but her own grandfather's life's work was too, which nobody ever bothered to mention. If Jay didn't start acting like he gave a damn, Stefan was going to have no choice but to hand Wynter Estate over to Danielle and Cass. And if that happened, the second restaurant would be destined to fail.

Sure, Stefan would see to it that the restaurant went on as planned. Cass and Danielle would even be obligated to go along with it, but she wouldn't put it past them to sabotage the entire thing so they could say *I told you so* and move on to their own plans. They'd proven how conniving they could be at the solstice event.

Tears stung her eyes, but she set her hardened stare on her notebook, refusing to let them flow. She concentrated on breathing in and out slowly to keep her sobs locked in the back of her throat. When safely composed, she stole a glance at Stefan. From across the table, he gave her a sympathetic nod, and that was all she needed to understand that the meeting was adjourned.

* * *

The damn starter on his truck gave him grief for nearly a half hour, and by the time Jay made it back to Wynter Headquarters, he was beyond late. Foregoing the elevator, he climbed the wide carpeted stairs two at a time, hoping the meeting had gone ahead and everyone was still gathered in the conference room.

Indeed they were. Pop, Leyna, his mom, and Cass were all clearing the table, placing their notes into their laptop bags.

"Good, you're all still here," he said plowing through the doorway, out of breath. "The starter on my truck set me back."

Stefan didn't turn around. Leyna didn't meet his gaze, either.

Jay shifted from one foot to the other. "I know I'm late, and I'm sorry, but—"

Stefan yanked the cord out of his laptop, and Wynter Estate's bright logo disappeared from the projection screen. "Jason, today's meeting was the most important to date, and you just couldn't be bothered to check the time or pick up the damn phone? Leyna's been sending you messages all afternoon, for Christ's sake."

His phone. Shit. He hadn't charged it. Anger festered down low, and Jay drew in a long hard breath. "I *told* you, I—"

"I don't need the excuses," Stefan snapped. "Leyna was depending on you to be here. I was counting on you, and you failed."

Jay stumbled back a step, and his breath caught in his throat. Few words could knock his esteem down to the level it had been before Stefan became his legal guardian and got his dyslexia diagnosed, but any insinuation that he'd failed transported him back to that little boy who constantly wondered what was wrong with him. Not this time. Squashing the memory, he took a step forward, determined to rise above it.

Cass's fingers clicked across the screen of his phone. "By any chance were you off talking to Frank about his recent job offer in France?"

All the oxygen was sucked from the room. Son of a bitch. Jay nearly lost his footing for a split second. He gripped the back of the nearest chair as Leyna's eyes grew wide and Stefan slowly turned toward him. Even his mother's mouth dropped open. "How…"

Cass's hand covered his mouth. "Whoops, was it a secret?"

Stefan's tanned face paled to a grim gray. His mouth formed a tight line, and he hung his head. With trembling hands, he zipped his laptop into its bag.

Jay pushed past his parents. "Pop, I haven't taken the job."

"Just asked for more time to decide," Cass put in, hands on his hips.

"Cass, enough." Danielle stepped forward.

Jay reached for Stefan's arm. "I just wanted to wait until after this meeting to make up my mind and talk to Frank in person. Let's just have the meeting now, and I'll explain everything," Jay pleaded, ignoring Cass. He raised his brows at Stefan. "I made some headway on our mystery."

"We can't discuss it right now." Stefan huffed. "I had other commitments today besides this meeting. For one, I'm meeting with my lawyer to solidify the changes happening with this company." Stefan's voice was on the brink of shaking. "And for the life of me, I'm trying to figure out what the hell to do with it."

Speechless, Jay retreated. The anger he could handle. It didn't take much to get a rise out of Stefan anyway. But the disappointment… The hurt… Jay swallowed hard.

Stefan spun on his heel and headed down the hall, with his mother and Cass hurrying after him.

Jay let him go and turned to Leyna, who'd remained silent throughout the argument, her chest rising and falling at top speed.

She folded her arms and hugged them into her body.

"Before you say anything, just hear me out," he said, gently closing the door. "I went to Mark's."

Her eyes immediately filled with tears, and her voice was barely above a whisper. "I don't care about Mark right now. We've been spending every spare minute together, Jay. I've let you in, like I've never let in anyone. How could you not bother to mention you had a backup plan in France?"

Jay bit his lip. "It just happened. I'm not going to take the job."

"But you did ask for more time to decide."

He reached for her arm, but she pulled it away and stalked out of the room.

Jay knew better than to go after her. She needed time to blow off steam. Everyone did. When the dust settled, he'd go talk to her, make things right. For now, he'd go back to the vineyard—the only place on the planet he didn't seem to screw up every way he turned.

When he parked his truck at the Renaissance Road vineyard, it occurred to Jay that he'd been so lost in thought, that he didn't remember a single detail about the drive from headquarters. Moving blindly, he grabbed pruning shears from a tool shed and headed for the rows to clear some of the leaf growth so the light could reach the fruit. He snapped out of his daze when his phone vibrated in his back pocket.

His grandfather's lawyer's name appeared on the caller ID, so he answered. "Jay Wynter."

"Mr. Wynter, I'm calling from Appleton's law office. Your grandfather collapsed in the middle of his meeting. We've called the ambulance."

* * *

Snippets of Sapphire Springs in its regular afternoon routine flashed by the truck window, but Jay barely registered the tourists crowding the sidewalks or kids zipping by on their bikes. Instead he was confronted with a montage of images: Stefan placing his strong hands over Jay's and showing him how to prune a vine when he was ten years old; Stefan passing him a cigar for the first time when Jay was sixteen, his laughter bellowing when Jay inhaled. They took the truck out to the old Tower Road once so Jay could learn to drive a stick shift, and who could forget the night Stefan told him he convinced the winery in Burgundy to take Jay on as an apprentice. He practically burst at the seams with the news.

Remnants of telephone conversations over the years coursed through him, along with fragments from letters they wrote, containing bits of wisdom Jay had grown to refer to as *Stefanisms*.

Somewhere in the world was a father he'd never known. His mother had checked out on him long before Cass Nixon came along and swept her off her feet. Stefan Wynter was the closest thing to a parent Jay had. He couldn't lose him. Not yet.

He pulled into the ER parking lot, leapt from the car, and bolted toward the entrance. When the double glass doors slid open, a wave of nausea nearly crushed him, a bold reminder of how much he hated the sterile smell of hospitals. His mother was losing her shit on some poor woman at the nurse's station. Cass offered apologies and tried to calm Danielle while the nurse explained Stefan had suffered a heart attack.

Another nurse in pink scrubs stepped out from behind the desk. "Are you Jay? He keeps asking for you."

Ignoring his mother's red tear-streaked face and tuning out her wailing, Jay followed the nurse into the trauma room, where his grandfather lay motionless, covered by a generic blue blanket. He froze in the doorway. Tubes dangled from machines to where they were strapped to Stefan's thin, feeble arms and monitors beeped with information Jay couldn't even begin to understand. Choking back the swelling lump in his throat, he took a deep breath and forced himself to cross the room. At the edge of the bed he covered his grandfather's frail hand with his own.

At what point had their roles reversed?

Stefan's eyes opened halfway,and his voice was nothing more than a whisper. "Jason."

Jay's legs buckled and his heartbeat thudded in his ears as he grasped the cold metal bed rails to keep from collapsing to his knees. "Pop, you don't have to talk," he managed in a voice that sounded nothing like his own.

Stefan's eyes were unfocused and his pupils were overdilated. He shook his head and spoke slowly, each word seeming to take more effort than the last. "I want to tell you…Raising you has been the greatest gift of my life and I'm…" He took a labored breath, "Proud of you. I've got it all figured out. If you want the job in France, take it. I'll understand."

"Pop, I—" He halted when Stefan lifted his trembling hand.

"No matter what happens, this year's vintage will be special. My hands…To your hands." He squeezed Jay's hand with little strength.

Christ, what had he done? Pop actually believed he wanted the job in France over Wynter Estate. The lump in Jay's throat erupted into a ball of fire. "Don't say that. Come on, this is crazy talk, you're getting better. I'm not taking the job. I'll stay in Sapphire Springs, but you've gotta be here with me, because I'm not ready for any of this on my own." His voice gave out.

"It's about what you want, not being ready, because you *are*, Jason. You were born ready." He gave Jay's hand a final squeeze before his eyes closed and his body went limp.

Monitors went haywire, their shrilling beeps ringing in his ears. “No!” Jay screamed, lunging toward Stefan’s lifeless body, grabbing both his arms as though he could keep him alive simply by hanging on. He nearly jumped backward, horrified by how frail Stefan’s arms were in his hands.

Nurses and doctors rushed into the room, pushing past Jay and sending a cart crashing into the wall. Somebody grabbed him by the back of his shirt and hauled him out of the way. As they began performing CPR, the room spiraled into a blur.

Near the doorway, Jay leaned against the wall, sliding all the way down to the floor, while the whole scene played out in front of him in slow motion.

And then all the noise ceased.

The doctor’s shoulders sagged, and he raised his gaze to the clock on the wall. His lips moved, but Jay couldn’t hear over the ringing in his ears. From the other end of a long dark tunnel, the young nurse in pink turned to him, eyes flooded with sympathy. “I’m sorry Mr. Wynter. I’m so very sorry.”

Jay grabbed onto the vinyl chair next to him and pulled himself up. He turned on his heel and stumbled from the room, past his sobbing mother, nearly colliding with Leyna in the main entrance.

Leyna chased after him. “Jay, I just got your text,” she called. His legs wouldn’t move fast enough and she caught up with him and grabbed his arm. “Wait.”

He'd known loneliness. He'd known inadequacy and failure, but never in his whole life had he experienced such helplessness, such defeat. He spun around, and when he met Leyna's wide teary eyes, his lower lip trembled. His throat was almost too tight to speak, but he managed a gruff response.

"He's gone."

# Chapter Eighteen

Days passed in a blur. Exhaustion took over as Jay dealt with the practicalities of keeping Wynter Estate running while the rest of his life spun out of control.

His mother and Cass were staying at the main house, which wasn't ideal, but what could he do? He couldn't exactly tell them they weren't welcome. His mother spent the majority of her time barking orders at poor Maria, who was as grief-stricken as the rest of them. Cass made a pale attempt to smooth over the events of the meeting from hell, apologizing for blurting out the news of his job offer. He said he'd overheard the phone call through the kitchen window and didn't realize nobody knew, which of course was bullshit.

Even his mother, a grieving mess, called Cass out for his tactless announcement.

Neighbors had stopped by at all hours over the past

couple of days to offer condolences, but the constant flow of visitors had petered out. Today, the quiet consumed him and reality came to a crash landing. He'd never bicker with his grandfather again. He'd never laugh with him, or hug him, or share a cigar.

How could he go back to the life he'd grown used to since coming back to Sapphire Springs, when his grandfather would never wander up to him in the vineyard for a chat or inundate him with all the urgent phone calls and emails he'd grown so accustomed to? How could he function in a world that didn't include Stefan Wynter?

How could he live with himself, knowing his grandfather had been so disappointed in him, so hurt by his actions, or lack thereof, that he'd suffered a massive heart attack?

If he'd just agreed to take over Wynter from day one, none of this would have happened. If he would've just *committed* instead of hovering on the fence, questioning everything. If he'd shown up to the damn meeting instead of confronting Mark.

If, if, if.

The sudden hum of the refrigerator cycling nearly knocked him off his stool, so he pushed away from the island and flicked on the radio.

Platters lined his kitchen counter. Whatever dishes they contained were likely delicious, but the blend of aromas combined was nauseating. John and Nina had sent an enormous dish of lasagna—Jay's favorite when he was a kid, and the only actual meal he'd consumed the past two days. Cards filled with touching notes and fond memories cluttered the island alongside random vases of flowers. One of the neighboring vineyards, Valley View, if he remembered correctly, had sent an enormous fruit basket he'd probably never touch.

He and Leyna had been slated to work a booth together during the Cultural Expressions Festival on the weekend, but they'd backed out, given the circumstances. Luckily she offered to help him write an official statement from Wynter Estate, announcing Stefan's passing. Jay was drowning in the emails pinging his phone at all hours. People bombarded him with everything from budget issues to inventory questions now that Stefan was gone. He didn't resent them for it—the show had to go on, but having to decipher documents and paperwork was difficult enough for him on a good day, without grieving along with it.

Despite what had happened at the meeting, Leyna stayed with him the night Stefan passed. Just having her there was a comfort he'd grown accustomed to. It also gave him an opportunity to explain the job offer. Once he told her Frank had been holding it over him long before he ever came back to Sapphire Springs, and that he hadn't in any way actually accepted the offer, she came around some. Still, Jay had asked for some space to try to clear his head, and since they parted ways the morning after, they'd kept a reasonable distance.

He needed time to figure out what the hell he was going to do after the dust settled and Cass and his Mom inevitably took over Wynter Estate. Given how disappointed Stefan had been at the meeting and what he said in the hospital, it was a serious possibility. With him gone, Rosalia's second location would probably never see the light of day. Joe and Stefan's dream would never happen, and it was on him.

Just like the aftermath of the meeting—upsetting his grandfather so badly that he had a heart attack.

He poured himself a glass of wine from the open bottle on the counter and glanced at the time on the microwave.

Five o'clock somewhere, and all that.

Shit. Cass crossed the courtyard with his damn clipboard and headed straight for Jay's house. When he appeared at the door, Jay sighed and reluctantly waved him in.

"Am I catching you at a bad time?"

What exactly constituted a *good* time these days? Jay shook his head and used his foot to shove a nearby stool in Cass's direction. "What's up?"

Cass laid his clipboard on the island and lowered onto the stool. "We've finalized the arrangements, so it looks like everything is pretty much set for the service tomorrow. Maria is preparing a roast beef dinner for tonight. I hope you'll come."

Jay bit his lip and tapped his foot against the leg of the stool. "That's probably not a great idea, but thank you for the offer." No point in opening the gates for another sparring match with everyone. His mom feigned innocence about Cass's outburst at the meeting, but it confirmed what Jay knew all along—they'd stop at nothing to get what they wanted. Even throw him under the bus.

"Jay, try to bear with us right now, okay?" Cass rubbed the shadow of silver-speckled scruff Jay had never seen him with before. "We all upset Stefan that afternoon, and everyone is carrying guilt. Danielle is grieving. We all are. Your mom loves you very much and would like it if you'd come."

Jay squeezed his hand open and shut.

"Which brings me to the other purpose of my visit." Cass met his gaze. "We'd love it if you'd consider giving the eulogy."

His hand froze, mid-flex, while music from the radio drifted over the kitchen. He drew his brows together and heaved a sigh. Give the eulogy? He hadn't expected that. "I...I wouldn't know where to begin."

Cass peered at him over tented fingers. "Your distance never changed the relationship you had with your grandfather. The fact is, you were closer with him than anyone, even Danielle." He shifted his stool and straightened his posture before going on. "When your mom and I got married, she wanted desperately for you to come back to the city and live with us. We could've put you in private school and hired tutors to help with your dyslexia. But you'd gotten a taste of the vineyard, and everyone could see where your heart was. That was a lot tougher on your mother than you probably realize." He opened his hands into a shrug. "It'll be too hard on your mom to do it. I can give the eulogy if you're not up for it, but Stefan and I really weren't that close." He stared at the floor. "I wish we had all been closer."

Speaking in front of a church full of people about

losing the closest family member he'd ever had would be torture. But a rush of pride swelled inside Jay's chest. After all the arguments, guilt, and regret, this was one last thing he could do to honor his grandfather's memory. "I'll do it," he said, before he could talk himself out of it.

Cass's set jaw relaxed into a grin and he slapped Jay on the shoulder. "Good. We both know your grandfather would rather you speak about him than me."

Understatement of the year.

Cass stood and crossed something off the list on his clipboard. "I'll get out of your way so you can collect your thoughts. If you change your mind about dinner, the offer stands."

Yeah, wouldn't happen. Everybody gathering around a big table for a family meal on the eve of Stefan's funeral was a pretty picture, if your family was close like the Milans, but Jay's presence would do nothing but stoke the fire.

He'd caused enough problems already.

So he plucked a napkin out of the drawer, grabbed the fancy pen Cass had left behind, and tried to come up with something worthy to say about the man who took him in when nobody else wanted him. Nothing useful came to him. Since Stefan had passed, the memories had almost been too much to bear, and every time Jay thought about the years he chose to stay away, he hated himself a little more.

Willing the words to come, he rolled the sleek silver pen between his thumb and index finger. His eyes narrowed on the logo etched on the side.

Toner Law Firm.

* * *

Leyna was up to her elbows in dishwater when Emily surfaced at the screen door.

"Hey." She pulled the door closed behind her, glancing from Leyna's sparkling faucet to her gleaming floors. "It's spotless in here. Wanna come do my apartment next?"

Leyna rubbed at a mark on the countertop, and then remembered the scratch wouldn't come off. "I needed a distraction. I purged two bags of clothes I never wear and a bag of shoes that I've always considered too New York to wear in Sapphire Springs."

"Dibs." Emily held up a pink box from Tesoro. "Can I interest you in some cake? It's got the vanilla bean frosting I've been tweaking."

Mother of God, who would turn that down? Even Felix abandoned his post on the back of the sofa to come sniffing. Leyna got plates from the upper cabinet while Emily sliced the cake. "Just what the doctor ordered."

Emily ran her finger along the flat side of the knife and then licked the creamy frosting before passing Leyna a serving. "I used the other half of the batter for cupcakes. Just dropped them off at Jay's before I came here. He looks like hell."

Leyna hadn't heard from him since she left his house two days ago. He'd apologized for not telling anyone about the job offer. He didn't think it was worth upsetting everyone. It seemed logical enough now. Still, he could've been upfront about it, considering how close they'd gotten.

The last thing she wanted was for him to go through the loss of his closest family member alone, but he had asked for space, so what else could she do other than back off? The first bite of cake sent Leyna's eyes rolling back. She pointed to it with her fork. "That's damn decadent."

"Thanks. I think I finally got it right." Emily speared the cake with her fork. "I feel so bad for Jay. It's like he's lost."

Leyna flicked on the kettle and got two tea bags out of the pottery jar on the counter. "He is lost. He probably hasn't slept or had a decent meal." Keeping her distance was driving her crazy, and even though she was still angry about him dropping the ball on the meeting, she wanted to comfort him, help with arrangements, anything to feel useful. But he was retreating, and the significance of that pressed harder on her chest with each passing hour.

"You're worried he'll leave Sapphire Springs now that Stefan is gone." Emily took the jar of honey out of the cupboard. God forbid she drink anything without sweetener. "I don't think you need to be. Sure, he came back because of Stefan, but you're enough to keep him here."

Leyna sighed, pushed the plate of crumbs away, and absently rubbed her bare foot over Felix's outstretched belly while he purred to no end. "I don't know. The meeting was bad, Em. And apparently some of Stefan's last words gave Jay his blessing to take the job in France if he wants it, which leads Jay to believe Cass and Danielle will take over Wynter Estate. If that's the case, Jay's going to bolt for sure."

If that happened, things would go one of two ways—

either Danielle and Cass would try to find a way to contest the partnership, or they'd accept that they were legally bound but would go along with the agreement only long enough to save face, until they inevitably found a way to undermine the restaurant.

She got up to turn off the whistling kettle and poured water into their cups. Tears flooded her eyes, and she didn't bother to try to hold them back. She leaned against the counter and hugged her arms tight to her body. "Jay won't have the heart to stick around and witness whatever they do." Her voice morphed into something sounding like an angry wet cat, and then she broke into a sob.

"Hey, you don't know that. Give him the benefit of the doubt. He hasn't taken the job." Emily's arm circled Leyna's waist and guided her to the chair at the end of the table. She set Leyna's mug in front of her. "Jay might surprise you."

Emily, the eternal optimist. But she hadn't been there to bear witness to the disappointment in Stefan eyes or Jay's determination to pin Rosalia's financial woes on Mark. He just couldn't drop it, no matter how much she tried to convince him. Even Rob had taken Jay's side last night on the phone when she'd called him midway through a pint of Ben and Jerry's.

"I appreciate what you're trying to do, Em, but I have this gut feeling that he's going to leave. What if he gets on a plane and I never see him again?" Worse yet, what if she spent her entire life never again feeling the way she felt when she was with him? Her hands started to tremble. She pushed away from the table, snapped a tissue from the box on top of the microwave, and gave her nose a loud blow.

"You need to go talk to him," Emily said gently. "Be honest about your fears."

"I can't, because he asked for space." Leyna sniffed and tossed the tissue into the garbage. "He's slipping away, and there's nothing I can do, because if I come on too strong, it'll only push him further away." The offer in France didn't come with any baggage, and Sapphire Springs had more baggage than JFK airport. "God, what was I thinking? I knew better than to trust him, to let myself fall for him again, but I threw caution to the wind. That's not who I am anymore—"

"You took a chance on love," Emily cut in. "That's very brave and a huge step for you."

Brave or stupid? She'd find out soon enough. Leyna's gaze drifted to the luminous lake beyond the front windows, and she shook her head to try to forget about all things Jay. She wiped away her tears and squared her shoulders. "Let's talk about something else. Fill me in on the election campaign and Officer Hottie."

Emily rubbed her lips together before the smile took over. "*Todd* is damn decadent. Busy though, with shift work. We're just having fun for now. I'm not getting my hopes up that it'll go anywhere, but it sure beats yearning for a guy who's already taken."

Leyna reached across the table and squeezed Emily's hand. "It's good to see you happy."

"As for the campaign," Emily continued, sipping her tea, "the election is still months away, but so many people tell me they'll be voting for me. I think I might actually have a shot at snagging one of the seats."

Word on the street was that Emily was a very strong candidate. In fact, Fuzzy yammered on about it just this morning at Jolt. Twelve people were running, including four who already held seats. There were six seats in total, and the favored contenders were Emily and Tim.

Best not to bring it up, though. Emily was finally interested in someone else. No point in discussing a hypothetical situation where she and Tim both end up on town council together.

# Chapter Nineteen

Friends, family, and an entire community paid their respects. Organ music droned throughout the room, and candles cast a heavenly glow.

Danielle had carried Stefan's urn to the front of the church, Cass by her side. Jay had trailed behind, officially alone, trapped in a surreal dream.

Distant relatives filled the spaces in the pews around them. Wynter staff occupied the rows behind. Leyna sat across the aisle with her parents and Rob. Tim was there, and so was Emily, along with practically everyone else in town. He hadn't realized how many lives his grandfather had touched.

After the priest welcomed everyone and read a piece from the Bible, the vocalists took their places at the microphone and began singing the hymn "Be Not Afraid." Leyna had suggested it because Nina remembered it from Jay's grandmother's funeral. They had such a knack for those subtle yet meaningful touches. When Danielle asked him why he chose the song, he'd just shrugged. No need to tell her Leyna chose it—she'd probably demand something else simply to flex her control.

The longing in his grandfather's eyes when he spoke about love their last day in the cellar surfaced. At least his grandparents were together again. He could be grateful for that, if nothing else.

Hell, who was he kidding? He had nearly thirty years to be thankful for. From the time his mother dropped him off at Wynter Estate, Stefan put him first, as nobody ever had.

Considering he'd had a grown child of his own, a smart-mouthed eight-year-old was probably the last thing on the planet most men would've had the time or patience for. If that was the case, his grandfather had never let it show. Instead, he took Jay everywhere. *My little grandson can prune a vine alongside the best of them*, he'd boast to his friends down at Moe's Bakery.

Tears pierced the backs of his eyes, and his throat tightened. The three vocalists at the microphone blurred together with the pots of plants and flowers adorning the altar. Jay lowered his head and concentrated on the woodgrain on the seat of his pew with more attention than he'd ever given anything in his entire life. A tear dropped onto the seat, and the reflection of colors from the stained glass window fused together like a kaleidoscope in the tiny pool of water.

He tried to block out the harmonizing singers and the

sniffling of the people around him. Being in a church for anything other than checking out the architecture was a new concept. It'd been years since he'd attended an actual mass. The song came to an end, and the priest nodded at him. Time to give the eulogy. He composed himself and stood, surprisingly steady. He buttoned the jacket of his black suit and moved toward the altar like a puppet with someone else guiding his strings.

Facing the congregation, he was taken aback by the number of people who stared back at him. With not an empty seat left, many stood in the back of the church. He scanned the faces and paused on Leyna, who gave an encouraging smile through tear-coated lashes.

"I didn't know what to say today." He cleared his throat, folded his carefully crafted notes, and shoved them into the inside pocket of his jacket. They'd do nothing but trip him up. "How do you wrap up a life like Stefan Wynter's in the span of five minutes? But when I thought about the man we're all here to honor, I decided to do what he would do. So I'll speak about the vineyard, because my grandfather always found a way to make every conversation, even his final one, circle back to the place he loved the most.

"Each spring vines awaken. We foster them, nurture them, maybe even obsess over them, and when the conditions are right—warm temperatures, mixed with the right amount of sunlight and moderate rains—their buds flower, and eventually bear fruit. These young vines require meticulous attention, because the early days are the most vulnerable time in their life cycle."

Nina smiled from a few rows back and gave a slight nod, unknowingly confirming he was on the right track. Jay relaxed his shoulders and rocked back on his heels, falling into the rhythm of a topic as natural to him as buttoning a shirt. "As grapes grow, they're monitored to ensure they develop to their fullest potential. Conditions are studied, like soil characteristics, climate, sunlight, drainage, and slope of the land. All of these factors contribute to the terroir, which, for non–grape growers, is a term to sum up all of the natural conditions that conspire to give the grape its character." John placed an arm around Nina, and she leaned into his chest.

"You could say Pop created my terroir. He provided a strong foundation and the home where I grew up. He looked out for me, loved me, and taught me a whole lot of things about love and honor and respect." Jay paused to collect himself, pushing past the lump working up his throat when Leyna brushed tears from her cheek and clasped hands with Emily, who was sitting next to her.

"Stefan Wynter raised me single-handedly, from the time I was eight years old. He fought tirelessly with me when I was wrong and encouraged me relentlessly when I was right. He'd say the most profound things with an absent wave of his hand." Jay impersonated the gesture, earning an appreciative chuckle from most of the congregation. Despite her perfect poise, a tear rolled down his mother's cheek.

"Pop told me after his stroke, when he was struggling with the decision to retire, that he wasn't sure if he wouldn't let go of the vineyard, or if the vineyard wouldn't let go of him. And in the end, I'm still not sure, but the cycle goes on, even if we aren't ready for what lies ahead."

He stood a little straighter and squared his shoulders. Almost done. "Grapes are harvested every fall. The grower, who has worried about every stage of the process, like a doting parent, must let go and pass them on to the winemaker to create the phenomenon that is wine. The leaves left on the vine wither and fall to the ground, and the vines go dormant once again.

"This fall, as we work the rows, harvesting the grapes from those vines he planted with his own hands, I know he will be watching over us, guiding us, as he always has. He will live on in the wine. There will be a part of his soul in each and every bottle. And for that, I am eternally grateful."

He couldn't have added another word, even if he'd wanted to. Jay was spent. He steadied himself and returned to his seat at the front of the church, aware of all the eyes in the church following him. As the priest gave his final thoughts, Jay and his mother were presented with his grandfather's urn, a miniature oak barrel.

Stefan's ashes would be scattered in the vineyard, of course. Jay couldn't imagine a better place.

* * *

Leyna waited for Jay on the tailgate of his truck. She'd given him enough space. He needed her today, whether he'd admit it or not.

Cass ushered Danielle out the door of the church and down the stone steps into the back seat of a black Lincoln Town Car. Jay would probably be the next one out. Everyone else had already left.

A couple of hummingbirds competed for the same bed of pink geraniums beyond the parking lot that opened up into the cemetery. Finally, Jay surfaced, the thick wooden door of the church slamming behind him with an echo that likely scared off every living creature within a half-mile radius.

Back rigid, shoulders square, he shrugged out of his suit jacket, balling it up as he crossed the vacant parking lot. He threw it into the open window of his truck before unbuttoning his shirt cuffs and turning them up to the elbow.

She slid off the tailgate and smoothed the front of her black dress. "I just wanted to say that the eulogy—what you said—it was really beautiful."

"Thanks." He settled onto the tailgate and braced his elbows on his knees to cradle his head in his hands and rub his fingers over his dark-rimmed eyes.

Leyna hoisted herself back up so she was sitting next to him. She cleared her throat. "How are you?"

He was silent a long time, staring at the pavement through the spread of his fingers. Dread built with each painstakingly silent minute that passed. Leyna scratched the polish off her thumbnail. The manicure she'd splurged on two days ago hadn't stood a chance.

"This is all my fault," he finally whispered. Pressing his hands against his legs, he sat up straighter. "Pop is gone because of me."

"Jay, don't say that. It isn't true. I was there, remember? Everyone in the room was involved in that conversation. Sure, you pissed Stefan off, showing up late, but Cass is the one that blurted out you had another job offer." She grabbed his arm to make him look at her. "You can't blame yourself for that."

"All of this could have been prevented if I would've just manned up in the beginning. Because I couldn't get past my own inadequacies, I pussyfooted around the most important job offer of my life. The only one that ever mattered. I let Pop down, and he was so disappointed. What choice did I give him but to leave Wynter Estate in the hands of my mom and Cass?" Jay shoved off the tailgate before going on. "I can't stand by and watch that happen. I *can't*."

Tears welled in his eyes. "I screwed up, and the hardest thing of all is that I knew I couldn't pull this off. I *knew* I didn't have what it takes, and I tried to convince Pop, but he just..." A tear escaped Jay's lashes and rolled down his cheek. "He believed in me so much that I started to believe it, too."

Leyna's throat tightened, but she stood so he'd have to face her straight on. "You don't know he's left them the company. Not for sure. Stefan believed in you because you *do* have what it takes." She folded her arms, hugged them tight to her chest. "You're going to leave again aren't you?" Even as she said the words, a tear slipped down her cheek.

"I don't deserve you," he exclaimed, his lip quivering. "I don't deserve any of it." He got up and flung open the driver's side door and started the truck. His voice was little more than a whisper.

Leyna followed him to the open window. “You told me to trust you.” Her voice broke, and another tear rolled down her cheek.

“I don’t know what else to do.” His lips pulled down and he searched her face. “Just know that none of this is because of you. Please, believe me when I say that.” He reached through the window and pulled her toward the truck to trace his fingertips across her cheek. “When I left all those years ago, I said I didn’t love you, and that was a lie—we both know that. I won’t lie to you this time. I love you. I love you more than anything in this world. But sometimes love just isn’t enough.”

“Yes it is,” she cried. “Love is enough, if you stay here and fight.”

His lip quivered, and he simply shook his head.

She clenched her teeth so her bottom lip wouldn’t tremble. She didn’t dare open her mouth to speak. Taking a step back, she folded her arms. There was nothing left to say. If he was leaving town again, they were done.

He threw the truck into gear and sped away, leaving Leyna in a cloud of dust. When he rounded the turn at the end of the street she got inside her car, locked the doors, and curled over the steering wheel to give in to the sobs clawing their way up her throat.

Obligation had brought him back to Sapphire Springs. She was an idiot to believe things could’ve worked between them. *Trust me*, he’d said. And she had.

Stupid.

One thing was certain. Jay Wynter had left her in his rearview mirror for the last time.

# Chapter Twenty

Jay slammed the front door of the guesthouse and collapsed against it, his chest heaving. He couldn't recall a single detail about the drive from the church, up until he stopped at the Renaissance Road vineyard. The delicate vines that had been so vulnerable a few months ago were now lush and hanging with plump grapes starting to transform from green to purple.

From there he went to Wynter Estate. He walked through the cellar, running his hand over the dusty bottles racked on the wall before returning to the guesthouse to pack.

*You told me to trust you.* Leyna's words resurfaced in the pit of his stomach, where he figured they'd pool and ferment for the rest of his sorry life. Sweat beaded on his forehead, and hot tears stung the backs of his tired eyes. Unclenching his fist, he dropped the keys he'd been gripping onto the glass table in the foyer, then climbed the stairs two at a time to the bedroom.

The only thing more gut-wrenching was Leyna's disappointment and acceptance that yes, he was indeed letting her down again.

Leaving Sapphire Springs was the only thing to do. His place—or lack thereof—in the Wynter family was solidified when he chose to take a gamble and confront Mark instead of preparing for the meeting and showing up on time. When he chose to keep the job offer in France a secret.

Leyna sure as hell didn't need him around, complicating her life, screwing up at every turn. She deserved somebody reliable.

Throwing T-shirts into a duffel bag, his eyes fell on a delicate pair of silver earrings on the nightstand of what he'd come to think of in the last few weeks as Leyna's side of the bed. Rubbing his jaw, he let out a long shaky breath. At least he'd gotten her back for a little while. He'd gotten to see her smile again and take pleasure in the knowledge that he'd made her happy, brief as it was. He'd held her in his arms, whispered to her in the quiet of the night. He could carry those memories with him. They'd have to be enough.

He'd arrange the return of the earrings and anything else she'd left behind. He couldn't face Leyna again right now, if ever.

He changed from his dress clothes into jeans and a T-shirt and stepped out onto the terrace into the soft breeze rustling the trees to appreciate the view of the lake one final time before going back inside to clear his small selection of toiletries from the bathroom.

At the foot of the stairs, the grouping of photos of him and Pop caught his eye and drew him into the living room. Most of the best moments of his life were captured right there on that wall. He traced a fingertip over the picture of them in the pinot noir plot. Nothing but a field of promise back then. And now, an enterprise.

Someone else's.

He'd have the photos sent once he was settled back in France. Someday he might even have the heart to hang them on another wall in another house. For now, he'd work on putting Sapphire Springs as far from his mind as possible. Time to start over again. He should've been used to it by now, but this time was different. This time it hurt like hell, because he'd be plagued with the image of what could have been.

A soft knock pulled on his heart, and he craned his neck to look into the hallway. Mom. She'd changed out of her dress into leggings and a long top.

"I was actually on my way out," Jay said, opening the door. "Did you need something?"

She poked her head in the doorway, eyes searching the space. "Can I come in?"

With a nod, Jay led her into the kitchen, his back stiff. The sooner he got away from Wynter Estate, the better. Danielle sat at the island, but Jay simply leaned against the counter and crossed his arms. The conversation wouldn't be long enough to warrant sitting. Because there were no lights on, he turned and opened the blinds on the window over the sink, to let the sunlight filter through.

She cleared her throat. "Cass went to lie down for a couple of hours. A solid rest will do him good. With all the arrangements and everything, he's been going nonstop."

*Poor Cass.* Tough to feel bad for the bastard.

She tucked her hair behind her ear, revealing a large gold hoop earring. "Anyway, there are some things I wanted to say. First, that I'm sorry for the way Cass blurted out the news of your job offer. He had no right—"

"Water under the bridge." Jay waved his hand. "He's already apologized."

She nudged the unopened bottle of wine on the island. "Mind if I open that?"

The interruption cut into his plan to escape Sapphire Springs ASAP, but when was the last time he'd talked to his mother without Cass hovering by her side? He pulled two glasses from the overhead cabinets. "Not at all. Pour us both one."

With a few turns and a swift pull, she freed the cork and poured. His mother could maneuver a corkscrew with the best of them. For years, she'd worked as a hostess at Wynter Estate's tasting room. Until she'd decided it wasn't enough and left town.

She passed him a glass. "Jason, I've really botched this whole parenting thing."

He swirled the wine in his glass and braced one foot against the cupboard behind him. "If you're going to launch into some justification for decades-old mistakes, you don't have to. We're all grown-ups here now."

After a little sip of wine, she shook her head. "No, I really want to put the past behind us this time."

Silenced followed her statement, and Jay set his glass down and folded his arms, unsure of how to respond.

Danielle pushed her glass to the side and fiddled with the purple ribbon on the fruit basket a few seconds before flinging it away. She buried her face in her hands and looked at him through fanned fingers. “I have so many regrets, they eat me alive. That I left when you were young. That I didn’t come home more, and that I underestimated you and made you feel you weren’t good enough because you had a learning disability.”

Her gaze skated across the collection of vintage tin coffee signs hanging on the far wall. “I’m not going to make excuses, other than at seventeen, I didn’t quite grasp the level of responsibility that came with raising a child.” She sighed, tracing her finger along the curve of her wineglass. “I wanted to escape—to do more with my life than work in my dad’s tasting room.”

Wanting more than a position cherry-picked for her was something he could relate to. Jay moved to the island and took the seat opposite her.

“I never meant to abandon you, but every time I came back, you seemed so content here with Dad. And then when you were older, and dating Leyna, you had this whole new family, and I just felt like a nuisance whenever I was around. It became this constant ache in my chest—the guilt of missing out on so much with you.”

She dabbed at her eye, leaving a smudge of mascara on her finger. “I was so scared Leyna was going to hurt you, break your heart when she went off to school, and I never wanted you to feel that kind of heartache, of someone you're in love with turning their back on you."

Like his father had done to her. Jay reached for his glass and took a long gulp.

"I thought if I encouraged you to get out of Sapphire Springs and go to college—see the world like I was doing, we'd have something in common. That I could become some kind of friend to you, even though I'd blown it as your mother. The problem was, I'd already made my bed. You were doing just fine without me, and that was something I've had to live with."

He reached across the island and clasped her long, slender hand. "Mom, I appreciate you telling me all that. It does help me understand your perspective. We haven't had a perfect relationship, but there's no reason we can't try, moving forward. I think it would make Pop happy."

For what seemed like the hundredth time that day, a pang stabbed his chest at the knowledge his grandfather was really gone. He pushed back off the stool and went to look out the window. "I am going to be leaving town, but I'd like to stay in better touch."

She crossed the kitchen to stand at his shoulder. "You don't need to leave, Jay. That's not what anybody wants."

He kept his gaze fixed on the maple trees. "Pop as much as said I wasn't fit to run Wynter Estate in that meeting."

Danielle sighed, squeezing his arm. "That is not what he said."

Not in so many words, maybe, but it didn't need to be

spelled out. The disappointment on his grandfather's face had said it all.

An image of Leyna skipped through his mind, and he blinked it away. "There's nothing left for me here."

"That's not true. You're assuming Cass and I are going to end up with Wynter Estate, and we don't even know that yet. And even if we do, we're going to need help. Sure, Cass can run the day-to-day operations, but we don't have the vineyard knowledge you do."

"Then you'll have to hire somebody, or promote a crew member, because I'm not staying." Jay pushed off the counter and sauntered away. "I'm taking the job in France. I called Frank on the drive home from the church. It's best for everyone." Funny, how now that he was free and clear of all the responsibilities of running the company, going back to France was the last thing he wanted.

Danielle squinted from the late afternoon sunlight streaming through the blinds. "We'd match their offer, better it, even. We'll create a special position for you."

Exactly what he didn't want. More special treatment because of who he was. These plans probably hadn't even been run by Cass, because he wouldn't have cared less whether Jay stayed in Sapphire Springs or not. Resentment festered.

"We could work together to figure out the best plan for Wynter Estate." She was oblivious to Jay's building anger. "You and Leyna can continue whatever it is the two of you have going on. She'll probably be relieved to not have to go along with this restaurant scheme between Dad and Joe, and I'd like a chance to repair my relationship with her, too."

Jay tuned her out the moment she said they could work together to figure out a plan for Wynter Estate. Cass was all about profit, and Jay was all about quality of product. They'd never see eye to eye. His gaze roved around the room. The sunlight beaming across the kitchen glinted off the silver pen on the island, catching his eye. His eyes narrowed, and he picked up the pen and handed it to his mother. "Cass forgot this yesterday. Any particular reason he has a pen from Mark Toner's law firm?"

Danielle's brow wrinkled. She reached for the pen, inspecting the logo. She traced her manicured nail across the engraving. "Sure. He met with Mark a while back, said he wanted to have plans in place. We never know what could happen." She fidgeted with the pen a few more seconds before placing it on the counter.

Jay nodded. The theory of Mark ripping off Leyna along with Cass's financial desperation and his resulting ambitions to run Wynter Estate were like puzzle pieces that fit together better with every beat of the ticking hallway clock. Could the two actually be connected? What did he have to lose by pursuing it?

But his mom was still talking. "Dad was the picture of health for a man his age. The stroke was a swift reminder that none of us are promised tomorrow..." She trailed off with a longing shake of her head.

Jay lowered onto a stool to face her head-on. "Mark Toner was owed a lot of money after all of Joe Leone's meetings regarding his will. You and Cass should be careful. Time spent with him can really add up."

Danielle leaned back and drew in her perfectly arched

brows. "What does Leyna's grandfather's will have to do with anything?"

"Leyna's business is in jeopardy because of bills from Mark's firm. She dragged her heels on the deal with Wynter because she didn't have the financial backing to come to the partnership on an equal playing field. Cass has been meeting with Mark, and it's no secret he wants Wynter Estate." Come to think of it, Cass and Mark golfed at the same club and drank the same whiskey, too. Was the two of them getting their heads together such a stretch? Sure, he'd suspected Mark of being shady, but never that he'd had an accomplice right under his nose the entire time. A fire kindled in his stomach and flared all the way up his chest.

Danielle opened her mouth to speak, then closed it again. She glanced out the window and then back at Jay. "Are you suggesting Cass and Mark Toner…" She coiled her long hair around her finger, a line forming between her brows as she pondered the possibility. "No. You need to pour yourself another drink and relax, and so do I. It's been an exhausting few days for everyone. Get a solid night's sleep, and in the morning, when your head is clear, you'll realize how ridiculous this all sounds." She stood, smoothed her hair, and walked out.

Jay bit his bottom lip and shook his head. "I don't think so," he murmured, as the door clicked shut. "In fact, I may be seeing clearly for the first time in days."

* * *

Mark's office was on York Street, just around the corner from town square. Jay's tires squealed when he took the turn. He tapped the steering wheel, eyes peeled for a parking spot. The closest space was three doors down, in front of the hardware store. He swung into the spot, slammed the truck door, and marched down the street. He was getting answers, even if he had to drag them out of Mark.

Cool air washed over him when he pushed through the heavy wooden door. Mark's assistant lifted her head from a file and peered at him over her wire-framed glasses. "Can I help you?"

Jay stalked up to her desk. "I need to see Mark."

She removed her glasses and propped them on top of her curly blond hair. "I'm sorry, sir. Mr. Toner is not available at the moment. In fact, he's booked the remainder of the day." She put her glasses back on and thumbed through an appointment book on her desk. "I could get you an appointment the first week of August."

Jay towered over the desk, hands firmly planted on either side of an ivy plant. "I'm not a client, and I am most definitely not waiting until the first week of August. Can you tell him Jay Wynter is here?"

She arched a brow over the rim of her glasses, lifted the receiver of her phone, and pressed a few buttons, turning away to speak in a hushed voice. Mark's office door whipped open just as she was hanging up. His shoulders practically filled the doorway.

"Wynter, always a pleasure," he said dryly. "My condolences for your grandfather."

Jay stepped around the secretary's desk and met Mark in the doorway. "I think you better clear your schedule and let me in your office so we can speak privately."

"Funny, I don't recall you making an appointment. Giselle, does Mr. Wynter have an appointment?"

"He most certainly does not," she retorted, spinning her chair back to face her computer, her long nails clicking across the keyboard.

Mark dusted some lint off his sport coat. "Well then, I guess there's no cause for disruption—"

"Save the bigshot act, Mark," Jay cut in. "I know about your dealings with my stepfather." Mark paled, and when his eyes darted to the left, Jay knew he had him. He'd mentioned Cass only to bluff, but Mark's guilty expression said it all.

"Clear my schedule, Giselle."

He then turned to Jay and pointed his thumb to his office. When the door clicked shut behind them, Mark hurried to his desk, barking insults as fast as they came to him. "You're still playing detective? Don't you have anything better to do with your time? Who do you think you are, Perry Mason?"

Now that he was behind closed doors, Jay was much calmer. "I want to know everything. Start talking, and if I think for one second you're bullshitting me, I will go to the middle of town square and out you for the crook you are to everyone within a ten-mile radius."

Mark lifted his hands. "And then what, people are just going to believe you over me?"

Jay considered. "They may or may not believe me.

But the rumor will be planted and your reputation will suffer."

"I have no idea what you're trying to accuse me—"

"Mark," Jay interrupted. "I know everything. All I want to know is why."

After a long pause Mark pushed the chair away from the desk, rolling backward. "Fine. But I'm telling you the truth when I say that none of this was my idea, and I was ready to pull out altogether the day you showed up at my condo. The only reason I didn't come clean then is because I texted Cass after you left and he said he had it under control."

Jay's hand balled into a fist, but he kept it down by his side. "Was my mother in on this?"

Mark loosened his tie and opened his desk drawer. He took out two rocks glasses and poured them each a drink of whiskey. He tipped his own back and took a swig before answering. "No, and Cass was adamant she didn't find out."

Jay relaxed his cramping hand and expelled a sigh of relief.

"He came to me about a month after Joe Leone died. There was already lots of talk between the families about a Rosalia's and Wynter partnership. Cass and your mother apparently had some plans for Wynter Estate of their own, so he came up with a scheme to make Leyna look irresponsible. If Stefan believed Leyna blew through all the money Joe left her and had nothing left to cover her share, he'd back out. At least that's what he hoped."

Jay ignored the drink Mark poured and leaned forward, past a stack of file folders on Mark's desk. "Why?"

Mark shrugged and got up to pace. "I don't know, ask your gold-digging stepfather."

The plummeting stocks. Of course. Jay followed Mark around the desk. "What was in it for you? What made you go along with it?"

A few moments passed before Mark turned. "He offered me a stake in Wynter Estate."

Jay's chest broadened with every bit of air he sucked in and his hand coiled into a fist again. "Son of a—"

"I never had any intention of keeping Leyna's money." Mark lifted his hands and let them drop. "I told Cass that, and he said he didn't care what I did on my end, as long as I went along with the plan. So I did, because I saw Rosalia's as a good investment. I even tried to buy the Blackhorse because I knew she wanted it. I thought if I could convince Leyna to trust me, we'd get closer. Maybe eventually she'd develop feelings."

Of all the twisted things he'd ever heard…Jay went back to the chair. He needed to sit, so he could think straight. "So you were hung up on Leyna, and you thought the only way to get her to reciprocate was for her to be indebted to you?"

"Well, when you say it like that, it sounds kind of pathetic." Mark lowered back into his chair, too.

Man, did Mark ever misjudge Leyna.

"I'll give her back every cent," he was saying.

"You're damn right you will," Jay fired back, pointing his finger at Mark. "Give me one good reason why I shouldn't call the cops right now."

"Because," Mark said, rolling away from the desk

again, "on my end it's a computer glitch, a mistake in paperwork." He mimed air quotes. "I fully intend to give back the money and always have. The rest is all hearsay, and it's all of our words against each other's. Involving the police would only prolong the drama for everyone."

Spoken like a bona fide criminal. Leyna would decide whether she wanted to involve the police. Jay squeezed the bridge of his nose. "This has been weighing on Leyna for months. Do you have any idea how much stress she's been under, all because the two of you have been playing puppet master?"

"I was going to present Leyna with the mistake eventually," he said, again with the air quotes.

"I need to find Leyna," Jay said, rising from the chair.

Mark got up, too. "Let me tell her. Please. I owe her that much."

Jay's jaw was locked in place. He eyed Mark. "Fine. Tell her yourself." Seeing Leyna again would only make things harder anyway. Getting out of town was the smart thing to do. "If I find out that you didn't, or that you left a single detail out, I will make it my life's mission to smear your name across every newspaper in the country. I will ruin you. Do you understand me?"

Sweat beaded on Mark's brow, but he nodded. "Fine. But if I'm going down, Cass is coming with me."

# Chapter Twenty-One

Chances were good Ben and Jerry's stock was on the rise. Leyna was probably single-handedly keeping the company afloat. She tossed the empty ice cream carton into the garbage and set to work polishing glassware before the restaurant opened for the day.

The hours following Stefan's memorial service were foggy. At some point after she'd collected herself enough to drive, she'd gone home and the wallowing set in. She'd changed out of her dress clothes and into her comfiest yoga pants and cried her eyes out. Felix hopped onto the bed and pawed around her cave of tissues to curl into her. She'd allowed herself that indulgence, blasted depressing music, and drank a little too much wine, which was likely the cause of this morning's dull ache behind her eyes.

Today was a new day. Natural light poured in the windows, illuminating the scratches and scuffs on the wooden floors. Faint laughter from the kitchen, where staff prepped for the day ahead, brought with it a bit of clarity.

Life went on.

She wasn't eighteen years old, and she certainly was not going to fall into some depressive state because Jay Wynter left her again. She had bigger problems right now, like running her restaurant and figuring out if this second one would ever see the light of day. Yes, the track Leyna had been on for so many years suffered a slight derailment when Jay came back to Sapphire Springs, but she had to get back up and keep on going, right?

Part of what had attracted her to Richard all those years ago was that he was settled. He had a stable career and knew exactly what he wanted in life. There were no guessing games. In hindsight, he'd been everything Jay wasn't, which should have been exactly what she needed to make her happy.

Except she hadn't been happy.

At some point during the thorough examination of her bedroom ceiling the previous night, she considered that maybe the reason Jay had been brought back into her life, albeit briefly, was to remind her what real love was like. There'd been times in her life when she'd looked back on those years with Jay and accused herself of romanticizing the past, but this summer with him proved her memories hadn't been embellished.

The thing was, though, this time had been different. They'd both grown and evolved, but the new Jay and Leyna worked as well as, if not better than, the old. "Jay and Leyna, version 2.0," somebody had joked the night of the street dance. New Jay made her happier than she ever thought she'd be again, and now that he was gone, a hole filled her heart.

Her eyes flickered over the black-and-white prints on the wall of her loving grandparents throughout various stages of their lives. At least she could take comfort in knowing she'd experienced true love, not once, but twice, with the same man. Every single time she'd ever met anyone else and that cautionary inner voice suggested something was missing, there had been. Settling for anything less would have been selling herself short. She'd always been right to trust her gut, and in time she'd be okay.

Just as soon as her chest stopped aching so hard she could barely breathe.

The wineglass Leyna polished slipped and shattered on the bar. For the love of God, where was her head?

That was the trouble with love. In the end it blinded you, and it always let you down. She'd sworn up and down she'd never open herself up to that kind of vulnerability again, and here she was too nauseous to eat anything other than ice cream for breakfast, her mind too cluttered to sleep, and unable to even look across the bar without the image of him leaning there, peeling the label off his beer, giving her that knee-buckling smile, like she was the only woman in the entire world he wanted.

She blew out a heavy breath. Because she needed something else to occupy her mind, she started to turn up the volume on the music, but she paused when she spotted someone outside, knocking on the front door. "Not in the mood," she muttered, waving Mark off. No more than she'd been in the mood to return his calls or texts the night before.

He persisted, tapping louder.

She pulled the door open just enough to stick her head out. Bloodshot eyes gaped at her. "What do you need, Mark?"

"I, um, I have something really important to talk to you about, Leyna. Can I come in?"

She noticed that he smelled like a whiskey-infused ashtray as he passed her in the doorway.

Leyna folded her arms. "I'd appreciate it if you make this quick. I've got a lot on my mind this morning."

Mark pulled a chair from a nearby table and motioned for her to sit before taking the seat opposite her. He raised his gaze from his grip on the edge of the table, and his eyes welled with tears.

Leyna stiffened. "Mark, is someone hurt? Did something happen?" Her parents...Rob...Jay...She'd just seen everyone yesterday.

"Nobody's hurt." He wiped his eyes with the heels of his hands before continuing. "I came here to tell you that you don't really owe all that money to my firm." There were a few beats of silence before he kept going, his voice hoarse. "Cass propositioned me to fix the numbers so you'd be in no position to open another restaurant."

Clearly this was a dream. Her subconscious was trying to give her something to obsess over besides Jay leaving Sapphire Springs. But the words *fix the numbers* rattled her ears. Leyna gripped the table with both hands and straightened her spine. "Come again?"

He blew a breath upward, ruffling his hair. "Cass had plans for Wynter Estate. He wanted to put an inn on the property where Stefan wanted the restaurant. He figured if you were broke, there'd be no way you'd be able to afford to open a new restaurant."

Mark reached across the table, but Leyna pulled her hand away before he could touch her. "Leyna, I am so sorry I went along with it. I was never going to keep your money, you've got to believe me. I kept trying to give it back to you by investing, but you wouldn't—"

She could barely hear him over the pounding in her ears. "Are you telling me that all those invoices you hand-delivered were falsified documents? That I've been racking my brain for a year trying to come up with a way to afford this second restaurant?" That Jay had been on the right track all long? Her hand covered her mouth and hair rose on the back of her neck. Goose bumps dotted her arms and her hands trembled. Oh God, she might vomit Ben & Jerry's all over table thirteen.

Mark's eyes filled again, and he flew into a sob story about how he'd always had a thing for her and he thought that if he could make her see how far out on a limb he'd go to help her save her restaurant that in time his feelings would be reciprocated. "I wanted you to see that I've changed. That I'm more than the quarterback who bullied people in high school."

Leyna rose from the chair and paced, shaking her hands vigorously to try to stop them from trembling. "So you and Cass, what, just got your heads together one day and decided to steal thousands of dollars from my inheritance?"

"We didn't steal it," Mark cut in. "We *withheld* it for a while. It was never about the money. I tried to give it back to you in my own way."

"That does not make any of this okay!" Leyna yelled, digging her nails into her palms. When the chef poked his head out the kitchen door, she simply shook her head and lowered her voice. "The two of you committed fraud, and I will most certainly be pressing charges."

Mark got up and started toward her.

"Don't." She stabbed a finger at him.

He stopped in his tracks and held up his shaking hands. "Leyna, I was hoping that by coming to you with the truth we could speak rationally about this. Please don't go to the police." His voice cracked. "Because of one error in judgment, my career will be toast." He fumbled in his suit pocket and produced an envelope. "I've got a check with me for every single cent I owe you, with interest added on."

Mark clasped his hands together in prayer position.

Her mind raced too much to process. Why couldn't Jay be here with her? He'd know exactly how to handle it. She met Mark's gaze and her voice shook. "Jay was onto you. He confronted you, and you denied everything. I accused him of being irrational and jumping to conclusions." Her breath caught. "Does he know about this?"

"Jay came to see me late yesterday afternoon." Mark hung his head. "He figured out Cass's involvement and was pretty much ready to yell the news from the rooftops. I convinced him to let me tell you myself, since it's your money and your place to decide what to do. He was fired up as hell, but agreed. I got the impression he was leaving town."

Leyna's stomach sank. What did she expect, he'd come dashing in on a white horse, with her check from Mark, and they'd ride off into the sunset? Please. She slumped at the table again. "I can't think straight right now."

Mark gave a slight nod, then set the envelope he still held on the table. "It's all there. Every cent, and then some. If you need anything else, you just ask. No strings attached, I swear. Please," he pleaded. "Don't go to the police over this."

She remained silent, glaring at him across the table.

"I'm going to go... give you some time."

As he walked out of the restaurant, Leyna squeezed her eyes shut to ward off tears until she locked the door behind him. She slid her index finger under the lip of the envelope, tore it open, and the check fluttered out onto the table. Everything around her blurred as her shoulders began to shake with sobs. All the worrying, the self-doubt... It hadn't been her fault. The restaurant... her grandparents' legacy would live to see another generation.

So why did she feel so empty?

* * *

Just before the restaurant opened for the day, another soft knock tapped on the door.

Moving to the front of the restaurant, Leyna squinted for a better look. Wait, was that Danielle?

It was Jay's mother all right, but with dark-rimmed eyes and a baggy hoodie, Leyna instantly conjured up an image of a tabloid, covered in shots of celebrities without makeup. She unlocked the deadbolts and pulled back the heavy glass door.

Danielle pushed her hands into the pockets of her black hoodie. "I know you don't open for another hour, but…can I come in?" Her voice was raspy.

Leyna tucked a strand of hair behind her ear and moved to the side, letting her shuffle past. Danielle took a seat at the bar and motioned for her to sit, but Leyna chose to stand behind the bar. Her safe haven.

She'd spent the last two hours in a fog, mulling over all the new information, and trying to decide what to do about it. She poured two cups of coffee, added a shot of Irish cream to each, and slid one in Danielle's direction.

With a grateful nod, Danielle sipped the hot drink. "Thanks." She peered at Leyna through heavy-lidded eyes. "I don't know what to say."

Leyna cupped her mug in her hands and leaned on the bar. "I take it Cass came clean?"

With a far-off stare, Danielle nodded. "Mark came to the house last night after a confrontation with Jay. I was upstairs, but their discussion became heated and I overheard everything. I swear I didn't know. I was on board with Cass's idea to build an inn. I selfishly wanted to inherit everything, but I never knew he was full-on trying to sabotage you and Jay." Her forehead wrinkled, and her voice cracked into a sob.

Leyna gulped her coffee. Should've made it a double.

"I'm leaving Cass, and nobody would blame you if you went to the police."

Wow. It turned out Jay's mother had morals after all. On a deep breath, Leyna circled the bar and lowered into the stool beside Danielle. "I think I'm going to. They can't get away with it, even if Mark did pay me back every cent."

Danielle nodded, gripping her coffee with a trembling hand. "Good. Cass deserves it. To think he was using my father this whole time. Using me—" She broke off, and a sob escaped before she cupped her hand to cover her mouth. "How did this all become such a disaster?"

Leyna remained silent. She'd gotten her money back from Mark, and her family restaurant was no longer in jeopardy. Sure, there would be a trial, and the media would no doubt run with the story, but despite the ache in her heart that seemed to practically deprive her of oxygen, an enormous weight had been lifted.

Danielle was severing ties with her husband less than a week after she'd lost her father. Damn it, she kind of wanted to hug her, but she resisted the urge.

Because she felt closer to the woman than she ever had in her life, she turned to face her directly. "Can I ask you something?"

Danielle nodded, her diamond stud earrings gleaming under the lights over the bar. "Of course."

"All I ever did was love your son." Leyna's voice was raw, barely above a whisper. "What did I ever do to you to make you hate me so much?"

Danielle's chin crumpled. "I don't hate you, not like you think. I resented you and your family because you gave my son something I couldn't at the time. I'm working through that." Tears streamed down her face, and she rubbed them away with the back of her hand. "And I couldn't bear the thought of Jason being cast aside by someone he loved. I know all too well how that feels. I guess in my own twisted way, I was being overprotective."

She plucked a napkin off the bar and blew her nose. "I saw his dyslexia as something that would limit him in life, and I chose to let it define him instead of helping him excel despite it."

"This is all stuff you should be telling Jay." Leyna got up for more coffee. The walls were closing in, and she needed space to wrap her mind around everything that had been said in the last ten minutes. "It could go a long way toward repairing the relationship you have with your son."

"We had a good talk." Danielle clasped her hands together. "But he had his mind made up about leaving town." A tear slipped down her cheek. "While it's going to be a long road to repairing our relationship, I think he understands me a little better."

She stood and dried her tears. "For what it's worth, I know how it feels to watch somebody you love choose a life without you."

The image of a young single mother trying to make her own way choked off any response Leyna could've mustered, and all she could do was offer a slight nod.

# Chapter Twenty-Two

A midcentury pickup truck somehow didn't quite belong alongside the sports cars and hybrid SUVs parked in the paved driveways of Rob's cookie-cutter subdivision. Jay turned onto Canterbury Crescent and pulled up to the curb in front of the address Rob had given him. The two-story semidetached home was identical to every house on the block. A few toys were scattered across the manicured lawn, and as he approached the house, a deep *woof* came from behind the front door.

Before Jay had a chance to ring the bell, the door flew open and Rob tried to block the massive chocolate lab from lunging at Jay, but the dog was too fast. "Down, Guinness," Rob commanded from the doorway.

The shock of a hundred-pound animal's paws on his chest knocked Jay back a couple of steps. He let Guinness sniff his hands a few seconds. "Easy, boy." The dog's panting slowed down, and his wagging tail seemed to deem Jay an acceptable guest.

Rob leaned against the door jamb. "I thought I might see you today."

Jay rubbed Guinness's velvety ears. "I take it you've spoken to Leyna?"

"Multiple times. She went to the police." Rob took a step back and held the door open—a silent invitation to enter. Jay removed his shoes and Guinness trotted ahead, leading them down the hallway. They wound around random dolls and other toys, and when Jay stepped on a piece of Lego, pain shot straight up his leg. He caught himself before a string of curse words spilled from his mouth. By the time they reached the kitchen, the pain had subsided to a throb. The kettle sputtered and whistled on the stove, and a woman bribed the two rambunctious little girls from Leyna's refrigerator pictures to eat their tuna casserole.

Jay's stomach lurched like a dying fish at the smell of tuna. Guinness parked himself between the kids and tracked the forks' journeys to and from the girls' mouths. Rob popped the lid on the kettle, releasing a cloud of steam and silencing the whistle as he said, "Issey, this is Jay Wynter. Jay, this is my wife and our two girls, Carly and Sarah." Guinness thumped his tail against the tile floor. "And Guinness, who you've already met. Girls, can you say hello to Daddy's buddy?"

Issey set down the plate and extended a slim arm to shake Jay's hand. If she resented his timing, she hid it well. "It's a pleasure to meet you. Rob's always spoken highly of you. I've heard all kinds of stories from back when you guys were kids." She blew on a forkful of casserole before shoveling it into the younger girl's mouth. "Wynter is a pretty popular wine in this house. Don't mind the mess in here." She glanced at the spattered stove and the mountain of dishes in the sink.

Jay returned the handshake and then rubbed the back of his neck, embarrassed for dropping in on Rob and his family during what was obviously a chaotic time. "Thanks. It's a pleasure to meet you, too, and don't apologize. You must be a real saint to be married to this guy." He poked a thumb in Rob's direction.

That earned a laugh from her, and she raised her brows at Rob. "Why don't the two of you grab a couple of beers and go on out to the garage and catch up. I'll go up and bathe the girls, get them into bed."

Retrieving a beer from the fridge for each of them, Rob gestured for Jay to follow him out the side door to the garage. Guinness chose to hang out with the guys over tuna casserole, trotting along behind them.

"Your wife's got great intuition," Jay remarked as he and Rob took refuge on a couple of lawn chairs under the dartboard. "She's not hard on the eyes, either. You're a lucky man."

Rob clanked his beer bottle against Jay's and took a swig. "Start talking, brother."

Without drinking, Jay set his bottle down and ran both hands through his hair. A few seconds passed before he spoke. "Christ, Rob, I can't believe everything that's happened this past week. I'm sick over what my step—what

*Cass* did to Leyna, and what's going to happen to Wynter Estate. Mom says she's leaving him, but the damage is done. When that will is read, he might legally be entitled to my family's company. Even if she divorces him, he could still have a firm grip on all her assets."

Rob rocked his chair back on two legs. "The fact that he's a criminal has got to be grounds for an appeal. Don't let him get away with this."

Jay rose from his chair and kicked the tire of Rob's lawn mower. "I might not have any choice. Pop was so disappointed in me for missing that meeting. He met with his lawyer right afterward to finalize his will. He said he had it all figured out, and I should take the job in France if I wanted it. It all points to them being named his successors. Leyna deserves more than them or me, for that matter. She deserves a business partner she can rely on and put her faith in."

Rob was quiet for an eternity, rubbing his fingers over his clean-shaven chin. "Well, you're right about one thing. Leyna does deserve more than a guy who takes off the minute the going gets tough. She deserves someone with the balls to stand up and fight for the life he's meant to live."

Well, shit. Because words would betray him, Jay took a long drink, the cold liquid coating his throat while he paced around the clutter of tools, bicycles, and containers of toys the kids had likely outgrown.

Rob stood, too, the metal on his chair scraping against the concrete floor. "Nobody blames you for leaving Sapphire Springs the first time. Breaking up with Leyna opened doors for both of you that wouldn't have been possible if you'd stuck around here and settled down. But you've got a shot at a second chance with her. If you legitimately don't want that, then fine, get out of her way and take the job in France. But this is your one and only chance. You know that, right? If you blow it with Leyna this time, there's no do-over."

Jay's stomach dropped and he stared at the dartboard hanging on the wall. The truth in Rob's words forced him to blink back tears.

Rob pressed on. "The way I see it, eighteen years ago, you loved Leyna enough to let her go. Do you love her enough now to go back? There's no point in beating yourself up over the stuff that happened in between, or the things your snake of a stepfather did out of desperation and greed."

Rob paused to pet Guinness's head. "Besides, what Leyna deserves is a guy who will stand by her—have her back no matter what. A guy who trusts his gut so much that he's like a dog with a bone when he thinks someone is trying to pull a fast one on her. A guy who doesn't let up until he proves it, no matter how skeptical everybody else is. That's the kind of guy Leyna deserves." He pointed a finger at Jay and took a gulp of his beer.

Jay bit his lip and stared at the clutter. All his life he'd believed that the people you loved hurt you the most—that nobody stayed—not his father, his mother...He'd been so sure Leyna would leave him all those years ago that he'd gone ahead and beat her to the punch. But in reality, *he* was the one who'd taken off on everyone else—on his mother when she'd tried to make up for her shortcomings, on Stefan, on Leyna, even on his friends. And after everything, Leyna was still trying to stand by him. All he had to do was let her.

He loved her, always had. There wasn't a doubt in his mind that would ever change.

The door to the kitchen creaked open slightly, and Rob's oldest, Carly, craned her neck around it quizzically, then flashed a wide smile when she spotted them. "Daddy!"

Rob set his beer aside and met her in the doorway, scooping her into his arms. Kissing the top of her dark hair, he rubbed his hand on the back of her pink pajamas. Her fuzzy bunny slippers dangled at Rob's side. "Hi, angel," he whispered. "Where's your sister?"

"Mommy is tucking her in, but she said I could come down and say goodnight before it's my turn."

She had Leyna's dark expressive eyes. Rob's eyes, more accurately, Jay supposed. Tiny arms circled Rob's neck, and then she placed her little hands on his cheeks and rubbed noses with him before giving in to a high-pitched giggle. Rob's face lit up with the most genuine smile, his eyes creasing with so much joy and admiration that Jay's chest ached.

Would he ever know that kind of unconditional love?

"Goodnight, sweetheart, I love you." Rob planted a big loud kiss on her cheek that sent her into another fit of laughter. She scampered to the door and blew them each a kiss, causing another yearning pain in Jay's heart.

When she was out of earshot, Rob slapped Jay on the shoulder. "Let's go have another beer in the living room. You look like you could use a hot meal, too."

"I'm good. I don't want any tuna casserole," Jay replied, his stomach turning. "I need to get out of town and clear my head. I've got a lot to figure out."

"The hell with tuna casserole." Rob grinned. "I've got two steaks in the fridge I was marinating for tomorrow. We'll toss those on the grill and drink a few beers. And afterward," he continued, "you're going to have a good night's sleep on my couch."

"No fancy guest room at Casa Milan?" Jay joked.

"I'm in the guest room," Rob said, his eyes fixed on Jay's. "And that's a whole other story we aren't discussing tonight."

* * *

The next morning Jay and Rob exchanged an ancient handshake they'd made up as kids through the open window of Jay's truck.

Rob plucked his laptop bag off the hood of the truck. "So you're going back to France?"

Jay started up the truck. "At least until I can tie up loose ends, resign in person. I owe Frank that."

"I'll make some calls about the vineyard you mentioned is for sale in Sapphire Springs." Rob checked the time on his phone. "At least that way you've got a fallback if your mom and Cass inherit Wynter Estate."

The sun warmed Jay's arm, which hung out the truck window. "Good. But after our talk last night, I've decided I'll contest the will. My mom is going to need me by her side in this fight. Cass doesn't deserve a stake in Wynter

Estate after all that's happened. Pop wouldn't dream of it." He sat up a little straighter. "And if that doesn't work, I'll buy that other vineyard. Build something from the ground up, just like Pop did with Wynter. I'm going to prove to everyone I have what it takes. Hopefully Leyna will give me another chance, too."

"That's the best news I've heard in weeks." Rob leaned his elbows against the hood of the truck. "I could give you a hand for a bit with the finances. Consult or something."

Jay grinned. "Are you asking for a job?"

Rob craned his neck back and glanced around the neighborhood. "No, I have too much security at the bank. But a consulting gig would allow me to cut back my hours, have more time at home with the girls, so it's not always a constant scramble as to whose picking them up at daycare, or whatever."

"Music to my ears," Jay said, resting his hand on the steering wheel. "Thanks for the pep talk last night. I'm here if you ever need me to return the favor."

"I may take you up on that." Rob raised a brow.

Jay coasted through Rob's neighborhood. He had a plan to put in motion. All he needed to do was convince Leyna to go along with it.

# Chapter Twenty-Three

Leyna was certain her parents and Emily took turns checking in on her since Jay had vanished. All it took was mentioning in passing that she'd forgotten to eat breakfast one morning. Awareness had flashed in her mother's eyes. Leyna didn't forget meals, and everyone knew it. She plotted her next meal before she washed down the last, which meant the cat was out of the bag—Leyna was worse off than she let on.

Emily dropped in to her office at roughly the same time every day and dragged her to lunch so she couldn't skip meals. One of her parents called every night, granted, they always had a lame reason—*The Wi-Fi isn't working, could you come take a look?* Or, *What was the name of that book you suggested again?* She'd make small talk, tiptoeing around the topic of Jay, and it occurred to Leyna that the things left unsaid often demanded the most attention.

Tapping her pen on her desk, she pondered what project to tackle next. On the advice of their lawyers, Cass and Mark were apparently going to plead guilty to avoid a lengthy trial and make the whole fiasco go away faster. Their fate would be decided a few months from now at their sentencing. White-collar crimes didn't normally result in jail time for first-time offenders, so they'd probably get off with a light sentence.

Whether justice was served or not, their credibility was ruined. There was something deeply satisfying about that.

She had her money back, and though the details of the partnership remained uncertain, at least she didn't need to stress over her finances anymore. She'd even given in to the relief and excitement and started looking at realty sites again for potential concert venues. Everything was as she imagined it would be before Stefan and her grandfather ever started talking about another restaurant. In a way, she could pretend it had never happened, try to forget the last few months. This was what she'd wanted all along—the freedom to do everything on her own terms.

Rosalia's sales figures for the previous month were downright impressive. As for Wynter Estate, it remained to be seen. Danielle was leaving Cass, but who knew what he'd end up entitled to in the divorce? Hopefully she'd hang the bastard out to dry.

The image she'd allowed herself to paint of she and Jay together and transforming their family businesses faded with each hour that passed that she hadn't heard from him. Every once in a while she caught herself yearning a little, for what could have been, but as quickly as the thoughts crept up, she squashed them. Rosalia's would evolve in its own way. She didn't need Jay, or Wynter Estate, or anything else, to ensure that.

The light knock on her office door interrupted her thoughts.

"I hope you haven't eaten yet."

Mom's turn to check in. Little wonder, since Emily had already been by earlier with coffee and cinnamon buns from Jolt. "Hi, Mom. What's up?"

Nina could have walked off the pages of a 1950s fashion magazine, with her crisp cotton shirt topped with a sweater tied over her shoulders. She propped her sunglasses on her brown hair and placed a picnic basket on the corner of Leyna's desk. "I thought maybe I could convince you to take a walk across the street with me. Maybe have a picnic in the square. It's a beautiful day, and I don't even have to ask to know you've been cooped up in this office all morning."

Of course she didn't have to ask, because Emily already told her. They were hovering, likely afraid Leyna was going to slip into depression mode like she had when Jay left her the first time. Even though she was moping, Leyna Milan was not some weak, broken teenager who played sappy love songs on repeat anymore. She would hold her head high and handle the cards life dealt her.

Her mother had already launched into a description of the salads and chicken sandwiches she'd brought along, and Leyna knew trying to brush her off would only result in prying. Besides, she'd gone to a lot of bother.

She saved the document that was open on her laptop and plucked her purse out of her desk drawer. "I'd love to go to lunch, Mom."

They snagged a bench under an old oak tree that provided just the right amount of shade. While Nina unpacked the food, Leyna scrolled through her latest emails on her phone, stopping on one from Stefan's attorney. The subject line made her gasp softly: "Reading of Last Will and Testament."

The words hit hard. Shit. He was really gone.

"Are you all right, honey?" Her mother squinted, searching her face. "You look a little pale."

With the press of a button, the message disappeared, and Leyna stuffed the phone into her purse. "Just a message about Stefan's will. The reading is tomorrow at Wynter Estate. I'm not sure why I'm included on the email. Maybe there are a few loose ends." That was probably it. She'd read the email more thoroughly later.

Nina bit her lip, frowning. "I know this is hard for you. Do you think Jay will be there?"

"I'm really not sure, but if I had to guess, I'd say no." Leyna busied herself shaking a container of salad to distribute the dressing. "Rob was the last to talk to him. If Jay was coming back, I think he'd be here by now."

"Oh, honey." Nina reached across the bench and squeezed Leyna's hand. "Don't count him out yet."

Her mom's tenderness nearly led to tears. Leyna propped her elbow on the back of the bench. "Mom, are you actually still holding out hope that Jay is going to show up and whisk me off my feet? It's not happening.

It's over. If it had ever even begun." Though the words stung on the inside, the speech she'd been rehearsing came easier with each passing hour.

With a frown, Nina untied the sweater and hung it over the back of the bench.

Leyna kicked off her shoes and rubbed her feet against the cool grass. Jay had chosen once again to take off instead of sticking with her. No matter how much she missed his lame jokes or his warm, solid embrace, they couldn't go back from that. "Love shouldn't be this hard. Plain and simple."

Nina put down her chicken sandwich. She shifted her attention to the glass bottle of Perrier and sipped through her straw. Finally, she spoke. "Love has its ups and downs, Leyna. It isn't always perfect. In fact, most of the time it's not."

"Well, maybe not *perfect*, but what is?" Leyna waved her hand. "The bottom line is that when the going gets tough, you're able to count on each other. Like you and Dad."

"Your dad and I have been married almost forty-one years. We've come to a really good place, but our marriage has been far from perfect. In fact, there were times when I didn't know if we'd survive."

Leyna stared at her mother, blinking, unsure of what to say. She set down her plate. "Like when? I never saw you guys fight, or, or—"

"Of course you didn't see us fight. No matter what was going on in our marriage, we'd never fight in front of you kids. But that doesn't mean we didn't have our disagreements, trust me."

The food wasn't sitting well all of a sudden. Leyna

dropped her sandwich into the container, secured the cover, and returned it to the cooler. She waited for her mother to elaborate.

Nina patted her lips with a napkin and offered a polite smile to a woman walking by with a standard poodle. She lowered her voice before going on. “I didn’t think I’d ever tell you this, but your dad and I have had our share of problems. We even discussed separating once.”

What kind of alternate universe was this? Her parents talking divorce? A car alarm started honking from in front of town hall, and Leyna pressed a hand to her ear.

“It was years ago, of course,” Mom was saying. “Basically, we’d fallen into a rut. We both worked too much, and neither of us was tuning in to the other. At times it felt like we were just friends, living under the same roof, co-parenting. But when we got married, we vowed to never give up on each other. At least not without a fight.”

Grateful somebody silenced the alarm, Leyna shifted. “So what happened?”

“Your father never gave up on us. I was ready to walk, convinced the marriage had run its course. He persuaded me to give it one last shot, and so we went to counseling.” She leaned against the bench and turned her head toward Leyna. “I honestly didn’t see a thread of hope, but I owed it to you and Rob to at least try. In time we were able to recognize that even though starting over might have been easier than persevering, what we had was too important to walk away from.”

Mom zipped the lid on the cooler. “The reason I’m telling you this is because couples have to shoulder the weight for one another from time to time. One person has to step up and be the strong one, when the other is wavering—be patient when the other person needs to work through things on their own. Fight for each other when you've got something worth fighting for. That give and take is what makes a relationship work."

Her mom's hand covered hers, warm, wise, and full of comfort.

"I'd hate to see you to waste time holding out for the perfect relationship. There's no such thing. Not mine and your father's, or Rob and Issey's. The sooner you recognize that, the better shot you've got at making it work. If not with Jay, then with the next man who's lucky enough to earn a piece of your heart."

"How do I know it's worth fighting for?"

Nina smiled, and rubbed her fingers over the back of Leyna's hand. "I think you already know."

* * *

That evening Leyna mulled over the conversation with her mother. She'd worked the rest of the day, updating social media and planning fall menu changes, but she was distracted by her mother's advice.

Jay might have no interest in coming back to Sapphire Springs, but Leyna owed it to herself to see him one more time, face-to-face, and lay her feelings on the line. Otherwise, she'd never know what could have been.

She crossed the living room, grabbed her laptop off the coffee table, and searched flights to France.

She was ready to trust.

# Chapter Twenty-Four

The only positive thing Leyna could come up with about gathering around the Wynter Estate conference table for the reading of Stefan's will was that Maria was there, and she'd brought freshly baked banana muffins.

Pleased they were still warm, Leyna broke the top off one, and steam curled out. Maria had sat next to her and insisted she have one, as she was practically fading away. Danielle sat on her other side, chewing her nails in a frenzy, even though Cass wasn't present. As part of the legal proceedings, he had to obey a strict no-contact order.

Ross Newman, the lawyer, sat across the table. Rings of sweat dampened his blue dress shirt, and he checked the time on his phone again. Maria wrung her hands in her lap, eyes darting from Danielle to the lawyer and back again.

"Everything will be fine, Maria." Leyna spun her chair a quarter turn to whisper.

Maria shook her head. "Nothing is fine. Cass is a vulture. He practically pawed through the good silverware the last night he stayed in the house. Mercifully, Jason hasn't been around to witness his behavior."

Leyna checked the time for the tenth time that morning. In four hours she'd be at the airport boarding a plane, and she wasn't finished packing. What exactly did one wear to track down their lover in another country and lay their heart on the line, anyway?

The heart-to-heart with her mother the day before hit a nerve, and the hopelessness surrounding her situation with Jay had shifted. Perhaps she'd jumped the gun, though. Maybe a life with Jay simply wasn't meant to be. In any case, she was about to find out. If nothing else, seeing him would provide closure.

Danielle tapped her pen against the table. "Can we get on with it, Ross? I don't think he's going to show."

Ross shrugged and pulled his chair closer to the table. "Fine. We do have a lot to get through, and some of it could be complicated." He flipped open the file in front of him and began reading. "I, Stefan Wynter…"

Leyna was already bored by the terminology, as it seemed was everyone else at the table. Maria was a nervous wreck, idly twisting her chair from right to left. Throughout the reading, Danielle fidgeted with the few rings she still wore.

The lawyer glanced up from the document, took a sip of water, and sighed. "Why don't we save a lot of time and do this in layman's terms?"

"Yes," Danielle replied a tad too quickly, glancing at the rest of them for approval.

Ross nodded. “Okay. Stefan’s financial assets are to be divided equally between Mrs. Nixon and his grandson, Jason Wynter, who, as we can all see, is not present and, as such, will be notified with a letter. It’s pretty straightforward and likely as you’d expect. He glanced at Danielle, who tucked a strand of hair behind her ear and nodded. “We can discuss the specifics at the end of the meeting. Next,” he said, flipping a page, “to his good friend and longtime employee Maria, Stefan leaves the cottage in Muskoka.” Ross glanced across the table at Maria, his smile creasing his eyes. “He says to enjoy your retirement.”

Maria gasped, and her hand covered her mouth. “Oh, Stefan,” she murmured, her eyes filling with tears.

Leyna’s eyes welled up, but she forced the tears to retreat. Maria would likely miss Stefan more than anyone. Danielle winked at Maria and offered a tight smile.

Ross was still talking. “Danielle, in addition to the financial assets previously mentioned, you inherit the main house. The guesthouse will go to Jason.”

Danielle nodded, obviously expecting as much.

Flipping another page, Ross cleared his throat. “Mr. Wynter recently acquired some real estate, the former Blackhorse Theatre at 606 Queen Street, which he leaves to Leyna Milan.”

Leyna’s back stiffened. Convinced she’d misheard, she lifted her head and searched Ross’s face with wide eyes.

He returned the unspoken question with a warm smile and a slight nod. “His plan was to sign that over to you when everything fell into place.”

"I thought it sold to a doughnut franchise?" Danielle put in.

Ross looked up from his papers. "That was a rumor that Stefan never bothered to squash. He wanted the gift to be a surprise."

Leyna's eyes filled with tears again, and this time one trickled down her cheek. Of all the sweetest things Stefan had ever done. Seeing to it that she'd get her concert hall and make it on her own. She drew in a shaky breath and discreetly dabbed away the tear.

"Now the complicated part." Ross closed the folder and sighed. "Stefan amended this shortly before his heart attack occurred."

A hush fell over the room, the whoosh of the ceiling fan oscillating the only sound to be heard. Danielle surprised Leyna by reaching for her hand and clasping it. They'd come a long way.

"Regarding Wynter Estate Family Vineyards. All assets, equipment, and land go to Jason Wynter, but *only* if he is present at the reading of this will." He cleared his throat. "If Mr. Wynter is not present at the reading of this will, he forfeits the Wynter Estate portion of his inheritance. Under such circumstance, the company goes to Cass and Danielle Nixon."

"Oh my God." Danielle lowered her head into her hands and her voice was filled with dread.

Cass would be entitled to half.

The brief surge of excitement over the concert hall was quickly extinguished. Jay could have had the business after all. Clearly Stefan held out hope Jay would commit in the end. The little twist had been for Jay's benefit. If he was present, the company was his. If he didn't show up, he could walk away from the burden of something he didn't want, free and clear of any responsibility. Unfortunately walking away meant Jay would never prove to himself he could be capable, that he was worthy. It broke Leyna's heart to imagine anyone else taking over the business that Stefan always intended to be Jay's.

Danielle inched forward, her knuckles turning white with the grip she had on the table. "But I'm divorcing Cass Nixon. He's a criminal." Her voice shook with emotion and she gripped Leyna's hand. "Please. Ross, there has to be a loophole. My husband cannot be entitled to my father's company just because my son isn't here. Cass will change everything. It's all he's talked about for months—taking Wynter in a new direction. He'll hire all new staff and change the brand—"

"The hell he will."

Leyna, along with everyone else, spun around, her heart swelling in her chest. Jay stood in the doorway wearing a suit, clean-shaven, and not a hair out of place. Maria grasped her hand and Danielle squeezed the other.

"He's going to have to get through me." Jay unbuttoned the charcoal sport coat and crossed the threshold into the room. With each step closer, Leyna's heartbeat jackhammered in her ears.

"I have promises to keep, a legacy to live, and a future to build with the only woman I've ever loved. That is, if you'll still have me."

The tears again, and this time Leyna made no effort

to try to stop them. Her hands trembled too much to do anything.

"Leyna, I'm not perfect, and God knows I don't deserve you. But I know in my heart we can do this. We're better together."

She opened her mouth to speak, but the words wouldn't come. Too many thoughts were spiraling to the surface. Had she fantasized Stefan leaving her the concert hall and Jay showing up at the eleventh hour?

It would be entirely possible if not for the fact that Jay was crouched down, kneeling in front of her, close enough for her to reach out and touch his face.

"I'm not a business guy," he said, taking her hand in his. "In fact, I'm probably a complete liability as far as business partners go." His mouth spread into that irresistible grin. "I don't know the first thing about how to run a meeting or forecast finances. But Wynter Estate is my destiny. And so are you. Everything we've ever wanted is right in front of us. Can you trust me?"

A Wynter meeting was never what you expected, Leyna was learning.

Ross stood, collecting his papers. "I think it's safe to say we dodged one hell of a bullet here. The conditions are clear. Mr. Wynter is present, therefore his inheritance holds true. What he decides to do with it after this is entirely up to him." Ross turned to Jay. "You'll need to stop by my office so we can start the process on the transfer of ownership. Maria, if you've got time now, we can get the ball rolling on your ownership of the cottage. Danielle, same goes for you with the house. I've got a friend who's a divorce attorney and could help you keep your assets out of Cass's reach.

Maria bent down to kiss Jay's cheek before hurrying after the lawyer.

Danielle wiped a tear, placed a hand on Jay's shoulder, and squeezed. He met her gaze briefly and gave a slight nod before she followed Maria and Ross out of the room.

Jay's callused thumb rubbed across the back of Leyna's hand, reminding her she hadn't said a single thing to him since he walked through the door. She cleared her throat. "You're supposed to be in France." And in four hours she was supposed to be there, too.

"I was. I went back to officially quit."

She searched his face. "You quit? But how could you have known Stefan would leave you the company?"

"I didn't know the twist about the will until I was standing in the hallway," Jay said. He leaned back, glanced around the room. "But I was prepared to come back here and tell you that either way, I was contesting the will, and if that didn't work I was going to buy another vineyard in Sapphire Springs. That we could still put our plans in motion, even if it ended up not being Wynter Estate."

They had both given up on the partnership, but neither had given up on each other. Leyna brushed away a tear. "I came here with no clue as to why I was invited. Only that because of you, I got my money back from Mark. I could financially stand on my own. Because you wouldn't let it go, I no longer needed an investor. Then I find out your sneaky grandfather bought the Blackhorse right out from under me." Despite the brimming emotions, she laughed.

Jay drew a long breath in. "And now?"

"Now," Leyna said, lowering out of the chair onto one knee, then the other, so they were eye to eye. "I don't need to do it on my own."

His strong hands trailed up her back, toyed with the ends of her hair. "Do you remember what I said about pinot noir?"

*Okay, change of topic. All good, just roll with it.* She glanced toward the ceiling, trying to recall. "I believe you said the grapes are temperamental, vulnerable, and prone to disease. Or something to that effect."

His light laugh nearly made her knees buckle.

"Points for listening. But I also said it's seductive with a finish that won't let go." He pulled her closer, pressed his forehead to hers.

Leyna eased back, so she could take him all in. The boy she'd loved, the man he'd become. The years in between that shaped them in ways that somehow still fit. "You also said that making the perfect pinot noir was like finding the love of your life."

He tipped her chin up, kissed her softly, and whispered, "Completely worth the wait."

# Epilogue

September brought one of the earliest harvests the region had ever seen. By the third week of the month, pinot noirs, pinot gris, and chardonnays were already picked from the vines. The heavier malbec and cabernet sauvignon grapes would still need a bit more time to mature, but they, too, were well on their way.

Jay and his crew deliberated for days over when to start picking, testing the grape's sugar content and fretting over whether or not the time was right. Finally, Jay made the official call, and the grapes began their journey from the vineyards to the tanks.

Crews worked endless hours, arriving at dawn to begin picking and hovering over the crush pad into the early morning, sorting through the berries to ensure only the best moved on to be processed into wine. The next day, they did it all again, sometimes bringing in up to five or six tons of grapes in a day. They survived on a lot of coffee, and each evening had a meal together to celebrate the day's work.

Critics agreed across the boards that this vintage was primed to go on record as one of the best in Niagara's history. Jay had been up to his neck in grapes since he was eight years old, and he couldn't remember a season in his lifetime that progressed so quickly, and where the stars seemed so perfectly aligned.

Nothing surprised him anymore.

Full of apprehension, he watched the last of the year's pinot noir fall into the de-stemmer. Time to put his faith into the hands of Wynter's chief winemaker.

Stefan said months earlier, when the buds had barely broken, that he had a good feeling about this year's pinot noir, and Jay carried that faith with him throughout the entire season. Challenges were plenty, both in the vineyard and out of it, but they'd had one of the driest, hottest years on record, and he was given a second chance with the love of his life.

As far as seasons went, a guy like him couldn't do much better than that.

If they were lucky, the critics and writers would give this vintage good reviews, and the world would buy it and hopefully understand and appreciate even an ounce of the grunt work required to put that bottle of wine onto their table.

The grape…it endured quite a journey, when you thought about it.

"Hey, stranger."

Leyna's voice interrupted Jay's thoughts. She wandered toward him, a sweater wrapped around her shoulders, and her jeans stuffed into a pair of red rubber boots.

God, he loved her.

"Hey yourself," he took her hand and pulled her into an embrace. "I feel like I haven't seen you in weeks."

"Well, mostly, you haven't." She reached up to rub the beard he'd been growing since the day they began picking. "Since the rain let up, I thought I'd steal you away for a quick visit."

He needed to be stolen away, and for longer than a quick visit, but unfortunately, that was all the time he'd be able to spare until the harvest was complete. They fell into a lazy pace, walking the rows, now bare in most places, and preparing for dormancy.

The sun broke through the heavy clouds and beamed gold across the vineyard, still damp from the day's rain.

"We've come a long way, haven't we?" Jay draped his arm across Leyna's shoulders.

She leaned into his side and wrapped her arms around his waist. "We sure have. When you first moved back, I was so horrible to you. I really never thought this partnership would see the light of day."

It almost didn't. Thankfully after all was said and done, Cass and Mark were both looking at a hefty punishment for their scheme, and his mother had a shark of a lawyer, who was confident Cass wouldn't touch Danielle's inheritance. She'd permanently moved back into the main house and accepted a position managing the tasting room until things with the divorce were finalized and she decided on long-term plans.

"Look, there's a rainbow," Jay said, pointing to the sky.

Bold and bright, its vivid colors glowed against the thick slate-colored clouds.

"What a perfect end to a rainy day," Leyna whispered.

"What a perfect end to a season."

She looked up into his eyes. "You think it's a sign?"

He grinned, tightening his hold on her. "Absolutely."

LOOK FOR EMILY AND TIM'S HEARTWARMING ROMANCE IN THE NEXT SAPPHIRE SPRINGS STORY

**ONLY FOR YOU**

AVAILABLE SUMMER 2021

# About the Author

A happily-ever-after-crafter at heart, Barb Curtis discovered her love for writing with a quick-witted style column, and her background in marketing led to stints writing print and web copy, newsletters, and grant proposals. The switch to fiction came with the decision to pair her creativity with her love for words and crafting characters and settings in which she could truly get lost.

Barb happily lives in a bubble in rural New Brunswick, Canada, with her husband, daughter, and dog. You'll find her restoring the century-old family homestead, weeding the garden, and no doubt whistling the same song all day long.

You can learn more at:

www.barbcurtiswrites.com

Twitter @Barb_Curtis

*Fall in love with these charming contemporary romances!*

***A VERY MERRY MATCH***
**by Melinda Curtis**

Mary Margaret Sneed usually spends her holiday baking and caroling with her students. But this year, she's swapped shortbread and sleigh bells to take a second job—one she can never admit to when the town mayor starts courting her. Only the town's meddling matchmakers have determined there's nothing a little mistletoe can't fix... and if the Widows Club has its way, Mary Margaret and the mayor may just get the best Christmas gift of all this year. Includes a bonus story by Hope Ramsay!

***THE TWELVE DOGS OF CHRISTMAS***
**by Lizzie Shane**

Ally Gilmore has only four weeks to find homes for a dozen dogs in her family's rescue shelter. But when she confronts the Scroogey councilman who pulled their funding, Ally finds he's far more reasonable—and handsome—than she ever expected... especially after he promises to help her. As they spend more time together, the Pine Hollow gossip mill is convinced that the Grinch might show Ally that Pine Hollow is her home for more than just the holidays.

*Find more great reads on Instagram with @ReadForeverPub*

***CHRISTMAS ON REINDEER ROAD***
**by Debbie Mason**

After his wife died, Gabriel Buchanan left his job as a New York City homicide detective to focus on raising his three sons. But back in Highland Falls, he doesn't have to go looking for trouble. It finds him—in the form of Mallory Maitland, a beautiful neighbor struggling to raise her misbehaving stepsons. When they must work together to give their boys the Christmas their hearts desire, they may find that the best gift they can give them is a family together.

***SEASON OF JOY***
**by Annie Rains**

For single father Granger Fields, Christmas is his busiest—and most profitable—time of the year. But when a fire devastates his tree farm, Granger convinces free spirit Joy Benson to care for his daughters while he focuses on saving his business. Soon Joy's festive ideas and merrymaking convince Granger he needs a business partner. As crowds return to the farm, life with Joy begins to feel like home. Can Granger convince Joy that this is where she belongs? Includes a bonus story by Melinda Curtis!

*Connect with us at*
*Facebook.com/ReadForeverPub*

***HER AMISH WEDDING QUILT***
**by Winnie Griggs**

When the man she thought she would wed chooses another woman, Greta Eicher pours her energy into crafting beautiful quilts at her shop and helping widower Noah Stoll care for his adorable young children. But when her feelings for Noah grow into something even deeper, will she be able to convince him to have enough faith to give love another chance?

***THE AMISH MIDWIFE'S HOPE***
**by Barbara Cameron**

Widow Rebecca Zook adores her work, but the young midwife secretly wonders if she'll ever find love again or have a family of her own. When she meets handsome newcomer Samuel Miller, her connection with the single father is immediate—Rebecca even bonds with his sweet little girl. It feels like a perfect match, and Rebecca is ready to embrace the future…if only Samuel can open his heart once more.